Advance Praise for *Obvious in Hindsight*

"If you want to know what politics and tech are really like and you want to laugh, this is your book. Bradley gets it right and makes it fun."

—Gary Vaynerchuk (commonly known as Gary Vee) Serial Entrepreneur, Chairman of VaynerX, CEO of VaynerMedia, CEO of VeeFriends, and 5X *New York Times* Bestselling Author

"No one in America is better positioned than Bradley Tusk to write an entertaining and biting satire of what happens when politics collide with government and both collide with the tech industry and its opponents. *Obvious in Hindsight* pulls the curtain back—enjoy the ride."

—Mike Bloomberg, Founder and CEO Bloomberg LP, Three-Time Mayor of New York City

"This dazzling comic stew of power, policy, and tech reads like Jonathan Swift trapped inside a pinball machine, but Bradley Tusk keeps piling up authentic human insights alongside the laughs so that the more outrageous it becomes, the more real it feels. It's a must-read if you live in the actual world with other people."

—Steven Soderbergh, Filmmaker, Director of *Ocean's Thirteen*, *Erin Brockovich*, *Traffic*, and *Magic Mike*

"Bradley Tusk wrote the best kind of book: a rollicking propulsive satire about power so dark that you take assurance in the label of 'fiction,' even though, really, you know every page is truer than you could imagine. We don't yet live in the time of flying cars, but

Bradley already looks at the world from a bird's eye view—revealing exactly who we are with caustic and incisive wit."

—Brian Koppelman, American Showrunner,
Co-Writer of *Ocean's Thirteen* and *Rounders*
and Co-Creator of Showtime's *Billions*

"The way politics actually works—especially local politics—and the way most people think it works are often two very different things. I don't know when we'll actually have to decide whether to legalize flying cars, but Tusk's take on how it'll go down is probably right."

—Reverend Al Sharpton, Civil Rights Leader, Founder,
and President of the National Action Network (NAN)

"If good fiction is a reflection of the known world, then *Obvious in Hindsight* is something even more impressive—a rare glimpse of the world behind that world, where the real power is wielded, the real fortunes amassed. With a Sedaris-like penchant for humor and a Tom Wolfian knowledge of the Zeitgeist, Tusk's satiric tale of a flying car start-up gone awry is a story only he could tell. But to call it satire isn't quite right, because time and again its ingenious absurdities skew a little too close to plausible, resulting in something entirely new: a rollicking thriller, a riotous comedy, and a not-so-subtle warning to the complacent among us: it's time to start paying attention."

—David Goodwillie, Author of *Kings County* and *American Subversive*

"A funny, eye-popping novel about what it would take to get flying cars off the ground (literally) and into the skies of, say, New York City. Bradley Tusk pulls back the curtain on tech start-ups to reveal the money-driven, highly conflicted characters operating behind the scenes: loan sharks and CEOs, FBI agents and venture capitalists, pundits and politicians. Who is pushing innovation, who is slamming on the brakes... and why? A fascinating read!"

—Amy Poeppel, Author of *The Sweet Spot*, *Musical Chairs*, *Limelight*, and *Small Admissions*

"*Obvious in Hindsight* is a brilliant, biting political satire that pulls back the curtain on government, politicians, Big Tech, and lobbyists—and reveals just how absurd the system really is. It gets a whole lot funnier—and maybe even a little scary—when you realize Tusk has spent a lifetime around politics. This is like if *Schoolhouse Rock* actually told the truth about how a bill becomes (or doesn't become) law. If you want to know how the system actually works, read this book."

—Rob Hart, Author of *The Warehouse* and *The Paradox Hotel*

"*Obvious in Hindsight* gives readers a peek into the world of the political consultants trying to help push the future forward, while managing the often (ahem) strong personalities of their visionary clients. It's fun, fast-paced and entirely believable to anyone in the startup ecosystem."

—Connie Loizos, Silicon Valley Editor of *TechCrunch*

"Beneath the satire, the humor, and the flying cars, Tusk nails how politics really work. If you want to understand why politicians make decisions and what you can do about it, read this book."

—Corey Johnson, Speaker of the New York City Council, 2013–2021

OBVIOUS IN HINDSIGHT

a novel

BRADLEY TUSK

A REGALO PRESS BOOK
An Imprint of Post Hill Press
ISBN: 979-8-88845-220-2
ISBN (eBook): 979-8-88845-221-9

Cover Design by Hannah Tjaden

Post Hill Press
New York • Nashville
posthillpress.com

Published in the United States of America
1 2 3 4 5 6 7 8 9 10

For Abigail and Lyle

NOTE FROM THE AUTHOR

Look, I don't know you. I don't know what you believe in. I don't know where you live, what you care about, or who you voted for in the last election (assuming you even vote to begin with; statistically speaking, you don't). But I know you'll agree with this: America's politics are completely, wildly, devastatingly broken.

I spent the first fifteen years of my career working in city, state, and federal government—in the executive and legislative branches and running political campaigns. I've held jobs ranging from Mike Bloomberg's campaign manager to Chuck Schumer's communications director to four very long years as the deputy governor of Illinois. I saw it from every angle. I have since spent the last dozen years working with tech startups, beginning with running the campaigns nationally to legalize Uber, and then creating my own venture capital fund that invests in early-stage startups in highly regulated industries.

When you need something done in government—at any level—you have to understand what motivates the people you need to persuade. The good news is they're all solely focused on one thing and one thing only—reelection. Ninety-nine percent of politicians are desperately insecure, self-loathing people who can't live without the validation of holding office. They will never prioritize solving any problem ahead of reelection. Ever. If they did, we wouldn't have school shootings. Or an opioid epidemic. One out of every ten Americans wouldn't go hungry. Our roads and bridges wouldn't be on the verge of collapse. (Feel free to insert your own catastrophe here.)

That's a sad thought but not completely hopeless. Because if you can make politicians believe that doing what you want will help them win their next election, or if not doing what you want could cost them the next election, your chances of getting whatever it is you need done—passing a bill, blocking a bill, promulgating new regulations, preventing new regulations, securing government grants, landing lucrative contracts, receiving permits, even getting the city/state/feds to look the other way—are actually pretty good.

That's what we'll see over the next 312 pages or so of this novel. How decisions are really made. How the tech community uses politics to legalize its products, and how the tech community also sometimes misunderstands politics and watches their startups go broke as a result. My hope here is to share with readers one of the few things I know with 100 percent certainty to be true: every policy output is the result of a political input.

Flying cars may seem fantastical, but they are actually not that far away at all. Over 117 startups are working on the idea right now. They've already received over $8.4 billion in total investment from venture capitalists like me (though not me specifically in this case). Flying cars are coming a lot sooner than you think. So are the political battles to allow them and to stop them. Here's how one (fictional) flying car startup approached the problem.

PART ONE

CHAPTER ONE

BROOKLYN, NY

1 MetroTech Center

Lisa Lim emerges from the F train at MetroTech Plaza in Brooklyn and braces her jacket against the biting January wind. She looks down at her phone. The first thing she notices is the usual array of missed calls, texts, and voicemails whenever she loses reception for even a few minutes: Her lobbyist in Tallahassee updating Lisa on the Seminoles' mounting opposition to her client's lottery privatization bill. A state senator in Nevada asking Lisa to raise $50k for her next campaign. A reporter in Columbus wondering what Lisa knows about threats from the owner of the local hockey team to move to Fresno if the city doesn't pony up for a new arena.

An instantaneous response pops into her head for each one, but lately she's been trying to do her work a little differently, be more thoughtful and a little less reactive. Not go all in on whatever task is directly in front of her. So she pockets her phone.

The second thing she notices, which makes her forget all about the first, are the people dressed up like birds.

Dozens of them mill around outside 1 MetroTech, a gray, blocky building that looks like a half-finished Lego set.

It's New York, so weird shit like this happens all the time—normally, it's why Lisa loves living here. When she was a kid growing up in Alexandria, Virginia, mid-morning gatherings featuring human beings decked out as Australian king parrots and toco toucans didn't tend to happen all that often.

The problem is, the birds are here for her.

More specifically, for her client.

Lisa is meeting Susan Howard, the founder and CEO of FlightDeck—a heavily funded and much-hyped flying car startup. Susan is here to record the first media hit for their campaign to legalize flying cars. Because dealing with security at MetroTech is even more painful than most office buildings—and from what Lisa can tell so far, anything involving Susan seems to be inherently painful—Lisa figured that meeting Susan right outside the building would reduce the chances of a run-in with the invariably annoyed security guard at the desk who just wants to read his *Daily News* and be left in peace.

The bird-people certainly complicate things.

As Lisa scans the crowd for Susan, she notices a sign held by a lady in a richly textured yellow-and-black goldfinch costume. "The sky belongs to birds—not tech oligarchs!" Next to the goldfinch is a particularly fetching flamingo with shapely legs, and a costume that seems too tight and thin for the cold weather. "Say no to privatizing our skies!"

There are dozens more, but she knows none of them are pro-flying cars.

This can't be good, she thinks, as she finally spots Susan furiously pacing right outside the lobby, seemingly unbothered by the cold. She has AirPods in both ears, hands moving wildly, unquestionably yelling at whoever's on the other end of the line. Susan doesn't seem to notice the giant birds or the angry signs. Which is probably for the best before appearing on a top-rated podcast that's widely influential with female listeners in the coveted thirty-two-to-fifty-four age range.

Lisa heads over to Susan, who holds up a finger in the universal signal for "give me a minute." Lisa points to herself and mouths, "Lisa! From Firewall! For the podcast!" She points frantically towards the top of the building as if it's the universal signal for "I'm here to make sure you don't fuck up this podcast." Whether she understands or not, Susan nods and then resumes yelling into her phone.

Lisa heads into the lobby, politely gets their passes from the front desk, and waits for Susan to join her, using the free 164 seconds to catch up on unread Signal and Telegram messages. She considers, for the third time that week, whether she should re-download Hinge or Bumble, but decides not to. Given all the idiots she's met so far, the effort alone in putting together a decent, up-to-date profile takes more time than it's worth.

Susan canceled the first call to prep for the podcast and then didn't show up for the second. Lisa thought she might quickly try to brief Susan before they enter the studio, but Susan seems more interested in yelling at people. Susan used to have an in-house communications person who, in theory, could have helped keep her on track. She's had several, actually. Each one of them quit within months. After one former comms employee broke her NDA and spilled the beans on Glassdoor, filling the role has been challenging.

As they exit the elevator, Rachel Culkin-Ramirez, the host of *Leaning In, Branching Out*, breezes into the reception area, reusable polypropylene coffee cup in hand, wearing the uniform borrowed from New York's private-school stay-at-home-mom mafia: gray camo Lululemon pants and a new, but deliberately faded, Nirvana T-shirt under a black James Perse hoodie.

"Hi guys!" Rachel says, ushering them down the narrow, maroon-carpeted hallway and into the recording studio. "Thanks so much for doing this. Susan, I am such a huge fan. I've been following your career ever since Bad Shit Insurance. So impressive. Such a good idea. Really excited to have you on the show."

Even though Susan didn't bother with the briefing, the flattery should help her performance, Lisa thinks. And if she's raised over $80 million from sophisticated venture capitalist types, she must know what she's talking about, right?

Susan beams, always eager for affirmation, and finally pockets her phone. "Thanks so much for having me. Ever since it leaked last week that we're almost ready to launch, there have been so many misconceptions about what we're doing. All we want to do is give consumers the coolest and most meaningful technology since, I don't know...probably since the hoverboard."

Rachel nods sympathetically as they step into the cozy recording studio, which is decorated with posters that Rachel probably finds motivational and Lisa finds a little pathetic. One is simply a picture of a desert vista with the word "Motivate" written underneath. What the hell does that even mean? Motivate who? The camels?

"That's why we're here today," Rachel says, putting on a pair of chunky black headphones. "We'll clear all that up. Our audience is mainly women like us seeking career guidance and inspiration. Stories like yours are really popular. And look, this is all very informal. Super casual. Should be the easiest interview you ever do."

Lisa heads over to the window to check on the circus below. The protest keeps growing. By her very rough estimate, the crowd is now more than three hundred strong, despite the frigid mid-January temperatures. The speaking program is underway. Lisa can't hear them clearly from twenty-three floors up, and she needs to know what they're saying. She signals to the producer that she needs to head out for a moment, steps out into the damp maroon hallway, jumps onto Facebook Live, and finds the protest.

The goldfinch lady is at the podium, spewing hellfire. "They're destroying our planet, piece by piece! Species by species! Thanks to the wonderful people who brought us climate change, there are already three billion fewer birds in the sky. Three billion! And now this? All in the name of what? Flying cars? Take the subway! I mean, tell me this: are people even supposed to fly?"

The crowd roars back the desired "No!"

"Whose sky is it?"

"Birds!"

"Who are we fighting for?"

"Birds!"

"If flying cars win, who loses their God-given right to fly?"

"Birds!"

"So let's hear it! And let's make sure that vicious predator Susan Howard up there hears it too. One! Two! Three!" The entire crowd—including a guy in a black-and-yellow cockatoo outfit doing cartwheels—starts yelling, "Ca-caw! Ca-caw!"

Jesus, Lisa thinks, *this is even worse than the electric scooter protests of 2019.*

She hustles back into the studio as they're starting to record. Fortunately, so far, it's just been softballs.

"So did you always know you wanted to be an entrepreneur?" Rachel asks.

"Absolutely," Susan says. "Really for as long as I can remember. I started wearing my mom's HBS sweatshirt—that's Harvard Business School, obviously—when I was five. Once her parking lot company grew into a billion-dollar, multinational business, I knew I wanted to follow in her footsteps. But with my own thing."

"Tell me about your first company."

"Bad Shit Insurance?" Susan feigns surprise, though it's not clear for whose benefit or why. "The idea was pretty simple. It came out of a group project in my Advanced Entrepreneurship and Innovation course in business school. Wharton. Based on wherever you were traveling, you could buy insurance on-demand for whatever bad shit could happen to you. Earthquakes. Flight cancellations. Fjord explosions. All with dynamic pricing. We were using behavioral economics to set the pricing to maximize revenue in every situation. Even had two of my b-school professors on the advisory board."

"And you could purchase the insurance when you were booking your trip?"

"You could purchase it anytime you wanted, from anywhere in the world. All from your phone."

"I'm a little embarrassed to admit this," Rachel says, "but full disclosure, I got Montezuma's Revenge on spring break in Cancun during my junior year at Michigan. Should have dry-swallowed those Excedrins instead of washing them down with tap water. Spent half the trip in the bathroom. It would have been nice to get some of that money back—"

"Of course it would have been," Susan interrupts. "You know that. The entire venture capital community up and down

Sand Hill Road knew it. But all these imbecile regulators somehow couldn't wrap their heads around it. It was just too innovative, too unconventional, too intelligent, quite frankly, and I know I probably shouldn't say this—"

"Say it!" Rachel commands.

Lisa winces. *Whatever it is, please don't say it!* she thinks. But she already knows there's no way Susan doesn't take the bait—even if she had shown up for the briefing.

And she does. "Okay, I will. Honestly? They were in the tank for the industry. The big insurance companies started complaining to the regulators because they didn't want new competition and we got shut down in twenty-seven different states. We got screwed by corruption. The entrenched interests. Regulatory capture. Rent seeking." Susan likes throwing out vaguely abstract terms that make her sound smart.

Occam's razor, the Pareto principle, the Fibonacci sequence, and Sturgeon's law are her go-tos. She incorporated all four into her TEDx talk.

Susan pauses for effect. "But we're not making the same mistake with FlightDeck. No way, no how. We are not going to just sit around and naively assume again that the politicians and regulators are looking out for the consumer. We understand how the game works now. That's why we hired the smartest, sharpest, most ruthless political consultants out there. And that's why this is the year we make flying cars legal."

As soundbites go, that could've been worse, Lisa thinks.

Rachel tilts her head gravely, as if she too has given deep consideration to the politics and regulation of flying cars and come to the same conclusion. "So when did you come up with the idea for FlightDeck, your flying car startup?"

"Well, after we wound down Bad Shit Insurance, I took a few months off with my then fiancé to hike the Outback. No guide, obviously. Defeats the whole purpose. That was the trip before the trip where, if you go by the official Disney standards as detailed on their SEC legal disclosures, I set the record for the most theme park rides in one day—even though they still claim that the Swiss Family Treehouse is an attraction and not a ride. They're wrong. Now I have to come up with some other way to get into the Guinness Book of World Records. So annoying." Susan shakes her head, filled with sorrow and empathy for herself.

The cries of "ca-caw" suddenly get louder. Rachel looks up, confused. "What is that?"

"What's what?" Susan asks, though Lisa can't tell if she doesn't hear it or she's just ignoring it. "Theme parks? You know. Places with rides. And merch. Like Disney. Busch Gardens. Knott's Berry Farm."

So much for getting along with the host, Lisa thinks.

"I mean that noise," Rachel says. "From outside. It's so distracting."

She's right. Despite being on the top floor, the sound of the protest down below is getting louder.

Still hoping to salvage the interview, Lisa tries to play it off as nothing. "Oh, you know. Just the usual malcontents complaining about the future. Nothing important. We can ignore it."

Rachel gets up, takes off her headphones, and walks to the window. "Who are those people? And what are they wearing?"

No one speaks for a few seconds. It's clear to Lisa that Susan has finally realized something bad is happening twenty-three floors below.

Susan breaks first. "Their fear is our inspiration."

Lisa tries not to roll her eyes.

The din keeps growing.

"It's pretty loud," Rachel continues. "I don't know that we can—"

"People have been dreaming about flying cars for nearly a century," Susan tries. "Imagine soaring—"

Rachel shakes her head. "I don't think it's going to work. It's too loud. It's going to interfere with production—right, Ralph?"

For the first time since they entered the studio, the producer sitting in the glass booth across from them moves, taking off his headphones, which sends his long gray hair cascading around his shoulders. "Sound quality is definitely gonna be a problem," he says with an unmistakable Long Island accent. "We should reschedule."

"No!" Susan says a little too loud, not wanting—never wanting—to leave a sale half-made. "This is a recording studio, isn't it? Didn't you have it soundproofed? That's standard industry practice." Susan, of course, has no idea about standard industry practice for podcasts, or pretty much anything else, but she knows that when she says something with authority, people usually believe it.

"We're on the twenty-third floor," the producer says. "Noise from the street usually isn't an issue."

The protest keeps getting louder.

The window-washing platform is now level with the studio window. Rachel screams as the guy dressed as a cockatoo yells, "Ca-caw! Ca-caw!" and pounds on the window, hard enough to shake the glass. The window washer's hands and feet are bound. An older man with kind eyes, he's struggling against his restraints and looks terrified.

This just went from not-great to oh-fuck real quick, Lisa thinks. "You know what, Ralph?" she says to the producer. "You're right. Why don't we reschedule? Rachel, I'll text you."

She grabs Susan and hustles her out of the studio and back to reception. When they get in the elevator, Lisa hits B for basement. She has no clue where the basement leads, but there's probably a back door somewhere. It may set off a fire alarm or two, perhaps even cause the entire building to be evacuated in the middle of the workday, but anything is better than direct engagement with the bird mob—a confrontation that would be filmed and uploaded to YouTube, TikTok, and Instagram within nanoseconds.

Lisa watches the numbers on the display tick down, half-expecting the doors to open on a mob of birds.

"I wish Carol were here," Susan says between the eleventh and tenth floors. "Her kid's strep throat is ruining everything. Again. Fucking kids." Susan shakes her head in dismay.

Carol? Lisa thinks. "Who's Carol?"

"My executive coach."

"Oh. She usually travels with you?"

"Of course." Susan seems surprised by the question.

Lisa knows she should stop here, but she can't resist. "How often do you see her?"

"Every day."

"Every day?"

"Every day."

Every day, Lisa thinks. Susan pays someone to hang out with her and tell her positive things about herself every day. That's next-level insecurity. That makes most of the politicians they manipulate seem secure.

When the elevator reaches the basement, the doors open to an underground garage. As Lisa, holding Susan by the elbow, looks around frantically for the exit, a white Escalade with dark tinted windows rolls up. The backseat window slides down.

Nick Denevito, the CEO of Firewall, and Lisa's boss, sticks his head out, a big grin plastered on his "handsome for politics" face—which is, admittedly, a very low bar. But together with innate charm and at least the appearance of money, it's more than enough to generate a steady stream of notifications on Raya.

His eyes narrow on Lisa, noticing the mustard stains on her jacket. "Did you work the morning shift at the hot dog cart?" His tone says he's joking, but Lisa still winces. Offhand barbs from Nick aren't new, but even after four years working together, the mild insults still always cut through, at least a little. Even though she knows Nick would say that he's just fucking around because he's fond of her, she still has to get through each day.

Nick addresses both of them, bringing Lisa back to reality. "This is amazing! The protest made it on CNN. You can't *buy* this kind of press. Jump in!"

CHAPTER TWO

LOS ANGELES, CA

FlightDeck HQ

Yevgeny cups his hands around his mouth and raises his voice so he can be heard throughout the cavernous FlightDeck space—half open-concept cubicles and half airport hangar/testing lab. "She is unhappy with the prototype again! She says one more explosion and we are all going to be rotating tires and doing oil changes at the local gas station. Her words, not mine!"

He's met with a few shouts of "What else is new?" and "Please fire us!"

Most of the crew—the ones who aren't distracted by work or lost in chunky headphones—pantomime doing a shot. Murmurs of the same refrains and drinking game come a few seconds later from the stragglers on the lab floor.

Yevgeny Kolnikoff, FlightDeck's heavily bearded, even heavier-set chief engineer, had hoped for fewer jokes and more hustle, but at this point, everyone is bone-tired trying to make this flying car thing work.

He briefly wonders if he would command more respect if he switched up his wardrobe—give up the Fear of God jeans, the limited-edition Supreme hoodie, and the silver-and-white Jordan 4s in favor of something more business casual.

But that isn't really his style. Yevgeny likes to forge his own path.

Like when he gave up code monkey work and came to the U.S. from Estonia on an H-1B visa in 2009 to take a job at Boeing in Chicago. It wasn't long before he realized that only a masochist would choose to live in a city with eight winter months over Southern California, so he moved to Los Angeles for an engineering role at SpaceX.

At first, the money was incredible, more than he ever dreamed of. Then he realized the engineers who'd gotten there only two years before him now owned partial timeshares in chalets at Zermatt and had (albeit Tuesday–Thursday only) access to mid-range domestic trips on NetJets. As employee number 5,347, he was never going to catch up.

But he distinguished himself enough to get his name circulating around town, and when Susan offered Yevgeny the chance to come in on the ground floor at FlightDeck, he jumped.

On his first day, after seeing how little actual technology stood behind Susan's compelling narrative and vision, he worried that he'd made a mistake.

Six months later, he knew he'd made one.

The problem was, he didn't know where to go from there: he'd already quit his job at SpaceX, bragged to everyone he knew that he'd be a billionaire by thirty-five, and moved into a way-too-expensive three-bedroom/two-and-a-half-bathroom spread in Santa Monica overlooking the water, not worrying about depleting his savings because so much money was just around the corner.

To her credit, Susan gave him the budget to hire the team he needed. And for a while, things were good. They were making tangible progress on a weekly basis, solving difficult problems like lift-off velocity and landing gear applications. Nothing made Yevgeny happier than crossing items off the long to-do list written in bright orange on the big white board hovering ominously in a corner of the lab.

Until they ran into the sensory problem.

If you could fly a car in a completely empty sky, the tech might work as is. But the sky is loaded with birds, airplanes, helicopters, drones, kites, and a dozen other risks and irritants. And if a flying car can't sense or detect any of them, that flying car probably won't make it to its destination in one piece. And while self-driving cars are starting to make real progress with LIDAR technology, Yevgeny and crew haven't figured out yet how to apply it to the air.

Yevgeny needs a breakthrough. Fast. It's not like Susan's patience has worn off, because she never had any in the first place, but the daily beratings have been getting nastier and more personal as the problem goes unsolved. Yevgeny keeps hoping to reach the mystical Carol and have her whisper a few magic words to rein Susan in, but the executive coach remains elusive.

The good news, he thinks, as he tries to reassure himself after Susan's latest diatribe, is that even if they can't fly more than a few feet before hitting something and careening to the ground before erupting into flames, the cars at least look pretty cool.

The latest model, which the team unofficially dubbed the Quinjet—after the tactical aircraft that carted around the Avengers—sits gleaming in the middle of the lab. It looks like a military cargo helicopter, only with more rows of leather seats, more landing gear, a coat of shiny black metallic paint, and

FlightDeck's logo of a person of indeterminate gender wearing giant angel wings emblazoned everywhere.

The aesthetic is like Soho House meets the Israeli Air Force, even though the engineering team nearly doubled the car's weight capacity to account for the likely girth of many of their far-less-chic American passengers, especially once they start offering a cheaper version of the product to middle America, which, as Susan likes to say, is where the scale and real money is.

His only regret is not making the cars smaller and sleeker. They tried, but there wasn't enough room for the fuel cells. Something they can figure out by the third or fourth generation, like how the iPhone went from an oblong chunk of metal to a smooth, slim slice of glass.

Despite Susan's promise to her investors that the product would be ready in full by the end of Q1, so far, looking cool is all they really have to keep the board from plotting to unload their shares on the secondary market.

Yevgeny thinks back to the first conversation he had with that political consultant from New York, Lisa L-something. He knows it started with an L because she had the same kind of comic book name alliteration as Peter Parker and Lois Lane. The firm has a weird name too…Firewall. He googles "Lisa L Firewall" and her name pops up. A quick search of her posts shows that she must know what she's talking about. Four years as a top staffer in the U.S. Senate, running communications for Dianne Feinstein. Three in the governor's office of Virginia under McAuliffe overseeing legislative strategy. Ran six successful House races across the southeast for the DCCC and one winning mayoral race in Charlotte (her bio doesn't list the campaigns she lost). Made the move to New York and to consulting around four years ago.

Lisa had reached out soon after her firm signed the contract to run FlightDeck's campaign to legalize flying cars. She said she wanted to understand the product better, but Yevgeny could tell she was looking for more than Susan's word.

Yevgeny started the call like Susan taught him for all conversations with outsiders: say whatever you think they want to hear. But unlike their investors, Lisa seemed unconvinced. "Really? What Susan said is true? You guys will be able to launch self-flying cars in any city in just a few months?"

Yevgeny knows nothing about U.S. politics, but he guessed her radar detector for bullshit was probably pretty sharp. A little unsure what to say, he started dissembling instead, not quite wanting to lie to Lisa, not quite wanting to risk getting himself in more trouble with Susan. "You know, mostly? Still some kinks to work out, ay?"

"Uh huh," Lisa replied skeptically.

"This is how it always goes. It is pretty common in tech. Every day it is tricky, tricky, tricky. Then, one day, you figure something out and that makes you realize something else, and that leads to another thing, and then all of a sudden, you are there."

"Moore's law," Lisa replied, invoking the oft-cited principle in Silicon Valley that a relentless focus on innovation and experimentation allows the speed of computing to double roughly every two years, meaning that no technical problem is truly unsolvable.

Shit, Yevgeny thought. She kind of sounds like Susan.

But then Lisa posed a direct question that Susan would know to never ask. "You think you're on the verge of a breakthrough then? Something we can work with publicly?"

"Maybe. I hope so. Probably. I think."

"Like in three months? Because that's what Susan keeps promising just about everyone we talk to. Launch by the end of Q1. That's right around the corner."

Yevgeny didn't respond, so Lisa kept pushing. "What would happen if you tried to launch by late March?" she asked.

Lisa clearly wasn't going to fall for Susan's fake-it-till-you-build-it routine. So Yevgeny figured he might as well try something new, maybe even kind of revolutionary in tech: complete honesty. "Based on where we are today? Crash and burn. The sensors." He smashed his two fists together to illustrate the point, even though they were on the phone, just like little kids do.

Then he tried turning the tables. "It is not just us. I mean, could you meet Susan's deadline for all your political things? Legislation and whatnot? I bet we are not the only ones behind schedule."

Trying to out-spin a topflight political consultant never works. "Dude, that's on you—it all depends on when you can get us a functional prototype," Lisa said.

"And once we do, you will make it legal everywhere? Like that? So easy?" Yevgeny snapped his fingers for effect.

"Everywhere right away? Of course not. This is a major normative shift. We do it by building support step by step. We've done it before. Helped legalize ridesharing and online sports betting. Got medicine prescribed via text. Reformed worker classification. We even stopped the Butler's Union from requiring that all iPhones come preinstalled with on-demand valet services."

Yevgeny thought he read something about those butlers in TechCrunch.

"But," Lisa clarified, "we need *something* to work with. Maybe we don't have to take every City Council member on a test flight, but asking them to legalize something that doesn't exist is a heavy lift. Even for us."

Yevgeny paused. "Well, hopefully we will have something very soon" was the best he could offer.

Now he wonders if he never should have taken Lisa's call. Going down a political rabbit hole in Estonian Eesti would be hard enough for him. Despite twelve years of intensive classes and lessons, what are his odds debating her in English?

Then he realizes it might be an opportunity.

Maybe Lisa could convince Susan to stop overpromising so much. Maybe that even gets FlightDeck and Yevgeny's many stock options back on track. It is optimistic, but it is something.

Then he could stay in the overpriced three-bedroom and successfully play the role of self-made big shot when his cousins visit from Tallinn in July.

Yevgeny sighs.

He looks at the floor of the main lab and sees the latest version of his badass flying car that can't stay airborne for more than fifty seconds without crashing into something and plummeting to the ground.

The visual alone gives him angina.

"Hey boss?"

Yevgeny turns to find his assistant, Bryon, a slight, nervous kid who, on a good day, seems to be shrinking into whatever hoodie he's wearing. Today, the hoodie is emerald green and it looks like he's disappearing into a black hole. Yevgeny vaguely wonders if the kid is afraid of him or another crash.

Probably both.

"The new sensor system is calibrated," Bryon says. "The team thinks we're good to go for the next attempt."

Yevgeny nods. "Then let us get the Quinjet in the air."

And, he thinks, *let's hope it stays there.*

CHAPTER THREE

SOMEWHERE OVER NEBRASKA

Chartered Private Jet

"What do you mean they have a few valid points?" Susan asks Nick. "They're the enemy! How can they be right about anything? Do you think my mother made her fortune by letting the other parking lot guys walk all over her?"

Nick sighs into his empty rocks glass. It's never fun talking to a brick wall, but at least when the brick wall has money, it comes with perks (a typical startup founder isn't chartering jets before the company goes public, but Susan's family already has a plane). Especially when your first flight was in the middle seat of the back of the plane next to a bathroom with very bad ventilation at the age of nineteen.

Nick and Lisa have spent the better part of the flight to LA preparing Susan for her inaugural press conference. Nick does most of the talking. Lisa is getting a crash course in how to deal with an especially difficult client, and she's paying close attention to everything. Every client gets subjected to a murder board of tough questions before any major public appearance. They're usually scared enough to pay attention and do what they're told.

But so far, despite Susan's dual Ivy League degrees and frequent mentions of her near-perfect ACT and GMAT scores, the notion that anyone could possibly have a different opinion from her own still seems unfathomable to her. And whenever Nick or Lisa has a good point, Susan claims Carol would disagree.

"Look, it helps to at least think about where they're coming from," Nick says. "It's not unreasonable that the transit unions are worried this could eliminate their jobs. It's not unreasonable that the taxi industry doesn't want competition. Same for Uber. They're barely breaking even without having to compete against flying cars. It's not even unreasonable that the Socialists hate anything that caters to the rich, because the Socialists are almost always unreasonable. That's half the reason they exist. Three quarters, maybe. The bird nuts, though? I can't even pretend to understand how they think."

Susan nods vigorously in agreement.

"But bird nuts aside, the rest of them are going to make their case pretty cogently," Nick says. "To the media, to regulators, to elected officials, advocates, pundits, TV and podcast audiences, the world of Twitter and Instagram, and pretty much anyone else who will listen. Which means even if every single reporter at our press conference is completely clueless, a few of them will still at least come prepared with tough questions that someone handed to them. Questions we can handle—but only if you're actually prepared to handle them. And right now, you're not."

Luckily, a few days earlier, Nick anticipated Susan's belief that nothing she says can ever be wrong. So he moved the press conference from New York to LA, hoping to soften the sharpness of the questions by maybe 10 percent. New York reporters are a particularly dangerous breed—competition in the world's biggest media market is exceptionally fierce. At least in Los

Angeles, moods are tempered by the incessant sunshine, and the market is spread out enough that reporters aren't constantly at each other's throats.

It isn't a panacea, but that 10 percent could be the difference between complete public humiliation and living to fight another day.

***

After landing at LAX, Nick and Lisa break away from Susan, grab a quick bite from In-N-Out, and make their way to the press conference.

Nick couldn't wait to ask. "Who the fuck is Carol?"

"Executive coach."

"And she weighs in on everything?"

"Apparently. Susan sees her every day. Talks about her all the time like she's Yoda or something."

"Every day?"

"Every day."

There's nothing to say after that, so they ride in silence until they arrive outside the Disney Concert Hall about half an hour before call time. Nick picked the location for a couple of reasons: downtown LA makes it easier for most of the press to get to and the Frank Gehry–designed building offers a futuristic backdrop that suggests a sweeping vision for the future—much better than the industrial parts of Burbank where FlightDeck is based. Nick and Lisa were a little unsure about holding an event outside in January, but in Los Angeles, it is a bright blue day hovering around seventy degrees.

The press is already arriving and getting situated. Turnout is looking good. It's not always easy to wrangle coverage, but when you introduce a controversial and visionary idea that people have been clamoring for since the 1950s, it gets attention.

By the time Susan arrives, close to twenty-five reporters, bloggers, cameramen, and photographers are gathered around the makeshift stage. The Audubon Society is there in full force, but the French barricades the LAPD erected are keeping the birdcalls mainly out of earshot.

Susan steps to the podium. She has an air of being in total control, which Nick hopes the press interprets as confidence and not pomposity. She starts going through her talking points, delivering them exactly as written by Nick, only better than Nick ever could. He still can't decide if Susan is attractive. Objectively she is—perfectly highlighted blonde hair, fit, nice teeth, expensive clothes, and clear skin tone—but if it requires every advantage money and discipline can buy, does it still count? Kind of the opposite of Lisa, he thinks, who doesn't try hard at all and almost seems to look better for it.

"And that's why what your grandparents were promised, what your parents were promised, what you dreamed about as a kid is finally—finally—here." Susan bangs on the podium for emphasis. "Flying cars aren't just an idea. They're not just a fantasy. If the Los Angeles City Council allows it, they'll be operational here in LA in just three short months. Same for New York. Same for Austin. All those jobs. All that excitement. Just a simple statute away."

Nick and Lisa debated whether to get a teleprompter for the event, but Susan clearly doesn't need one.

Probably why she was able to raise so much funding for a product that didn't technically exist yet. She can sell.

"Any questions?"

The reporters start jumping up and down like first graders in a slowly deflating bouncy castle. The hometown reporter's hand goes up. Susan calls on him first. Nick's been talking to him on background for the last week, making the case that FlightDeck, as a born-and-bred LA company, would help galvanize the local tech scene. Right before the event, he told Susan to let the local guy kick things off.

"Ms. Howard? Duncan Buford from the *LA Times*. Do you seriously expect people to believe that they'll be able to just jump in a car and fly themselves across the sky three months from now?"

So much for the hometown discount. But Susan isn't fazed.

"Absolutely. I see no reason people shouldn't be able to use the technology to its fullest potential. Although I should correct you on one point—no one's flying anything. The vehicles are fully autonomous. And even better, once they're in flight, they're completely silent. Even if one of our cars flies right by your window and the window is wide open, you'll never notice."

Not bad, Nick thinks. Maybe she can handle this. Sometimes the client simply is that talented.

Derek Hines from the *Wall Street Journal* jumps in. "There aren't even fully autonomous self-driving cars on the road yet. And how do you do this without federal approval?"

"We can fly locally all we want if the city says so. It's their call. We just can't cross state lines." Seems like Susan learned at least something about jurisdictional authority from the murder board, although the authorities at the FAA may have something to say about her analysis.

Anika Nash from NPR goes next. "Are you conducting a demo today? When can we see one?"

"Not just yet," says Susan, perhaps a little too smugly. "Today's the day we unveil the concept, start socializing it with the public. Demo comes next."

Zoe Michaels from Slate doesn't wait to get called on. "Ms. Howard, your competitors say that you have an unfair advantage. Your mother is the biggest parking lot owner in the entire nation. And you have all of her facilities in almost every major city to use for takeoff and landing. They say that gives you a leg up, only furthering inequity. How do you respond to that? Will you agree to limit your use of family property to even the playing field?"

Susan looks at the reporter like she's just grown eight heads. "Why would I do that? This isn't kindergarten. This is business. If I have resources my competitors don't, that's another reason to support our efforts, not to try to tie a hand behind our backs. And if they don't like this, wait until they see the vertiports we're building."

Susan calls on a priggish-looking man with an English public-school accent. "Malcolm Hartwell of *The Economist*. Why is this the right time to pursue something like flying cars? Don't our elected leaders have more immediate issues to deal with? Abortion? Immigration? Gun violence? War? The political climate in Washington? The actual climate?"

Nick prepared her for this exact question. Talk about the importance of innovation. About how it all feeds into the same goal. About rising tides lifting ships.

But she gives a different answer.

"The bubonic plague killed fifty million people in the fourteenth century," she says. "They invented the clock that century too. And eyeglasses. I think we can all agree that we're better off having both of them in our lives. Would you prefer not to be able to see? We can't stop moving forward because things get a little hard. I know you all write about what other people do, and don't do anything yourselves, but still, I mean, come on. Get some perspective."

Lisa, who's hanging out in the back, starts furiously tapping at her phone. Nick's phone vibrates in his pocket. He whips it out and watches the messages pile up.

WTF
does she need to attack the entire press corps?
now they're out for blood
and calling the bubonic plague "a little hard"?
this is going off the rails
we should wrap up now

"How do we know your tech is even real?" asks Connie Bakal of the *San Francisco Chronicle.*

The press has now turned fully hostile, everyone asking a version of the same question. Nick tries to get Susan's attention. He holds up his index finger to signal "last question" to her.

"We've got time for one more question," Susan says. "Lior, how about you?"

She immediately realizes her mistake. Lior Longworth from the *New York Times* is the biggest asshole in the group. Yes, she knows him from the Bad Shit Insurance days. Yes, he wrote a halfway-decent story about their innovative insurance techniques. But familiarity is not nearly enough. "Isn't this precisely the same rhetoric we heard from Theranos?" Longworth asks.

Exactly the question Nick was afraid of.

It lands harder than the last FlightDeck test vehicle. Now Susan is Elizabeth Holmes with cars instead of blood. She starts backing away from the podium, not sure how to respond, or how to actually end a press conference. Of course, Lisa and Nick raised the Theranos issue a dozen times in prep, but despite remembering the bits about autonomous flights and about not crossing state lines, Susan apparently never registered the whole fraud line of questioning.

After twenty-five years in and around politics, Nick knows when to let the client figure things out on their own—and when direct intervention is necessary. He maneuvers around the shouting, jumping, bouncing reporters, steps directly in front of Susan, and as cheerily as possible declares, "Thank you, everyone." He leads Susan backstage, and they make a break for it before reporters can surround them with more questions.

As Nick and Lisa follow Susan into her idling, slate-gray Porsche Taycan, he prepares himself for a tongue lashing. Clients hire consultants, in part, to be able to have someone to blame when things go wrong. It's a cost of doing business.

And this definitely went wrong.

But Susan turns to him and says, "Not bad, right? Lots of energy there. Had them eating out of my hand until the very end. Overall, I think it was a net plus."

Nick knows better than to disagree.

CHAPTER FOUR

NEW YORK CITY

Inside City Hall, NY1 Studios

The lights come up on a local news station studio that's got some money to spend—but clearly nowhere near network-news money. The walls are covered with flatscreens showing clips from the events of the day: a three-hour backup on the BQE; a new bookstore and podcast studio on the Lower East Side called, for some reason, P&T Knitwear; a groundhog who bit the mayor again. The carpet is a brilliant French blue. In the center is a glass table, around which are seated three people, all of them anxiously waiting for their turn to speak and not listening to a word anyone else says.

Kirsten White, a former parks commissioner turned newscaster, wears a powder-blue blazer and white blouse, her auburn hair teased around her shoulders. The camera zooms in on her attentive stare and megawatt smile. "Welcome to *Inside City Hall.* The topic tonight: flying cars. Are they about to take off in the Big Apple, or will they crash and burn? Susan Howard, the controversial CEO of FlightDeck, seems to think we're ready for it, and has even enlisted the heavyweight lobbying firm Firewall to try and make it happen. With us tonight on this topic are Graciela Vazquez, president of the New York Democratic Socialists, and Roland Hodges, the former Republican state senator from Staten Island."

White turns to Hodges, in his dark suit jacket and white button-down shirt. He's not a politician anymore, so he doesn't wear a tie. He's one of those rare legislators with movie-star looks—square jaw and a full head of salt-and-pepper hair. He'd have made it further than the statehouse if not for that pesky secret second family (or the pesky blogger who figured it all out).

"Senator Hodges," White says, "you spent ten years representing residents with some of the longest commute times in the city. Is this something you think we need?"

"Absolutely, Kirsten," he says, flashing teeth so whitened they make Joe Biden's teeth look a little yellow. "First off, innovation is never a bad thing. It means jobs. It means tax revenue. It fosters even more innovation. I spent my entire tenure trying to bring fast ferry service to the south shore of Staten Island, where the average commute times are around an hour. The city shut us down over and over again because they didn't want to spend the money on dredging. If private industry wants to come in and offer a better option, I say let them."

Vazquez clears her throat and adjusts her red blazer, which matches her red lipstick, both of which stand out against her jet-black hair, pulled back into a tight ponytail. "That's if the technology even works."

"Time and patience," Hodges says to her. "If I learned anything, it's worth it in the end."

White chimes in. "Ms. Vazquez, you've said that this isn't what City Hall needs to be focusing on right now..."

Vazquez doesn't give her a chance to finish. "That's exactly right. Even if they can pull this off, should they? Are flying cars really what we need? The mayor's job is to reduce income inequality, not approve new ways for rich people to avoid traffic. Subway violence is out of control. Let's worry about keeping people safe underground before we start launching them into the air."

"Funny to hear you talk about more policing," Hodges says—light-hearted, but with a little bit of an edge.

Vazquez isn't thrown. "It's not about policing. It's about homeless and mental health support services. But that's a separate conversation. No matter what, this idea means more time, money, and energy to create space for the one percent to play with some new toys."

"FlightDeck's CEO..." White starts.

"Susan Howard," Vazquez finishes. "She talks a good game, but look at what we've seen so far: a disastrous press conference in LA where she couldn't answer any tough questions. A whole lot of promises and ideas but no actual tests or evidence of how these things would work. It feels like the sequel to Theranos: a brilliant idea with nothing to back it up."

"I'm glad we can at least agree that it's brilliant," Hodges says.

"Look, I get it," Vazquez continues. "In a perfect world, if these things are low-emission like they say, and it takes cars off the road, and it cuts down on greenhouse gases and commute times, I'm in favor of all that. But the last thing I want to see is this city dedicating an outsized amount of time and resources and infrastructure to an issue that feels more like a vanity project."

"No one's saying the government should fund flying cars over school lunches," Hodges says. "But if a private company and its investors want to spend their own money to create something new? You've got all those groups in Silicon Valley pouring money into stuff like this left and right. It doesn't take anything away from us."

Vazquez gives a little smirk, enjoying the back and forth. "It's still time and resources and distractions. Look at everyone lining up to oppose this. Taxi. Uber. The DSA. The Transport Workers Union. The Audubon Society. How do you overcome all of that? If Susan Howard genuinely wants to help people, she can donate her money to food banks or homeless shelters."

Hodges raises his voice, getting flustered, gesturing with his hands. "We're not talking about City budget money. We're talking about private money. You're deliberately conflating the two. Although you probably believe that all money should be government money."

Sensing the rising tension, White jumps in. "FlightDeck has enlisted Firewall to try and make this happen. The head of Firewall, Nick Denevito, has a reputation for making the impossible possible."

"Denevito and his team have pulled rabbits out of hats before," Vazquez says. "But this is gonna be tough. I just don't see it."

"I know Nick," Hodges says. "He doesn't bet on losers, and on the rare occasions he does lose, he puts up one hell of a fight. He made esports betting legal in sixteen states. Stopped Phoenix from banning *Pokémon Go*. Took down the Butler's Union. Made mini golf an Olympic sport. I wouldn't underestimate him."

"So how do they make this happen?" White asks.

Hodges nods solemnly. "If I were running the campaign? The opposition is steep. They're connected. The taxi guys alone have a disproportionate amount of power—especially over Mayor Navarro. But c'mon, we're talking about flying cars. I can tell you this—a lot of my former colleagues are going to say what they have to say to make the unions happy, and then get on the elevator and talk about how cool it would be if this passed. I hope they show a little backbone. Whatever Firewall does, they have to make the whole thing so exciting, so innovative, so attractive that the normal political rules of gravity don't apply."

"Speaking of Navarro, where does he land on this?" White asks.

"Navarro is termed out, so he doesn't have all that much riding on this either way," Hodges says. "We all know he got worked over by Uber and wouldn't mind getting a little revenge. That said, he's spent years doing business with the unions and he's close with some of the big taxi medallion owners. So I guess that's a long way of saying: we'll see."

"I know this much," Vazquez says. "He hasn't delivered on even a tenth of his promises. And what happens when one of these cars crashes into a school, or into the crowd in Times Square?"

"Gracey, c'mon. You're telling me that you wouldn't jump at the chance to hop into one of these? In a city where it can take an hour to travel six miles?"

Vazquez throws a sharp eyebrow at Hodges, not comfortable with the familiarity, but she doesn't pursue it. "If this was real, Susan Howard would have touched down at that press conference in a working car, and we wouldn't be having this conversation. But history tells the tale. All these Silicon Valley types—they come up with big ideas and they beta test them on us, and they don't care who gets hurt in the process."

Hodges is turning red now. The discussion has turned into a debate, and it's not going his way. He's about to interject when White jumps in. "Well, if anything can defy gravity, it should be flying cars."

Vazquez and Hodges pretend to laugh.

"We'll be following this closely. Now you tell us, New York. Text the numbers at the bottom of the screen to let us know if you support flying cars. Results when we come back. And up next on *Inside City Hall*, we ask our panel of experts, what's that chocolate smell?"

CHAPTER FIVE

NEW YORK CITY

Firewall HQ

Lisa rolls into the office at 6:32 a.m., a good two hours before her usual arrival time. She normally walks to the office, but given the hour and a charcoal-and piss-colored mix of slush and schmutz clogging the streets, she took a cab. The lights are still off, and there isn't a soul anywhere in sight. From the front doors, she can see nearly the entire place—Nick favors an open-office bullpen and likes using the wall space to show off his photorealism art collection. Even the conference rooms are enclosed with four walls of glass, so you get privacy of sound but not sight.

Some people don't like it; they feel like they're always being watched. But that's not Nick's goal—he just likes the energy and being able to occasionally stand at his desk in the center of the room to survey his domain. Lisa catches him doing it sometimes, always with a big smile on his face. It still tickles him that all these people work for him.

She wishes she wasn't there so early, but she couldn't sleep. It wasn't just the garbage trucks outside loading what seemed like endless bins of empty beer bottles that kept her awake.

FlightDeck is starting to feel like a failing campaign.

The protest, the press conference, and the lack of a testable product are bad enough. Seeing Hodges floundering on NY1 didn't help. If that was a debate, Vazquez was the winner.

But this is a campaign Lisa believes in. Cut carbon emissions, reduce traffic, create jobs and tax revenue. All great things. And more than that, Nick's starting to treat her as an equal on this one. She's been at Firewall for four years, and this is the first high-profile campaign that feels like it truly belongs to both her and Nick, not just something she's helping with.

Lisa briefly thinks that her mom would have been disappointed with her performance on this campaign so far. Then again, when was her mom ever not disappointed? Or focused on anyone's needs but her own? Even when she was alive, her whole "we lived through the Cultural Revolution so you have to do great things in America" narrative was really meant to get Lisa to make choices that would impress the other members of her mom's church choir. Fuck that. What does Mao's purge in 1966 have to do with taking advanced calculus in suburban Virginia anyway? Her mom was like ten when that happened.

Sure, Lisa's life would be wildly different—and probably far worse—if her parents hadn't made so many sacrifices to get to the U.S. and raise a family here, but that doesn't have to dictate her every choice for eternity.

Lisa still has the text from her mom from ten years ago that finally made her realize that if she wanted someone to look out for her, it wasn't going to be her parents. "Janice Yao's daughter is going to Harvard Law School. Melinda Shumaker's son is going to Columbia for his MBA. Amy Mendick's daughter got a 522 on the MCATs. And what do I have to tell them about you? Nothing good. So I say nothing at all."

Lisa actually thought about doing interviews with McKinsey and Goldman during her senior year solely for the purpose of getting offers and turning them down, but decided it wasn't worth the effort, especially since getting jobs in the field in which she actually did want to work—politics—not only wasn't simple, but was also totally ad hoc. There was no on-campus recruiting, no headhunters, no digital marketplaces for politics. You just found someone who knew someone, or you decided you wanted to work somewhere, figured out who was in charge, and harassed the living shit out of them until they gave you a chance.

Lisa cringes as she remembers the conversation when she finally tried explaining her logic to her parents. They were sitting in her parents' small, too-dark living room, overcrowded with too much heavy wooden furniture. The plastic cushions, as always, were on the paisley couch.

"Look, you have your views. You have your opinions. That's fine. But they're not my views. It's my life we're talking about, not yours," Lisa told them.

Her mom jumped right in. "Your life is my life. My life is your life. There's no difference." Lisa couldn't tell from her dad's expression if he agreed, but even if he didn't, there was no chance of him jumping in to defend her.

"I know that's how you see it. But it's not how I see it. From my perspective, you get one shot here on this earth. One." Lisa holds up a finger for emphasis, fighting every urge to make it her middle one.

She looked her mom right in the eye and kept going. "I know you believe in heaven and an afterlife and all that, but I don't. Nor do I believe in reincarnation. So this is it. One shot to get it right. And for me, getting it right is different than what it is for you—"

"You're too young to know what you want," her mom snapped.

No young person has ever heard that and reacted well. Lisa was no exception. "It's my life! Mine, not yours! Okay? And honestly, I think your version of life is a little pathetic. The whole goal is to make six figures at some boring job, gain some status that doesn't even matter, have some kids, live in a half-dead place like this and then rinse and repeat again and again until you die? Fuck that."

"Language," her dad said.

"No. Not language. You need to hear this. Why is it so bad that I want to do more than just come and go? Unlike you, I want my life to mean something. That's why I want to get into politics. The decisions you make impact millions, sometimes billions, of people. You can make things better. You can make them worse. But either way, you're actually doing something. Unlike most of your friends' kids—especially the one at Columbia who's going to get rich moving numbers from one column to another and skimming some off the top for the next forty years."

The blank look on both of her parents' faces confirmed that the conversation was pointless. They couldn't see anything wrong with moving numbers or getting rich. After some manipulative crying by her mom, it ended with her dad recommending she consider orthodonture or podiatry if medical school sounded too hard. He was still talking when Lisa left the room.

She settles into her desk and takes a half-eaten box of Cinnamon Toast Crunch out of the bottom drawer. She's wondering if she should risk tangling with the new pod coffee maker when she hears the glass doors at the front of the office yawn open. She pokes her head above her computer and sees Nick walk in. Nick's hours are never routine, but he never comes in *this* early.

Of course he's wearing a freshly pressed suit. His shoes are shiny and clean despite the miserable weather.

"If I'd have known you'd be here, I'd have gotten you a bagel. Hey, did you see that Kosher Mexican Korean food truck parked outside? I can't decide if it sounds terrible or delicious. Maybe we should hit it at lunch."

At least someone has gotten a dose or two of caffeine. She struggles to keep up, her head still tired and muddy. She does recall seeing the truck when she got out of the cab.

"Yeah, I'll let you take the first crack on that one," she says.

Lisa scans her desk, which looks a lot like her apartment. Sparse. White. Clean. Absent the laptop and multiple chargers and devices on the table, it would be empty altogether. Nick's desk is the exact opposite. His obsession with his appearance does not extend to his work environment. Papers everywhere. Business cards scattered. Half-finished drinks. Half-eaten food. Random wads of cash. Framed photos of a 2018 trip to Deer Valley with his then seventeen-year-old daughter and twelve-year-old son and his second ex-wife. Dog-racing forms on every surface. It's so bad, he rarely sits there anymore. Mostly, he paces around the conference room, pounding a mini orange Mets bat in and out of his palm.

Nick drops his bag on top of the pile and returns to Lisa's desk, staring at his phone and jabbing at it with his index finger, as if hitting it harder will somehow change the outcome of what's on the screen.

"Hodges really dropped the ball," Nick says.

Realization dawns on Lisa. "You put him there?"

"Of course," Nick says. "Guy is good-looking, pro-business, not crazy conservative. Been long enough since family number two–gate that people have mostly forgotten. Generally, he's good on TV. But Vazquez is better." He sighs. "What happened? A week ago, we were running the coolest campaign in the country. Every consultant in New York and DC was giving me shit about it. So jealous. It was great. Now we're the laughingstock of the internet?"

"Things go downhill fast when your CEO gets compared to Elizabeth Holmes."

"At least they didn't call her the next Adam Neumann. I'll take Theranos over WeWork any day. That guy was a full-on cult leader."

"Those two have third marriage written all over them."

"Susan and Neumann?" Nick asks.

"I was thinking Holmes and Neumann, but any combination there probably works. Maybe they can have a throuple. Throw Sam Bankman-Fried somewhere in there too." Lisa smiles and shakes her head briefly. "It's all about timing. Five, six years ago? The press would have lapped this whole thing up. But that was before so many things went wrong on the tech side. Google, Huawei, Facebook, Instagram, WeWork, Theranos, TikTok, FTX, and every other fucking tech scandal out there? Anyone with an idea is now automatically suspect."

Nick points to his phone. "Tell me about it. The taxi guys and Uber are holding a joint press conference this afternoon calling for government protection from flying cars. The fucking hypocrisy. The balls on these guys. The fucking Socialists are organizing a rally. The transit unions are scheduling a strike vote. I had to rescue you from those birds of prey."

Lisa smiles. "Nice metaphor. Really rounded out the narrative there." *I didn't need you to rescue me* is what she's actually thinking.

"Thanks. Was hoping you'd notice."

"So what if we're a little off track," Lisa says, waking up a bit now. "It's a campaign. Things always go wrong. Fine. We've been here before. I couldn't sleep. Kept thinking about this. So I put all my ideas in Notion. Let me show you."

Lisa taps a few buttons and hands her phone to Nick. It's all there—earned media, social media, digital ads, TV ads, lobbying, polling, grassroots, opposition research. Lisa proudly thinks she's covered everything.

"You're right. It's all here. Every tactic. But these are just tactics. They're useless without the right message behind them, something that gives elected officials the cover to support our bill. Because if they think we can help them win the next election or hurt them in the next election, they'll pay attention."

I know, I know, Lisa thinks.

But Nick keeps going. "What's rule number five?"

Nick Denevito's ten rules of demystifying politics. She's read them a hundred times and knows them all by heart—but it's hard to remember the order because they're all pretty similar. She thinks hard for a moment. "It's what you just said. Politicians will do what you want in one of two cases: they think you can help them win their next election or lose their next election."

"Precisely. And rule number one…"

"Every policy output is the result of a political input." Lisa smiles as she says this, happy to remember that one quickly.

When she first heard it, she thought it was a little too basic. Now that she's seen Nick's philosophy borne out in campaign after campaign, in city after city and state after state, she believes it too.

"Very good, grasshopper," Nick says. "In New York City alone, we've got fifty-one members of the Council. Every one of them is eyeing Albany or Congress when they're term-limited out of here. You could probably tell me half of their plans off the top of your head. Then we've got the mayor. Navarro is solely focused on the next move. Whatever that is. Probably making money. Same deal in LA. Same in Texas."

"We're gonna need to overwhelm them with money," Nick continues. "The more they think we have a bottomless pit of it, the less enthusiastic they're gonna be about going up against us, lest we exact retribution in their next primary."

Lisa nods again. "Got it. We nail the message. Get TV spots in production. Get digital ads up ASAP. What if we went old school and put up subway and bus ads? It'd be a nice fuck-you to the transit workers."

"I like that," Nick says, snapping his fingers. "Need a bunch of influencers on the payroll too. It won't reach triple prime Council voters, but all the young staffers will see it, and once this issue is in their feed, it'll make them nervous."

"What about the pundits? We need more than Hodges, right?"

"Yeah, but not yet. Hold off on the editorial boards. If the *Times* supports us, then every Republican around the country automatically hates us. On the other hand, if we go to the ed board of the *Journal*, we've got the opposite problem—we're fucked in New York and LA."

"You can't win either way," Lisa says.

"Not if we do things the way everyone else does. Look, this isn't a campaign we're going to win by convincing the pundits and all the assholes who hang around Two-Fifty Broadway all day. It's a campaign where we overwhelm them, where we make them think that making us their enemy is the dumbest career move they could ever make."

"Exactly," Lisa says, shifting forward in her seat. "And speaking of, I think we really need to lean into Los Angeles and Austin. Play the cities against each other. No one wants something until someone else wants it—and then everyone wants it. We turn this into a horse race and make them all think they have to beat the other one out."

"Like that Amazon HQ2 thing until the local pols in Queens fucked it all up," Nick says.

"Exactly! Best case scenario, our bill passes in all three cities. Worst case, it passes in one for now, we show it works, and then go after the rest."

Nick smiles. "I love the way you think."

"Shock and awe," Lisa says, remembering her high school days when she kept trying to write about the invasion of Iraq for the school newspaper. (They wanted her to focus on the college acceptance beat. *As if where you go to college makes any difference,* Lisa thinks. *Especially in politics.*) "But how are we going to find the budget to do all this? In three major cities with really expensive TV markets? Even Austin's pricey these days."

"Susan keeps telling me we'll have whatever we need."

Lisa raises an eyebrow. "You really believe her?"

"If it means she can't launch, yeah, she'll come up with the money. Plus, beyond what she's raised, she clearly has a ton of family money too. And..." Nick trails off.

"And?

"You ever notice how much she brings up her mom?"

Lisa nods.

"Susan doesn't need the money. She doesn't need to work. She needs to show she's worthy. Whether to her mom or herself or maybe to Carol, whoever she is, I don't know. But it's good for us because it means she'll spend any amount of money to prove it. And at a fifteen percent commission for every TV ad, every digital spot, every podcast placement, her mommy issues are our profits."

Nick is about to say something else when he takes out his phone. He stares at the screen for a second, and something flashes across his face. Concern? Fear? Then he pockets the phone and smiles.

"Everything okay, boss?" Lisa asks. She's almost never seen Nick look nervous before. About anything.

"Yup, all good," he says. "Want a cup of coffee? I think Blue Bottle should be open by now."

"That'd be great."

Nick stands for a moment, almost like he's confused, and then snaps out of it and heads toward the elevator.

Lisa wonders what that was about. Maybe something with his son? The kid's a teenager now, so there's probably plenty of problems to deal with. Drugs maybe. Hopefully not the hard stuff. Terrifying, with fentanyl laced in everything these days. Whatever. As long as he's not mad at her, it doesn't matter. She pushes it aside.

It's probably nothing. And she has a lot of work to do. More than that, she's excited to dig in. This is when the job gets really fun.

CHAPTER SIX

LOS ANGELES, CA
FlightDeck HQ

Yevgeny and his team are huddled around a big desktop monitor, Zooming with Susan, who is dialing in from her family's weekend place in Malibu, as opposed to her regular five-bedroom spread in Los Feliz (the Howards have come a long way from opening self-serve parking lots in Reno, moving into the big time in Los Angeles when Susan was twelve and acquiring homes in New York, London, Tuscany, Park City, Costa Rica, and more ever since).

Must be nice, Yevgeny thinks.

A fresh batch of scratch-off lottery tickets covers his desk. The Presidents' Day edition. He uncovers some of Theodore Roosevelt's face with a quarter. Another loser. People with advanced math skills tend not to get suckered like this. But for someone from Eastern Europe, even in today's age of on-demand commerce, the pure volume of consumer choice can be overwhelming, sometimes leading to illogical decisions—like playing the lottery.

With the stress he's been under lately, he'll take any indulgence he can get.

"We need to show those smug little assholes in the press that our cars are operational right now," Susan demands. "Today." Given the view behind Susan's angry image, it's too bad none of the engineers are capable of noting the juxtaposition of the simmering ocean and Susan's barely controlled rage.

"Sure, sure," Yevgeny says, nodding. "We have some good videos of a few flights, before things went south. We can splice some of those together. Or maybe do something cool with animated Legos, for storytelling purposes. I recently finished building the Millennium Falcon. You know, the really big one from *Empire* that they re-released with *The Mandalorian*, and..."

"No!" says Susan, pounding on the glass coffee table in front of her and sending a huge vase filled with wildflowers tumbling onto the carpet. She doesn't miss a beat. "Aren't you listening? A video won't cut it. They need to see the real thing."

Yevgeny draws a long, deep breath, closes his eyes, and tries to picture himself relaxing on a riverboat casino, *Wheel of Fortune* slot machines serenading him every step of the way, a cocktail waitress handing him a fresh whiskey sour before he's even done with the one he's holding.

The other engineers all look at each other, brows furrowed, lips pursed. Most of them have lived through something like this before—the hot-headed founder making irrational demands is a staple of the tech world. But it's usually for something fundamentally harmless, like finding a job for their inept best friend from the eighth grade or ordering a mango lassi at 4 a.m.—not something that will put actual lives in danger.

Yevgeny opens his eyes and regretfully returns from his gambling paradise. "You know that is impossible, right?"

"I don't fucking care," Susan says, her face turning splotchy. "Make it happen! I have two voicemails from Marc Andreessen. Two! I didn't even know he uses the phone. Emails from the guys at General Catalyst, Sequoia, and USV. Texts from almost everyone on the board. My DMs are bombarded by reporters. I'm getting crushed on Twitter. I can't even bring myself to look at Reddit. This is getting way out ahead of us, and if we don't rein it back in soon, we're going to lose the whole thing. I can't afford that." She tries to stare down the engineers over Zoom. "And neither can any of you."

"Well, maybe can you tell everyone to calm down? Buy us some time?" Yevgeny asks. The moment the words come out he wishes he could scoop them back in. Maybe he can blame the language barrier.

"Tell them to calm down?" Susan says, her voice acid. "What about this do you not get? They gave us a huge amount of funding—more than eighty million dollars—based on the promise that we'd produce a flying car this year. This year. Every extra day we take to launch, their IRR goes down."

"But the engineering..."

"Your department, not mine." Susan pauses. "Look, Yevgeny, just get it done. Because if we don't get this thing off the ground—literally and figuratively? Your equity will be worth as much as those goddamn lottery tickets on your desk."

Impressive, Yevgeny thinks. The scratch-off cards aren't even in the frame. It's a good reminder that just because Susan may be difficult or even more than a little amoral, she's paying attention. Even when it looks like she isn't.

"But what about the sensory problem?" one of Yevgeny's deputies asks. Loud enough that Susan can hear. Yevgeny cringes as the words come out.

Posing unexpected questions, as any lawyer can tell you, is always dangerous. Posing them to Susan is borderline lunacy.

"I've been thinking about that," Susan says, "and I think Carol and I came up with something: bats."

"Bats?" Yevgeny asks.

"How do bats fly?" Susan asks.

Yevgeny leans back in his chair, the lightbulb in his head sputtering to life. "Echolocation…emitting high-frequency sounds and listening for the echo…it helps them determine the size, shape, and location of objects…"

Susan smiles a little ruefully. "Exactly. Right now, our sensors are collecting information based on visual cues only. Maybe if we added another layer, like sound, they'd be a little more sensitive. Better able to read the environment."

Yevgeny's instinct is to brush it off—this is his specialty, not hers.

But it's also something they haven't tried, and there is some logic to it. More than anything, he's annoyed he didn't think of it first.

"Okay," Yevgeny says. "Certainly worth our exploring."

"I know it is—that's why I told you," Susan says. Then she seems to regain her composure. The wildflowers are somehow back in the vase. He keeps looking for signs of Carol in the background, but all he sees is Susan's mom's world-renowned collection of Chihuly glass sculptures. "Look—I get it. Our car can't detect other objects in the air, and that's a safety risk. What we need right now is time. In a totally controlled environment, what's the difference? If we can find a place to demo that has no birds, no drones, no airplanes, no nothing—we should be able to fly safely, right? No crashes? And that'll give us the runway we need to test out the bats idea and see if it works."

Yevgeny watches the screen as his entire engineering team turns to each other, nodding. He's too afraid to look away from Susan. In theory, she's right. In practice, they probably could conduct a completely safe test. But implying the car is ready to go when they know they could never launch it in the real world is a no-no.

All those faces turn to Yevgeny, waiting for him to tell Susan no.

"Well," he starts, trying to figure out what to say. "I mean, yes. Theoretically, you are right. We could construct a neutral environment. But that is a little…I don't know, wrong? Won't everyone then think we are ready to fly?"

"No. Not at all. This is just to show how far you guys have come. We won't misstate anything. We're just giving our investors and the media a sneak peek and giving you and the team some credit for all of your great work so far. There's still a long way to go. Everyone knows that. This buys you the time you need."

Yevgeny knows she's lying but doesn't know how to counter it. He glances down at the lottery tickets. This latest batch brought in about $75 in winnings. Far less than the $165 he actually spent.

He knows he should stop buying them.

He knows that.

But the urge to gamble is strong.

"Okay, sounds good," he says. "We will get working on it."

CHAPTER SEVEN

LOS ANGELES, CA

City Hall

Nick's version of having a girl in every port is having a top-notch political operative in every major jurisdiction. In Los Angeles, it's Jimmy Van Meter.

Jimmy meets Nick outside the entrance to City Hall. Jimmy looks like the LA stereotype: chiseled jaw, blue eyes, windswept hair—and like he's carrying a stack of headshots in his briefcase, just in case he runs across a casting agent looking for someone to play a dashing lobbyist.

"Ready to launch?" Jimmy asks.

"Funny," Nick says. "You brought your 'A' material today."

They enter the building and cross the lobby that's perpetually under some kind of construction that will ultimately never be finished. Both of them silently think, *Union jobs.*

They get in the elevator and before Nick can reach for the buttons, Jimmy taps B.

"Isn't the mayor's office on three?" Nick asks.

"We're not meeting with the mayor's official staff."

Jimmy leads Nick into the basement cafeteria. It was built by whichever contractor builds the most depressing cafeterias in elementary schools across LA County, so almost no one ever stops in—which makes it the perfect spot for certain types of meetings. They stand in front of an ancient vending machine, where Jimmy fills three cups of lukewarm instant coffee.

"Who's the third coffee for?" Nick asks.

"Jenkins," Jimmy replies. Nick needs no other information. He's impressed Jimmy got the meeting.

Doug Jenkins is the best friend, former business partner, and permanent campaign manager of Los Angeles Mayor Julian Estes. The policy people upstairs in the mayor's office do research and write memos. But like everywhere, when it comes to actually making decisions, only the political people matter. And out of all the competing, varying, warring, conflicting members of the mayor's kitchen cabinet, Jenkins' voice speaks loudest.

Jenkins enters the room—an impossibly tall African-American man with a bald head and bushy mustache. Less of a leading man type and more of a memorable character actor. They settle into their seats, and Jenkins asks, "Nick, how's New York these days?"

"Cold. Snowy. Rainy. Slushy. Miserable. But I could never live anywhere else." The usual New York City response.

Jenkins just nods, so after a few seconds of silence, Nick dives straight into his spiel. Jenkins responds by sitting up straight and paying attention, but he's showing no expression whatsoever. It's making it hard for Nick to know which way to take the conversation.

When Nick finishes, Jenkins remains silent for a moment.

Then a few more moments.

It's clear this power dynamic is not a new thing for him. And it's clear he knows how to use silence as a weapon. Finally, he speaks. "What do we do if he asks if the car can actually fly? So far, there doesn't seem to be any evidence it can. All I read and hear and see are people criticizing your client Ms. Howard. A lot."

"The question isn't whether it can fly—it's where it flies first," Nick says. "And that's really your call, Doug. Do you want Austin to post the win? Looks pretty bad when an LA company has to search elsewhere to be allowed to make people's lives better. Especially if part of the deal is moving their headquarters to Texas."

Jenkins remains impassive at the threat, so Nick keeps talking.

"Look, it's pretty simple. You guys are looking hard at the next election. Governor and both Senate seats are all spoken for, meaning either Julian goes for the White House, or he ends up at a mid-tier law firm in Encino. He needs an edge. Being the first government official to make flying cars happen is completely unique. Changes everything. Everyone will know about it. No senator could do that. But you can. It turns Julian into America's mayor of innovation."

"If you don't have the narrative of being the candidate of tomorrow," Nick continues, feeling that heady rush of a pitch hitting exactly the right note, "you're just another boring guy in an extremely crowded Democratic primary. This is your chance to break through."

Ambition trumps everything in politics, so how could framing it around the biggest office of all not work?

Jenkins waits another twenty seconds, with a slightly sour look on his face.

"Nick, I hear what you're saying," Jenkins says. "In a perfect world, sure. It sounds great. We all hate sitting in traffic. But in the world we actually live in, if we're not the first choice of every major power broker here in LA, we'll never get the campaign off the ground. You know that. The national press will only take us seriously if we can rack up endorsements and cash. And the number-one guy we need is not only sitting right here in Los Angeles, he's the guy who hates your thing the most."

Jenkins is talking about Steve DeFrancesco, the longtime president of SMART—the local union representing the Sheet Metal, Air, Rail and Transportation sectors. Jimmy had already briefed Nick on exactly this—another advantage of having a dedicated person in the field.

DeFrancesco has been with the union his entire career, starting as a mechanic at the Burbank airport and working his way up through union leadership, then into its presidency in 1994. Whenever there's a list of the most powerful political leaders in California, he's on it. Whenever there's a list of the most powerful labor leaders in the country, he's on it. Whenever a Democratic presidential aspirant visits Los Angeles to raise money, they always make the pilgrimage to SMART's intentionally run-down headquarters in Studio City to seek DeFrancesco's blessing. DeFrancesco's short stature—five-foot-six on a good day—only heightens the perception of the power he wields.

DeFrancesco hasn't committed his support in the presidential race to anyone. But when Jenkins backchannelled the negotiation for SMART's most recent—and absurdly generous—municipal contract, reciprocal support was heavily implied.

"Nick, even if somehow all the coverage so far is wrong and your car can fly, think about all the local opposition to it. The same groups who came out in New York will come out here.

Hell, the environmentalists here will be even worse. Overcoming all that? That's too much political capital to spend on one thing."

"What if the opposition were eliminated? Or at least far less vocal?" Nick asks.

Jenkins leans back, then shrugs. "If you can deliver everyone or get them to just shut up, it's a different story. Maybe this works. Maybe. But if Steve doesn't either sign on, or at least stop complaining about this? There's nothing we can do. It lives or dies with him."

The meeting over, Jenkins excuses himself. They wait until he exits the cafeteria. Nick unwisely downs the rest of his coffee—the last sip always produces the most reflux—but he's in a fog from the time difference and needs the caffeine.

Nick asks, "What are the chances of getting DeFrancesco on board?"

Jimmy thinks for a moment. "You could offer to build a solid gold statue of him in front of the Hollywood Bowl. He'll still say no, but he might be polite about it."

Nick sighs. He knew this was coming, but that doesn't mean he has to feel good about it.

***

Nick knows better than to rent a car in Los Angeles (unless that car can fly), but he can't resist the image of driving down Santa Monica Boulevard in a convertible, sunglasses on, top down, surf music blaring.

His phone rings. Lucien. His fourteen-year-old son. Who almost never calls. At best, Nick gets a text reply once every few days, plus the occasional two-minute conversation when they're together every other weekend. Which is still more contact than he has with his nineteen-year-old libertarian daughter.

Nick hits the green button as fast as he possibly can. "Hi!"

"Hey, Dad."

"How's it going? How was school? What'd you have for lunch?"

"Fine, fine, tangerines."

"Just tangerines?"

"You know how bad the food is. That's why I asked you and Mom to get me a note from Dr. Kaufman saying I can bring in my own lunch." Nick was fine with the lunch workaround, even proud of his kid for finding the loophole, but his ex-wife was adamant they hold the line.

"Don't they have, like, sandwiches? Or a salad bar?" For sixty thousand a year, they'd better.

"It's all disgusting."

"What classes did you have today?" Nick asks, realizing the cafeteria conversation isn't going to get any better. "Is that Arabic teacher still giving you a hard time about your handwriting?"

"Always. It's so annoying. When will I ever need to write Arabic by hand?"

"Or anything by hand."

"Exactly!! You get it. So can you do something about it? You know, fix it. Like you do for everyone else?"

Nick's ex hadn't forbidden him from solving the Arabic problem—and Nick certainly wasn't going to ask for permission. But as he's about to lay out what they can do about it, another call comes through. Nick's instinct is to send it to voicemail. Keep talking to his son. But it's Susan. And if he doesn't answer, she'll call back again and again until he does.

Nick sighs. "Hey, buddy? I'm really sorry, but I've got to take this call. Can I call you back later?" Nick knows his call will go to voicemail and never be returned.

Nick doesn't wait for a reply as he punches the end-and-accept icon.

"Hey, Susan. I'm on my way to your place right now. Should be there in like fifteen minutes." Nick glances down at the GPS on his phone. "Maybe more like forty-five."

"I need you right now. I have the board on the other line. I'll connect you."

"Wait, what? The whole board?" Nick has dealt with presidents, heads of state, mob bosses, union leaders, academics, reporters, gadflies, and everything in between. He's met the Pope and the Dalai Lama. But as someone who didn't grow up around money and spent the first half of his career making government and political campaign salaries, talking to a room full of billionaires still produces anxiety. Especially when he can't see their faces.

"Okay. Nick, you've got everyone. Everyone, you've got Nick." Nick puts the car into autonomous mode so he can concentrate.

No one bothers with a polite greeting. "Nick, I know you're the political professional here and, of course, I completely defer to your expertise," says a board member whose voice Nick does not recognize. "But I have to say, we have some real concerns about the strategy. And while I don't have your political résumé, I have cohosted three different fundraising events for Chuck Schumer, so I clearly know my way around the block."

Here we go, Nick thinks.

"Look, guys, this is a big idea," Nick tells them. "Which means a big campaign. When you invested in FlightDeck, you knew it wasn't going to be easy. But you also knew that the toughest fights are the ones that produce the biggest returns. You want non-linear gains? Politics is a non-linear business."

"But Nick, there's been a lot of bad press already," another board member pipes up. "We were under the impression that the bills in all three cities would be well on their way by now. Our projections for the launch and expansion are based on that. Instead, the bills seem to be stuck, *and* we keep getting attacked by the opponents. People are saying rude things about us on Twitter. Even on Mastodon. Not just about Susan or you. About *us*. Someone on my security team even said that the Audubon Society might protest my annual ayahuasca retreat. This is the opposite of what we expected."

"They wouldn't do that, Nick, would they?" Susan interrupts.

"You don't mess with another man's ayahuasca," says someone else.

Nick has given up even trying to sort out who's who. "They can, and...honestly? They probably will." Nick's blood pressure rises as he anticipates the coming counterattack. "I'm just a political hack. What do I know about finance or technology? Nothing. But aren't you guys the ones who like to move fast and break things? Aren't you the great disrupters? Doesn't this come with the territory?"

"Well yes, but..." says someone, maybe the first guy again.

"Just to be clear, this is going to get worse before it gets better. A lot worse. Protests outside your homes, maybe even your beach homes. Weirdos in bird costumes showing up at your kid's birthday party."

"Ayahuasca disruptions," board member three helpfully offers.

"Exactly. But this is also exactly what you signed up for, and it's why you hired us."

"We…we get that," says yet another unfamiliar voice, probably some new board member who's worried about being judged for not having said anything on the call yet. "But this is not an auspicious beginning. We expected something…you know… Faster. Cheaper. Better… Different."

"Everyone wants things to be easy. But that's not how politics works. This is a rough business. They always try to knock you down in the first round. Strangle the baby in the crib. You gotta get back up. You think these guys are tough? Wait until Detroit comes at you."

"So what do we do?" Susan jumps in, sounding very pleased that Nick is more than holding his own.

"You? Nothing. Do absolutely nothing. Don't talk to the press. Don't give speeches. Don't tweet. Stay under the radar. All of you. I'm coming back from a meeting at City Hall right now and it's clear that our problem isn't a lack of attention."

"Then what is it?" a board member asks, cutting in.

"We need to turn our enemies into friends. Or, assuming that's not feasible, we need to make them so fucking toxic, their opposition actually helps us. That's doable. There's always something. But it's not an approach any of you should be associated with. So the less we discuss this, the better. For everyone."

While sparring with a gaggle of billionaires is not Nick's idea of a fun afternoon, the fact that they all suddenly have nothing to say feels gratifying.

The feeling doubles down when a text comes in from Susan.

"Well done. You handled those men—oh and one woman—really well. And they're not easy to handle. Trust me, I know."

And then a second text: "Carol agrees."

CHAPTER EIGHT

AUSTIN, TX

City Hall

Lisa uses a red light to steal a quick glance at Google Maps as she drives from her boutique hotel on South Congress Avenue across the bridge to City Hall. The roads are big, but somehow still confusing, and the GPS is slow to give instructions. So Lisa has to rely on her gut more than she would like. She's relieved when she sees Austin's very modern, very angular limestone City Hall pop up in the distance.

She doesn't want to be late. It's her first major solo meeting of the campaign. She's meeting with Hal Taylor, Deputy Mayor to Austin Mayor Don Pearce. Deputy Mayor Taylor's purview includes issues like zoning and aviation, so he's the guy for flying cars.

Lisa pulls into the parking garage next door, glad to find she's running a few minutes early. She hopes the meeting doesn't go on too long—it's her first time in Austin. The weather is great—sunny and mid-sixties—and the place gives off some cool college-town vibes. She'd like to explore a bit before Nick lands and they meet with some of Pearce's donors to see how they can grease the wheels.

But that will all be later.

Taylor's office is surprisingly large and well-appointed for a civil servant. Lots of photos of him and famous Texans like George W. Bush, Michael Dell, Jerry Jones, and Roger Clemens. Even more signed UT football helmets and a Texas Tech basketball ensconced in a glass case, signed by Bobby Knight. Everything is shiny and well-displayed, which tells her a lot about the kind of man he is.

Preoccupied with appearance.

Taylor, a heavyset yet handsome man in his fifties with a mop of brown hair, barely acknowledges her when she comes in. As Lisa ticks off all of the benefits of Austin legalizing flying cars, he's on his phone for most of it, hunting and pecking keys. At one point, a sound emerges and Lisa thinks he's watching TikTok videos.

"Hal," Lisa says, trying to salvage the meeting, "a lot of people like the mayor. In fact, based on our data, most people in Austin here love him. He polls well in the suburbs too, even does okay in the panhandle and a few parts of East Texas. But as soon as you run statewide next year for AG, we both know that's all going to change. The Republicans are going to paint your candidate as a typical Austin liberal who's totally out of touch with the rest of Texas. You need to get out ahead of that. And I think I have a way."

Taylor smiles, though more ruefully than anything else, and doesn't look up from his phone. "You're talking about politics. I do substance. Why are you bothering me with this?"

"Because you oversee zoning. And economic development. And aviation."

"Yes, we've established that's my portfolio. In the government, not political campaigns. Is there anything else I can do for you, Ms. Lim?" Taylor pushes his chair back from his desk and starts to rise.

"This is your one way to beat back the GOP attacks. Which are coming and will be rough. Really rough. And will set you back, regardless of your specific purview."

Taylor sits back down, at least a little bit intrigued. "How so?"

"We already know how they're going to come at you. Pearce is a disconnected liberal who hates business, hates jobs, and loves taxes. A mayor who prioritizes coastal progressive ideology, social justice, and critical race theory ahead of results for the people of Texas. Flying cars knocks out both of those arguments."

Taylor doesn't reply this time, but he raises an eyebrow, which Lisa takes as a sign to keep going.

"Pearce becomes the first mayor to legalize flying cars? Now you're the mayor of the future. Someone who can see around the corner. Further innovation. Make things happen."

"That says to me that we're good on tech. Fine. Everyone knows that already. But none of that means we're creating new jobs here in Austin."

"You are if FlightDeck moves its headquarters to Austin as part of the deal."

Taylor arches an eyebrow again. "They'd do that?"

"They want to show that it works. Just get it off the ground. Literally." Taylor doesn't laugh. Lisa isn't sure if he even has a sense of humor. "So if you can beat New York and LA to the punch, there's no reason they couldn't move their lab and engineers and designers and operational team down here." She pauses. "Of course, LA has the same offer on the table. Soon, New York will too."

Lisa pegged him the second she walked into the room and he decided his phone was more important than this meeting. He's not the type who wants to be told what to do—especially by a young Chinese-American woman from New York City.

Then he smirks, and Lisa doesn't like the shape of it. "I'll tell you what. Rather than sitting here debating, bring one of those flying cars here to Austin. We'll take a ride out to my ranch in the hill country. See if it's what you say. Get some nice pictures in the process. If it works out, I'll take this to the mayor and make your case. If not, then we'll both know just how real your technology is." With that, he pushes his chair back again, stands up, and excuses himself to head to another meeting. Probably so he can scroll through TikTok some more.

As Lisa takes the stairs to the street two at a time, she knows she needs to talk to Nick—fast. If they can call Taylor on his bluff and prove the car works, then Taylor may have no choice but to push hard to get the mayor on board and push the legislation through. And once the genie is out of the bottle, it never goes back in. If Austin starts allowing flying cars, within a few years, every city in the nation will too. Global domination is a few years behind that.

And if anyone was going to approve this thing fast, it'd be Texas, where "regulation" is a four-letter word.

There's a snarl of traffic at the mouth of the parking garage. Lisa doesn't want to have this conversation in public—there are too many City Hall employees milling around, and she doesn't know who works for whom. Plus, she still isn't sure how to get to her hotel, despite having just driven the exact route (in reverse) twenty-seven minutes ago. So she hops in a cab idling outside on West 2nd Street. She'll come back for the car later.

Lisa normally avoids regular cabs because too often they're dirty, they're slow, and their pricing system is so convoluted and opaque, the driver can basically charge whatever he wants. This taxi is no different. As the driver smokes a cigarette out the window and charges her $35 to drive three quarters of a mile, she thinks, *Fuck these guys. They're slow and lazy and arrogant. They rip people off. Their business deserves to die. We're going to pass this fucking bill. Everywhere.*

As soon as Lisa gets to her room, she FaceTimes Nick. When he answers, he's in the back seat of a car. It looks like a hostage video.

"Hey," she says. "What time does your flight land? We have a few items related to the campaign to discuss. Maybe we can grab a drink before our dinner with Pearce's major donors?"

"Oh. Right." He pauses for a second. "I can't make it to Austin tonight. Something came up."

Lisa waits for him to offer more information, but he doesn't. She racks her brain trying to figure out what he means. If it were a client emergency, she'd probably already know about it—or he'd at least tell her. He's not married at the moment, so there's no spouse he has to answer to. It's too early for spring break. Maybe one of his kids is sick?

But Nick once went on a six-day, all-expenses-paid junket to Singapore with half the casino industry while his son was having his tonsils removed.

Lisa starts to ask what's wrong, but then sees the opportunity and takes a big swing. "Since you seem pretty busy, what if I start running the FlightDeck campaign on my own? I'd still check in with you, but I feel like it's time. I'm ready."

It doesn't seem like Nick is even listening. He replies with a vague "Uh huh."

Lisa takes that as a yes. "Great! Thank you! I'll send you a daily update. Seven a.m. Every morning. And obviously, we can talk strategy any time you want."

Now Nick hears her. "Wait. What? I wasn't paying attention. Sorry. Tell me again what you were saying?"

"That I'd like to take over the campaign and run it on my own since you seem pretty busy."

"Oh. No. I'm not comfortable with that. At least not yet. Maybe the next one."

He clicks off without saying goodbye. Lisa falls back into her chair, regretting that she wasted $35 on the cab ride here and will waste more on the ride back, just to get the car and end up back at square one.

CHAPTER NINE

BROOKLYN, NY

Turgenev Nightclub

Nick's Uber pulls up in front of Turgenev, the infamous Russian nightclub located in the heart of Brighton Beach. The club is Eastern Bloc chic: From a distance, it's all crystal, red carpeting, and copious gold leaf, not unlike most casinos in Atlantic City. Look a little closer, and it's all flimsy and crumbling. Which works perfectly. The décor brings the locals in and gives them the illusion of luxury, and it keeps people from Manhattan out. For Nick, while his childhood corner of Maspeth in Northeast Queens has a decidedly different vibe than Brighton Beach, and while Nick's barely-break-even-in-a-good-year, small-drug-store-owning parents were very different from Viktor, the every-borough-against-Manhattan comradery still prevails.

When Nick walks inside the currently-empty nightclub, he finds Viktor Velonova standing by the front door to greet him. Viktor—silver-maned, barrel-chested, yellow fingers and teeth—is known to readers of the *Daily News* as the taxi medallion king of Brooklyn, though it's really just one piece of his empire. He also owns three nightclubs, six optical shops, eleven pharmacies, a renewable energy crypto mining outfit, and a mid-size chain of physical therapy centers on Staten Island. Under his tutelage, a couple of those PTs have become the highest-grossing Medicare fraudsters outside of South Florida.

The medallions, though—that's the biggest source of his power. In order for a cab to legally operate in New York City, it needs a medallion: a license from the city. There are about thirteen thousand medallions in circulation, and that number is capped. It keeps supply down and keeps the cab companies in business, which is why Uber was so disruptive. Suddenly anyone with a smartphone could become a cab driver, and cab companies didn't have the market cornered anymore.

Like any commodity, medallions can be sold on the private market.

Viktor owns 420 of them. Which at one time made him a half-billionaire on paper. Until the market collapsed and the price went from $1.3 million to $130,000.

Nick knew this conversation was inevitable. Given their history and Viktor's reach, they'd have to meet sooner or later. Turns out it's sooner. He was waiting at LAX with a ticket to meet Lisa in Austin when the text from Velonova instructed Nick to come by ASAP.

It's been so long, Nick's not even sure how Viktor got his number. And the text certainly didn't feel like a request. That gave the whole thing an unsettling tone.

Viktor's vibe is surprisingly friendly. He immediately embraces Nick. He reeks of Romanian cigars, menthol cigarettes, and Manischewitz. And despite decades of living in New York City, his Russian accent is still thick as an Odessan coffee. "My friend! How long have we known each other? I always try to remember. Since the Giuliani days? You were so good at carrying his briefcase."

Nick winces at the backhanded compliment and tries to smile. "Thanks again for delivering those last-minute votes. We needed them."

"Rudy and his client have always been loyal friends to the Russian people. But you? With this flying car thing? Maybe not so much."

Nick doesn't say anything. Viktor keeps going.

"My medallions took a beating when Uber came along. If people can now start taking flying cars everywhere," Viktor flaps his arms like wings, "who's going to want to use a yellow cab? They'll be dead. Kaput."

Nick nods. Time for the pitch he spent half the flight from LA rehearsing. "Look, Viktor, you're absolutely right. This could all be very, very bad for you guys. I'm not gonna pretend otherwise. Flying cars is a death knell for your medallions. But that assumes two things. First, that the flying car bill passes. And second, that you're on the wrong side of the trade. If you start moving assets from yellow cabs to flying cars now, maybe this all works out just fine for you."

"You can make that happen?"

"Which one?" Nick asks, testing the waters.

Viktor narrows his eyes. "I understand how you tell your client at FlightDeck that we join forces. Take me away as an opponent. Have me inside the tent pissing out. Makes sense. But how can you make the bill fail when you are the one running the campaign to pass it?"

"Viktor," Nick pauses for effect, "politics is sometimes a complicated business. Things don't always go according to plan.

And sometimes," Nick smiles and spreads out his hands, "even the best campaigns still come up a little short."

Viktor smiles. "Especially when you plan for them not to go as planned."

"Exactly."

"And what would it take to ensure that this...particular campaign comes up a little short?"

"FlightDeck is paying us a hundred and fifty a month, so..."

Nick hopes that Viktor gets what he's implying—and from the way his eyebrows dart up, yeah, he does.

"You seemed so...I don't know...idealistic in the Rudy days," Viktor says.

"I was twenty-six. And sometimes there are greater needs."

"Yes. I heard about that. But I don't pay retail."

Nick winces and wonders how much Viktor knows about his situation. More than he's comfortable with. Neither of them speaks for a good thirty seconds.

Finally, Viktor says, "I hear there are a lot of people looking for you."

Well then. He knows a lot. Nick shrugs. "I'm a popular guy."

"How about this?" Viktor asks. "If the bill were to fail, I could meet with these people. Tell them what a nice guy you are. See what kind of understanding we can come to. Maybe even... compound things for you, *da*?"

Nick's stomach twists into a knot. Viktor is offering to buy out his debt, which is good. But then he owes Viktor, which is the worst kind of bad.

The people he owes money to now—they're serious, but not Viktor serious.

Nick doesn't want to say too much. He doesn't trust Viktor, and he knows better than to push Viktor too hard. So instead, he offers his hand. They shake. A brief look flashes across Viktor's face. Disappointment? Nick isn't sure.

"Nice to catch up," Nick says.

"Very nice," Viktor says.

***

After a pro forma bro hug, Viktor watches Nick climb into an Uber—in any other neighborhood, taking a rideshare service would have been a clear fuck-you, but Viktor can give him a pass. It's not easy hailing a cab in South Brooklyn.

There's a shuffling sound behind him, and he turns to find a tough-but-handsome-looking white woman in her late thirties, her brunette hair in a pixie cut, wearing a boxy, cheap gray suit. She's eating a chicken shawarma and looks at Viktor like she's waiting for something.

"Think this one will be useful?" Viktor asks.

"We'll see," Agent Justine Wheeler of the FBI responds.

CHAPTER TEN

NEW YORK CITY

East Village, Madison Square Park

As Lisa walks out the front door of her Avenue B, marginally-converted-from-a-tenement apartment building and heads to the corner bodega to pick up her usual breakfast (two sugar-free Red Bulls and a toasted English muffin with butter), she notices the Kosher Mexican Korean food truck parked down the block.

Weird. Last she saw it, it was outside the Firewall office on Twentieth and Park. Lisa likes Mexican food. She knows her way around Korean food. She's not sure how the two cuisines fit together. The kosher part is even more confusing.

Who knows, maybe there's a demand among Orthodox Jews for Mexican Korean fusion cuisine? But if that were the case, wouldn't the truck do better business in someplace like Boro Park or Williamsburg or even the Upper West Side?

Guess that's New York, Lisa thinks, as she thanks Ernesto for breakfast and starts the half-hour walk to meet Nick and the team in Madison Square Park. To Lisa, walking not only saves money and burns calories, it also represents freedom. Growing up in the DC suburbs meant relying on her dad for a ride everywhere. If he remembered to pick her up.

The tradition of holding their new ideas meeting at the Madison Square Park dog run started before Lisa joined the firm. Apparently, the team was supposed to meet a client there about some dog-related insurance company. The client bailed, so they hung around and spitballed some new ideas. Three of the ideas turned into new revenue, so Nick considers it a good luck charm.

When Lisa arrives, her colleagues Allison Bernstein and Alphonso Lewis are already waiting. Allison, wearing a jet-blue Prada suit, her brown hair pulled back into an efficient bun, runs comms for the firm. *Allison looks good*, Lisa thinks. But in Lisa's experience, she knows what happens when she's too focused on her own appearance—everyone else focuses on it too. And then, instead of Lisa being a highly respected, badass political strategist, she's a very attractive woman. Before the subject of politics even comes up. Lisa knows the two are not mutually exclusive. Allison knows it too. They just reached different conclusions about whether leaning into it does more harm or good.

Alphonso, in his hipster sweater and striped slacks, oversees paid media. It's cold enough still for gloves and a hat, but both he and Allison seem opposed to opting for warmth. Maybe they're trying to show Nick how tough they are.

They've both been at Firewall a lot longer than Lisa, and her immediate closeness with Nick created some underlying tension. Fortunately, Lisa's self-aware enough to realize that, and she's worked hard to stay on their good sides.

Allison is texting furiously, and Alphonso is petting a pug puppy who's been eagerly saying hello to every person and dog in the vicinity. Nick walks in right behind Lisa, closing the gate to the dog run so that none of the animals can escape onto Broadway and into oncoming traffic.

"Okay," Nick announces. "New business meeting comes to order. Go." Nick usually starts with some chitchat, Lisa thinks. He seems stressed.

"Wait," Allison interrupts. "Don't we have our hands full with FlightDeck?"

Nick looks at her like she just grew a second head. "We always need more clients. Always. Especially now." Nick's mentality is no different from every founder of every business: no amount of revenue is enough.

Lisa jumps in first. "Okay, how about this? Facebook is everyone's least favorite social network, right? Or Meta now—whatever they're called. They're an easy target. Republicans hate them. Democrats hate them. Parents hate them. Kids don't even know Facebook exists. The media hates them. Congress is going to pummel them with new privacy laws, antitrust laws, liability laws. Beating up on Facebook may be the only bill that can get through the entire process in DC these days."

"You want us to pitch Facebook again?" Nick asks. "After the last time? I think I'm still banned from their Nashville office." Lisa wasn't there for Nick's legendary mid-afternoon bourbon bender on Lower Broadway. But she knows it was embarrassing enough for him to cut down on his drinking, even after he somehow got the YouTube video taken down.

"No. Not at all. I want to lean into their problem. Let's find some startups that have tech that actually enhances privacy. Sign them as clients. Make them the good guys in this fight. Mandate their product. Create the market for them. Just need to figure out who those startups are."

"Okay, not bad. What else? Alphonso?"

"We haven't done one of these in a while, so I came prepared." Alphonso pulls a mess of crumpled yellow legal papers out of his pocket. He's the most creative of the group, and he keeps a running list of ideas expressly for this meeting. Two more dogs come over to Alphonso to say hi and sniff his ankles. He gently pets both of them.

"Two words: online funeral. You plan the whole thing on your phone, soup to nuts. One app does it all. Burial services. Floral arrangements. Obituary placement in dozens of outlets instantaneously. 3D printed tombstones. Virtual cremations. Automatic cancellation of the dead guy's social accounts and streaming platforms. Launching ashes into outer space via satellite if that's your jam. You can use AI to write the eulogy. Livestream the whole service so that no one has to actually go anywhere. Convenient and emotionally moving—all in one."

"Die Easy?" Lisa offers.

Nick groans, though it's unclear if he's reacting to Lisa's corny name or Alphonso's crazy idea. "It feels like you're planning my funeral," he says to both of them.

"That's okay. I've got more." Alphonso scans his list. "Oh, this one is good. So Gene and I rescued this Corgi a few months ago? You know, much easier and much cheaper than having kids. Super cute, super friendly, doesn't poop in the bed. Just some skid marks from time to time—"

"Get to the point."

"Getting Gary around town isn't that easy."

"Wait," Allison asks. "Who's Gary?"

"The dog," Nick and Lisa say in unison.

"Right! Here's the problem," Alphonso continues. "The doggy spa we like is in Williamsburg. The trainer is in Bushwick.

The therapist is in Park Slope. It's a whole day affair. We barely have time to shop at the co-op by the time we're done."

Alphonso hands each of them a map of Brooklyn with the three locations and lines connecting each one to the next. Lisa looks at it incredulously.

"So think Uber, but for pets. Not just dogs. Not just cats. All pets. Chickens are big in Brooklyn these days. Pigeons too." Alphonso pauses. "I think the same thing could also work for small children."

"Puber?" Allison offers.

Lisa can't tell if Alphonso genuinely likes this idea or is just fucking with them.

Either way, Nick's had enough. "Uber barely even makes a profit. Now you want to expand it to small children and pets? How are these even revenue ideas?"

Nick looks at his phone, holds up a finger meant to tell everyone to hang on for a moment, and walks a few feet away, speaking loudly into his phone. "Sid! Sid! What do you mean dogs can't take Robitussin? It worked during World War II. Battle of the Bulge. They'll be fine. Don't cancel anything. The race goes on as planned."

Nick hangs up and rejoins the group. "I kind of like that Facebook idea." He looks at Alphonso. "Before I forget, Alphonso, how's the spot coming?"

"It's done." Alphonso whips out his iPhone to show the team the latest version of the FlightDeck intro ad.

"Shouldn't we watch this up in the office?" Lisa asks. "One of the bigger monitors?"

"Nah, it's like the car test," Nick says. "Before a band locks the mix on an album, they drive around listening to it in the car to see how it plays on shitty car speakers in the real world, rather than on expensive studio equipment. Gives you a more honest look at the quality. If the ad lands here, it can land anywhere. Alphonso? Fire it up."

Alphonso nods and hits play as they huddle around the screen.

> *VO: Life is hard. There are so many things to worry about.*
>
> *We see shots of Ukrainian refugees fleeing violence, of immigrant children held in detention centers on the Rio Grande, of gunshots reverberating in a south Texas school.*

"Wait," Allison says. "Pause it for a second. We got Obama to do the voiceover?"

"We got a guy who sounds like Obama," Alphonso clarifies.

"But then won't people think it's Obama?"

"I hope so," Nick says.

"It really sounds a lot like him," Allison says. "Seems risky. The Obama people might get upset. Then that becomes the story."

"Exactly," Lisa replies. "If they publicly demand we pull the ad, it'll drive tons of coverage. The more Twitter gets outraged that we hired someone to impersonate the president, the more people will search us out just to watch the ad. The left will get angry and the right will think it's funny. Works either way because they both drive eyeballs to the spot. And even better, the more Twitter gets outraged, the more print and TV reporters then think it's an important story and the more they cover it. Controversy over an Obama impersonator is probably better for us than if Obama himself actually did narrate the ad."

Nick smiles and says, “Nice work, grasshopper.”

Allison rolls her eyes a little. Alphonso doesn’t seem to register it. Aside from being called grasshopper again, Lisa takes it as a sign that, yeah, maybe things are okay.

Nick nods to Alphonso to click play.

> *VO: We just got past a global pandemic.*
>
> *We see hospitals overflowing with patients, beds in all the hallways. We see people waiting in their cars, backed up for miles, to get help from a food pantry.*
>
> *VO: For all we know, another could be right around the corner. We need something to look forward to. Something to give us hope that all the struggle, all the pain is somehow worth it. We need to believe that tomorrow truly can be better than today.*
>
> *We see footage of the FlightDeck vehicle lifting off.*

“Hold on. Pause,” Lisa says. “All of our headaches lately are related to these things *not* flying. Where did this come from?”

“This was the proof-of-concept video they showed us at the first meeting, remember?” Nick asks.

“I thought that was CGI,” Allison says.

Nick shrugs. “It’s good CGI. Keep going.”

> *VO: We need to believe that new ideas, new technology—that human ingenuity itself—can solve our darkest, deepest problems.*

We see simulated shots of FlightDeck's vehicle soaring in the air, with packed freeways below: shots of MoPac in Austin, the 405 in LA, the Cross-Bronx Expressway in NYC.

VO: It all has to start somewhere. It has to start with something. And that something is finally here.

We see shots of FlightDeck vehicles landing smoothly and dropping off happy passengers at key landmarks in New York City, Austin, and LA: the Flatiron Building, the Texas State Capitol, the Getty.

VO: Will some say it can't be done? Of course they will. They'll say it's too soon. They'll say it's not ready. That we need more time.

We see unflattering shots of Ted Cruz and Elizabeth Warren wagging their fingers interspersed with the indignant faces of Rachel Maddow and Sean Hannity sermonizing into the camera.

VO: People always say that. And history always leaves them behind.

We see shots of people turning off their TVs, closing their laptops, putting their phones back in their pockets.

VO: If there was ever a time to take a leap of faith—if there was ever a time to jump headfirst into the future—it's right now.

We see shots of rockets lifting off, of cars gliding through the air.

VO: Salvation is possible. The future is within reach. It always has been. We've just needed a way to get there.

Shots of the FlightDeck logo appear, before the screen fades to black.

Everyone turns and looks at Nick. "What do you think?" Alphonso asks.

"It's fucking great," Nick says. "I know it's a little last minute, but are there any sixties left for the NBA All-Star Game?"

"A couple of spots at halftime, one during the third quarter, and then a bunch more pre- and post-game," Alphonso replies. "You think Susan can afford it?"

"Yeah. I mean, it's not like it's the Super Bowl. How much can it be? Have the bill sent directly to Susan."

"So we're good to go?" Alphonso asks.

Most people in Nick's position would hedge and say, "Let's poll first," before signing off on a multimillion-dollar ad buy. Or they'd stall and say, "Let's do focus groups and see what they think of the ad." Some might even punt to, "Let's see what the client thinks." Not that they really care what the client thinks, because if the client knew what they wanted, Nick wouldn't have a job. But it's a way to delay having to make a decision.

Nick never does anything like that.

"Ship it," Nick says.

As the group heads back to the office, Lisa tries to get Nick's attention without it being too obvious. She finally does as they're turning left from Broadway onto Twentieth Street, the city's new restaurant row.

"Hey. Everything okay?"

Nick looks confused.

"Just, you know, dropping out of the Austin dinner..." Lisa says.

"Oh yeah," Nick says. "All good. You know how kids are. Crazy one moment, totally fine the next. Shit. I should've gotten Lucien something from LA. A LeBron jersey or something. I guess I can order it online. He'll never know the difference. And I still need to text the headmaster about that handwriting thing. He'll come through. He still owes me for cleaning up that zoning mess."

Lisa actually doesn't know how kids are or what land use problem Nick solved for the school, but she knows what Nick is saying doesn't sound right, doesn't sound like him. Didn't sound right when she was in Austin either.

Lisa waits, but Nick doesn't offer any further explanation. As they push through the revolving door into their lobby, Lisa wants to ask more questions. But that voice in her head—the one she ignores far too often—tells her not to.

"Listen," Nick says, "I'm off to see Joe in a few. Wish me luck, okay?"

Joe Navarro, the mayor of New York City. That ought to be a fun meeting. One that she'd like to be involved with, but since Nick doesn't offer an invitation, she doesn't want to push that either.

"Good luck," she says. "Hopefully he doesn't get so hung up on whether these things even work. You know, I'm starting to wonder..."

"Hey," Nick says, a sharpness to his voice that freezes Lisa in place. "That's what the engineers are for. Our job is to sell it and collect the checks, okay?"

Lisa wants to respond but finds that she can't. Nick's face turns down, like he's regretting what he said, or at least how he said it. For a moment, she thinks he's going to apologize. Then his phone buzzes in his hand.

"Gotta take this," he says, looking at the screen. "I'll be back in a few hours."

Nick stalks off to an alcove to answer the phone. Lisa doesn't like his answer. She cares if these things work. She's been wondering if it's all vaporware. Maybe legalizing something that doesn't actually exist is a better political accomplishment, or at least a better story at the secret lobbyist hangout, but it doesn't do much for society. And if this thing isn't real, long term, they're better off not being associated with it, no matter how much Susan's paying.

Lisa considers pushing the subject with Nick, but he obviously has something on his mind.

There's got to be someone with a realistic sense of this thing, she thinks. She digs out her phone, then absentmindedly scrolls contacts, until she lands on Y.

CHAPTER ELEVEN

LOS ANGELES, CA

FlightDeck HQ

"Wait," Yevgeny says, looking up from a pile of losing scratch-off tickets. "The echolocation thing is actually working? Seriously?"

His assistant, Bryon—today in a lime-green hoodie, nervous as ever—sheepishly nods, not quite sure if his boss wants Susan's idea to work or not. "Yes. Adding sound sensory capabilities to the vehicle seems to improve its ability to navigate obstacles."

"In theory."

"Well, yeah. This is all simulated. But I think we'd see the same thing in the real world."

Each test vehicle costs $1.8 million to build and assemble. Yevgeny's already burned through seven of them—four of them literally crashed and burned—so they switched to simulated testing in September.

He needs a moment to figure out how he feels about this.

Good, he decides. Progress is good, even if it will make Susan more unbearable for the foreseeable future. "Do you think we are ready to test it live?"

"Well..." Bryon stalls.

Yevgeny's been on the other end of this conversation enough times to know that tone. "Well what? Our problem has been the sensors. It sounds like we have developed a way to address the sensory issue. What is the problem now?"

"Well...it appears that the steering function is now having issues."

"What kinds of issues?" It's amazing how fast a good feeling can disappear.

"The vehicle doesn't always turn in the direction it's supposed to."

"I thought we solved the steering issue two months ago."

"So did we. Maybe it's a glitch that we haven't caught yet. But given that we can't control the flight path at the moment, I'm not sure a live test is a good idea."

Yevgeny nods distractedly, which Bryon takes as permission to leave the room as quickly as possible. Once he's alone, Yevgeny bangs his head on the desk. Once. Twice. Three times. Stops just shy of the fourth. He hasn't done this since he was nine and his parents were getting divorced.

He pulls out a legal pad and a pen and starts writing down the pros and cons of staying in a job that's now driving him to self-harm. Chance to make a lot of money—like tens of millions—if everything works out. Chance to make tech history as the guy who successfully built the first flying car. Those are both pretty appealing.

But then the other side. Susan is impossible to deal with, even before her batshit idea somehow turned out to be right. The tech still isn't working—and maybe it never will. Statistically speaking, most startups fail, so the odds of his equity going to zero are a lot higher than anything else. And engineers at his level can name their job, salary, and options at almost any tech company, so why suffer here?

Can't hurt to at least see what's out there, right? Worst case, he wastes a little time meeting with people, learns a thing or two. What was the name of that headhunter who used to bother him at SpaceX all the time? He's pretty sure it was Stan. Or Glenn. Probably Glenn.

Yevgeny takes out his phone, which has been in Do Not Disturb, so he has two dozen emails—mostly newsletters and spam—and a few notifications from Twitter and Duolingo (he feels like he's mastered English at this point but keeps forgetting to delete the app).

He's about to put the phone down again when he notices a text from Lisa, the political consultant in New York.

> *LISA: Hey Yevgeny. It's Lisa from Firewall. Just wanted to check in and see how things are coming along with getting those cars airborne. Need to get one to Texas ASAP.*

Yevgeny stares at it for a moment. *Not well,* he wants to say. But what does that help? If he tells her where things stand, does she disappear—and with her, their chance of passing this thing anyplace? And then his chance of this job actually working out?

Worse, will it get back to Susan?

Hell, is this a test *devised* by Susan?

Yevgeny doesn't know. All he can hear is Susan's voice ringing in his head.

He taps out a reply. What Susan would want him to say. *Very close! Expect good news soon.* Safer that way.

He wonders if the exclamation point feels a little too desperate, but instead of thinking on it too much, he puts his phone back in Do Not Disturb mode and turns to his desktop computer, where he starts pecking for Glenn the headhunter's email address.

CHAPTER TWELVE

ASTORIA, NEW YORK CITY

Neptune Diner

When Joe Navarro wants to meet with someone in a semi-private setting, he goes to Queens. Neptune Diner in Astoria not only serves some of the best Greek salads and BLTs in the city, it's also located right off the Triborough Bridge, which is a short drive from Gracie Mansion.

Nick has been summoned to Neptune Diner before (usually when Navarro wanted him to raise money), so even though Nick requested the meeting this time, the location doesn't surprise him. And having grown up in a neighborhood and a family where rare meals out of the house were all—and only—in diners like this, Nick feels at home. The mayor's security detail has cleared off a section in the back, giving the mayor both some privacy and the ability to walk through the entire diner, shaking hands and taking credit for leaving Manhattan, looking like a mayor of the people.

"Joe," Nick says as he approaches, "thanks for meeting me."

Navarro's in work mode, his tie shoved in between the buttons of his shirt so he doesn't get food on it, the sleeves of his baby-blue button-down rolled up. The job they say is the second hardest in politics must be especially stressful these days—Navarro's somehow not yet fully gray hair is unkempt, and he didn't shave this morning. Nick tries to remember if he caught anything in the newspapers the last few days that might be vexing him but can't recall seeing anything.

Navarro just nods at him as he takes his seat, and tears into a packet of packaged wheat toast, which he uses to mop up the remnants of egg yolk on the otherwise empty plate in front of him. The waiter comes over with a menu for Nick. Navarro waves him away.

So it's gonna be a quick meeting, Nick thinks.

"I know why you're here," Navarro says. "I checked into your flying car idea. You know I want to help you whenever I can. Always. But I gotta say, this thing's a fucking nightmare. How can I support this? The transit workers hate it—"

"What if I told you we had Sharpton on board?" Nick interrupts.

"Do you?"

"Well, no. But it's possible. We're trying."

"It's not enough," Navarro continues. "The taxi guys hate this bill. The whole progressive crowd sees this as their next crusade, and while I hate the fucking progressives, I also don't need them harassing me all day. And the bird nuts. Don't even get me started there. Plus, the experts at DOT say this is a really bad idea. They say it's dangerous."

"I thought danger was your middle name!"

Navarro shakes his head. "It's Herman."

Nick takes this all in. "Fine. Everything you said is probably true. Lots of powerful people hate flying cars. Some of them are your friends. But you know who else hates it? Uber."

"So?"

"What do you mean *so*? You're telling me you don't want revenge? After everything they did to you? The humiliation? The ads? The digital campaign? Turning the whole City Council against you? Cutting your favorability in half?"

"I've moved on. I've got bigger things to think about. Like what the fuck I'm going to do in ten months when my term ends."

"Come on," Nick says. "Who are you kidding? There's no way you're not still angry about this. This bill fucks Uber completely. Their whole message to Wall Street is that they're ten steps ahead of everyone else. Then some random tech company comes along and launches flying cars? What do you think that does to Uber's stock? It plummets."

"What makes you think we care?" Navarro asks.

Because if there are two things Joe Navarro cares about, it's money and power. When he proposed limiting the number of Uber drivers at the behest of his donors in the taxi industry (namely one Viktor Velonova), Uber hit back so hard, they not only killed Navarro's bill, they wrote the playbook on how every opponent should go after him ever since. It's hard to imagine Navarro wanting to leave office without evening the score.

"Unless you've gone really soft on us in your final year in office, Joe, we both know that you, personally, care. A lot. And given that you can't run again anyway, I'm not sure you're really all that scared of the Socialists or the unions or the bird nuts. It just gives you cover until you see which side benefits you more."

Navarro offers Nick a half-shrug.

"Look," Navarro says after a long pause. "It's a big idea. I like big ideas. I'm a big idea guy. So, you know, is there a world where this could work? I don't know. Possibly. Maybe. Too soon to say."

"Maybe" means "definitely" if the price is right, Nick thinks. Nick isn't sure if the price means more campaign money for whatever Navarro wants to pursue next, or something else.

Nick looks around to make sure there's no one within earshot and leans forward. "Look, Joe, it's you and me right now, okay? Let's be real. You've got so much shit hanging over you. The campaign finance allegations. That thing with your brother-in-law. You walk out of office today as the mayor who promised to unite the city and then spent his entire tenure showing up late for press conferences and handing out favors to his friends. You do this? You're the innovator. You get to rewrite your entire story."

Navarro leans forward, getting closer to Nick, and narrows his eyes. "I don't need a title. I don't need a narrative. I need a job. I'm not going to embarrass myself like every other mayor from this town who tried to run for president. That's a losing proposition. Anything else worth running for is already locked up. Right now, I just need money. All this," he waves his hand around, "is gonna disappear." He leans back in his seat. "Maybe you're hiring."

Nick laughs it off. "We're looking for a few interns, but I'm afraid you might be overqualified."

But Navarro just holds his stare.

Nick isn't sure if he's serious, so he fills the silence. "You know the law. You can't lobby your colleagues for a year after leaving office anyway, so even if you're serious, what good would you be?"

Navarro shrugs. "There are always ways."

Well, this is interesting. Navarro has come to him looking for favors before, but never one that bordered on the edge of illegal. What does he want? Some kind of off-the-books honorarium to be a consultant? Rather than explore it, or use it to push the car issue, Nick files it away.

Nick pushes things a little further to suss out the last piece of information he needs. "How's your relationship with Viktor these days?" Velonova was one of Navarro's biggest donors for years, until he pushed the mayor into a war with Uber. When the battle didn't go his way, Velonova lost favor.

Navarro nods his head. "You know. It's Viktor. So like everyone else. It's fine."

Nick smiles. "Fine" means Navarro hasn't gotten over it yet. "Fine" means Viktor has failed at restoring the relationship. It means that fucking over Uber is still a way to get Navarro on board—or at least get him to start listening.

CHAPTER THIRTEEN

NEW YORK CITY

East Village

Nothing had sat well with Lisa that day. Nick was clearly hiding something. The campaign was being attacked on all sides and, so far, they weren't really mounting an effective counterattack. The TV ad was…fine? Lisa wishes she'd been more vocal about it at the dog run. She has reservations. And when almost all of your self-worth comes from your career, when work isn't going well, nothing is.

But the day finally, thankfully, ends, and Lisa walks back to her East Village apartment to order in some pho from Hanoi House, drink a beer, and watch that reality show on Hulu about the sexy yacht crew and all the trouble they're constantly causing below deck.

As she approaches her apartment building, two women step out of the shadows and approach her. One is a white lady in her thirties, her hair pixie short. The other is a Latina woman in her fifties, her gray hair pulled into a loose bun atop her head. They're both wearing cheap gray suits. Lisa's never seen them before, but she's watched enough movies to know what's next.

"Ms. Lim?" the younger one asks.

"Yeah?"

"I'm Agent Justine Wheeler from the FBI. This is my partner, Agent Sarah Rosario. We need to talk."

Wheeler flashes a sympathetic smile. Lisa flashes a phony smile back, feigning calm. You have to be a sociopath not to be terrified by law enforcement agents waiting for you on your doorstep. But Lisa is level-headed enough to remember the golden rule of politics: never, ever talk to the FBI.

"They actually teach you this in orientation," she says. "When the FBI shows up at your door, take their card and have your lawyer call them back." She puts out her palm for their cards.

"They also teach you not to defraud your clients," says Rosario.

"Or at least not get caught," adds Wheeler.

Wow, hard-boiled agents, just like on Netflix, Lisa thinks. The cynicism brings her closer to her natural aura of intellectual superiority, helps her feel a little calmer. And standing up to the FBI isn't easy. She's proud of herself. She extends her arm again, palm open.

"Well," Wheeler says slowly, as if she's waiting for Lisa to come to her senses, "I admire your loyalty. If your boss had half as much, you probably wouldn't even be in this mess."

Lisa is starting to worry that one of her neighbors will see her being questioned. Not that she's ever spoken to her neighbors. She's grateful she doesn't have a doorman. She can only imagine how horrified her dad would be if he were here. The conversation with these two alone would validate everything he's ever said.

"Look, we can go arrest Nick right now for half a dozen different felonies," Rosario tries. "But then you and the rest of the team go right down with him."

"First off, I don't even know what you're referring to," Lisa says. "Second, even if any of this were true, you can't commit a crime by accident. They teach you that in orientation too. And I know I didn't do anything wrong on purpose."

"Sure," says Wheeler. "Who knows? Maybe the jury will believe that. You'll only be the ninety-ninth defendant to claim ignorance that morning alone. You know politics, Ms. Lim. Which is why you know there are times you fight, and there are times you come to the table."

"I also know that you don't make decisions like that after forty-five seconds, which is about how long I've known both of you." Lisa almost lands the line, but her voice quavers at the end.

"That's why we should talk," Rosario answers, trying out a slightly softer tone. "You're right—you don't know what we have on your boss. You don't know what we have on your colleagues. You don't know what we have on you. But you do know that whoever has less information usually loses."

"And right now, Ms. Lim, if you're as smart as they say you are," Wheeler adds, "you'll know what you don't know, and let us in."

Lisa stands there for another moment, her eyes darting back and forth between the two agents. If she sends them away and has a lawyer call them back, then it's a whole process. Files get opened. Retainers paid. Calls, meetings, document production, hourly rates. Hassles and expenses all around. But if she can resolve whatever the problem is right now? On the spot? Maybe it goes away.

Lisa reaches into her pocket, takes out her keys, and puts one in the lock. She pulls the front door open and steps inside. Then she holds it for another few seconds. Both agents follow her in.

***

There are only two chairs in Lisa's very stark kitchen. Wheeler grabs one of them, leaving Rosario standing. Despite being the younger one, Lisa pegs Wheeler as the alpha of the two.

Wheeler jumps right in. "Here's the issue, in a nutshell. Nick invested a lot of money in some risky tech startups. It looked smart when the valuations kept going up, but he didn't know what he was doing, he listened to the wrong people, most of it went to zero, he borrowed to cover his losses, and now he owes some people you really don't want to owe. So, in order to avoid losing his kneecaps, Nick has been double-dealing your clients. He signs one up for the traditional work your firm does. Then he quietly goes to the opponent and gets paid off for making sure the campaign loses. He collects on both sides, hoping no one notices. Plus, he only reports and pays taxes on half the total income."

"Wait, why would he do that?" Lisa asks. "The consulting firm makes tons of money. He's fine."

"If he were fine, we wouldn't be here," Wheeler replies.

"And you know this exactly how?" Lisa asks.

"Same as most investigations. Came up in the middle of something completely different. Usually, it goes nowhere. But sometimes it does. And when that happens, we jump in," Wheeler says.

"So this is all based on what some scummy informant told you?" Lisa asks.

"Initially, yes. And if we weren't able to confirm anything else, we wouldn't be here right now. We do have better things to do."

"But that was before we started talking to the alternate side of the street parking guys," Rosario jumps in. "They don't fuck around. Remember that campaign Firewall ran for them to suspend alternate side of the street parking on the day before and after every holiday?"

Lisa nods.

"How'd it turn out?"

Lisa winces, pained by the memory of losing anything. Ever. "We didn't get it through the City Council. Died at the last minute. Still not sure how we blew that one."

"I think you can figure it out now," Wheeler says.

"You think someone paid Nick to kill it?"

"We know someone did—the restaurant association. They want the space for outdoor seating. Their executive director already admitted it. Well, he was the executive director."

"But Nick miscalculated," Rosario continues. "The alternate side of the street guys knew something was off. The bill's last-minute failure didn't make sense. You had the votes. So they contacted the Department of Investigation. That led to an inquiry. When we stumbled across Nick in an unrelated investigation and asked them for info, they turned the case over to us."

"No," Lisa says, shaking her head. "I know Nick. This doesn't make sense. Starting with the tech investments. Nick's really smart. And he knows what he doesn't know. Why would he do that?"

"Well," Rosario says, "the way I see it, betting on startups is just another form of gambling. It only seems less desperate. Whether you're putting money on a horse or a stock or a tech startup, it's all the same thing. He needs the action. Isn't that why all of you are in politics in the first place?"

Lisa thinks of the dog-racing forms littering Nick's desk. She thought it was a hobby.

"You really believe that Nick is deep in debt because he lost a bunch of money betting on tech startups, and to cover the payments, he's running campaigns where everyone from each side pays him to make sure they win? And then he just strings them all along?"

"Yes!" says Wheeler. "Exactly."

"You mean someone in politics is telling both sides what they want to hear and asking for money all along the way?" Lisa asks. "What the fuck do you think the U.S. Congress is? And how is this even a federal crime?"

"Look," Rosario says, "if we're right and if Nick has been defrauding people on campaigns that you were working on, that's a crime. Mail fraud. Wire fraud. All kinds of fraud. All federal crimes. And why are we here in your living room? Honestly? Mostly luck—bad luck. Bad luck for Nick. Bad luck for you. Nick talked to the wrong guy while we happened to be listening."

"And once we charge Nick," Wheeler says, "there's really no reason to stop there. Seems pretty plausible to me that you and your colleagues were in on it too."

Lisa looks down at the table, then looks back up at the agents. "Okay, I'm not saying you're making this all up. But I'm not saying you're not either. I just...I need to know more. Nick's been good to me." She pauses and adds, "Mostly."

As Lisa speaks, Rosario is setting up a laptop on the counter, the screen opened to where Lisa can see it. There's a gray box with a play button on the bottom, already sized up to fill the screen. Rosario hits play.

Lisa watches a grainy black-and-white video of two men speaking. It's shot from above with a fish-eye lens. There's no mistaking that one of the men is Nick. She's sure of it when she hears his voice. "FlightDeck is paying us a hundred and fifty a month, so..."

"Recognize the other guy?" Rosario asks.

Lisa leans forward—and her heart drops in her chest. "Viktor Velonova."

Both agents nod.

"Biggest medallion owner in the city," Lisa says. "Among, from what I've heard, many other things. Flying cars win, he's fucked." Lisa pauses for a moment, then adds, "He's your guy. The one you're really looking at."

Neither agent reacts.

Rosario goes in for the kill. "So if Velonova's your biggest opponent, why is Nick asking him for a hundred and fifty grand a month to make sure the flying cars bill never sees the light of day?"

Nick didn't exactly ask for that. He just said how much FlightDeck was paying them. But the fact that he told Viktor... and Lisa recognizes that probing tone. It's the same one he uses when there's one donut left in the box and he asks if anyone wants it as he reaches for it himself.

Lisa doesn't want to let on how she feels in front of the agents, but it's hard to come to any conclusion other than that Nick is double-dealing. That's probably why he was so quick to shut down the idea of her taking over the campaign.

Lisa tries to shake it off. Nick is unpredictable. He's unorthodox. He's a good guy at heart. Overall, he's treated her pretty well. He returns her texts. He doesn't lecture her about the Red Guard like her mom or tell her to stay away from anything risky like her dad or make her feel like the firm's entire future depends on how much she's willing to sacrifice like both of her parents.

"Who knows?" she says. "Maybe he's fishing. Going undercover. Seeing how committed Velonova is to the fight..." Lisa wonders who would be crazy enough to inform on Viktor fucking Velonova.

Both agents give her a look. She tries one final, halfhearted angle. "Okay, let's say you're right. So what? The world's falling apart out there, people are dying in the streets, and you're worried about how Nick treats his clients? Who cares? Bunch of rich people fighting over getting even richer. Champagne problems."

Lisa studies the agents' faces and doesn't find a crack. She finally accepts reality and gives in. "Or...maybe he's playing both sides."

"Not maybe. He is. But we need more evidence to prove it," Wheeler says. She smiles, flashing what seems like all her teeth at once. "That's where you come in."

PART TWO

CHAPTER FOURTEEN

NEW YORK CITY

Uber NYC HQ

Leon Hamilton is Uber's lead political operative in New York. His job is simple: stop the taxi guys from pushing anti-Uber legislation and screw over Lyft whenever possible. The twelve years Leon spent as chief of staff to two City Council speakers and to one Assembly speaker taught him the dark arts of politics extremely well.

At one point, Leon had a burner Twitter account called @ NoFingerprints243, but then he decided that putting anything in writing was already going too far.

Leon is at his desk in the bullpen of Uber's NYC headquarters in far West Chelsea, a sprawling, open-concept space with a lot of glass and exposed red brick. Gorgeous, except the brickwork reminds him too much of his Tribeca apartment, so it feels like he's always in the same place. Leon used to manage half a dozen people, but then Uber adopted a strategy of non-aggression with regulators and now it's just him and the intern.

It's a slow day. He's lost track of how many times he's opened Tinder to see if Angelique responded. They'd had a nice opening conversation, but after telling her that the last good book he read was *Atlas Shrugged*, she didn't respond back. Too bad; she was a seven, easy. Nine once he had a few drinks in him. He puts it out of his head and stews on other things.

Like the rumor he heard from an FBI agent he plays pickleball with: that there may be something going on with a particularly dodgy political consultant in New York.

He isn't sure who or what it is or how advanced the investigation is. Leon named about thirty different local political consultants from lobbyists to pollsters, ad makers to opposition researchers, grassroots organizers to social media experts, hoping the agent would recognize a name—and hoping that name would be Nick Denevito. Uber-enemy number one. No such luck.

But he said it's someone big, someone who's been around for a while, someone high profile.

And more importantly, he also didn't say the subject of the investigation *isn't* Nick.

So Leon picks up the phone and dials a number he knows by heart. One that he calls at least once a week, if not to trade information, then at least to gossip. It answers on the fourth ring. "Julia," Leon says. "You guys hearing anything about the feds looking into Nick Denevito?"

***

Julia Alessi from the *New York Post* is walking back into Room 9 at City Hall when her cell phone rings. Leon Hamilton. She considers sending it to voicemail but figures it's a slow news day and she could use a lead, or at least a distraction. She steps into Room 9, the cramped, dilapidated office shoehorned into the corner of the building reserved for city government beat reporters. It's empty—which is good. She can talk freely, instead of finding a quiet alcove somewhere else in the building to avoid the prying ears of her colleagues. Except they're not really colleagues because they all work for competing papers.

After starting her tenure at the *Post* on the crime beat, and then almost a year manning the paper's regular series featuring female high school teachers sleeping with male students, Julia was named Metro Investigative Bureau Chief at the start of Navarro's first term. She's good at her job, mostly because she sees a conspiracy in every scenario, every situation, every story.

And because she knows to prioritize calls from people who've proven themselves.

Julia flops into her beaten roller chair and furrows her brow at Leon's mention of Nick Denevito. "What have you heard?"

"I only heard it, like, third hand," Leon says. "Not sure if it's solid or not. And look, don't attribute any of this to me—even on background. Please. But it seems like the FBI is asking around about him."

Julia gets up and paces. It helps her think. "Where'd you hear that?"

"A buddy at the Bureau."

"Care to be more specific?"

"No."

"And he said that Nick Denevito is a subject of an investigation?"

Leon pauses, which Julia finds interesting. "I had to read between the lines, but yes, that was my sense."

"Any bad blood between you and Nick?"

"No. Of course not. I love Nick."

"And the fact that he's running the flying cars campaign isn't a factor? Despite your vociferous opposition to the bill?"

"Me? Never."

Frank Jackson, the beat reporter for the *Daily News*, walks in, so Julia lowers her voice. "Okay, so, what are they looking at? Who's handling the case? Does Denevito know he's under investigation?"

"Look, I have no details here. I just heard that this may be happening. I owe you a favor from that Page Six item you helped me place about my boss's daughter's quinceañera, so I figured I'd pass it along. That's all I've got."

Julia opens up a new Google Doc and saves it under *Denevito / FBI*. "I'll look into it."

CHAPTER FIFTEEN

NEW YORK CITY

City Hall

Cy Berger, the spokesman for the U.S. Attorney's Office for the Southern District of New York, looks at the caller ID on his phone, exhales hard, and drops his head onto his desk hard enough that it hurts.

He hit his forehead harder than he intended, but at least the pain distracts from the roiling in his stomach. He hates talking to Julia Alessi. Julia thinks she's being lied to before the conversation even begins. And she's convinced that New York's true beacon of justice is not the prosecutors, not the police, not the courts, not even the fourth estate taken as a whole, but her—and her alone.

Cy considers letting it go to voicemail. But he knows he won't want to return the call. And then it'll nag at him in the back of his mind until he finally does. Assuming she doesn't call back a dozen times first. Better to just get it over with.

"Hey, Julia," Cy says, trying to sound cheerful.

"Nick Denevito."

"The political guy?"

"Yeah."

"So?"

"I'm hearing you're looking at him."

"Us?" Cy shakes his head, even though she can't see him.

"Yeah, you. I know you have agents working on something."

"Not that I've heard," Cy says, shuffling papers on his desk, hoping he didn't miss something.

"Not that you've heard because it hasn't reached your desk yet, or not that you've heard because it isn't happening?"

"I'm usually pretty up to speed on the political investigations. Haven't heard anything about this one."

"That's odd. I feel like you typically know what's going on."

Cy keeps shuffling papers on his desk, like an answer might suddenly appear. Truth is, he's been underwater lately. Nick is a decent-sized fish—enough that Cy knows him by name—but the guy isn't important enough to set off the klaxons.

"Right, I do," Cy says. "And that's why you're probably barking up the wrong tree."

"Or maybe you're out of the loop."

"You're the one calling me. So if there is a loop on this thing that I'm not in, you're not in it either."

"Then ask around. It may ring a bell or two. And when it does—"

"I know, I know," Cy says. "Call you first."

***

Abby Miller, Mayor Navarro's press secretary, answers her cell immediately and honestly. "Oh no."

"Why do you always assume it's bad news when I'm calling?" Julia asks.

"Because you're the archangel of corruption. Which means you see corruption everywhere. Even when it doesn't actually exist."

"Well, good news. This time it's not about your guy."

Abby twists her neck twice and reaches for the foam roller behind her desk. She got herself a Hypervolt for Christmas but then realized that she couldn't quite reach the spots in her back that needed pressure the most. Asking employees to massage her, even via a quasi-medical device, isn't really acceptable, so the foam roller is now in heavy rotation, especially whenever Julia calls.

Not having an immediate accusation to shoot down is a refreshing change of pace, but Abby doesn't really believe her. "Julia, I've been in this job for three-and-a-half years, and one way or another, between the Department of Buildings black market permits fiasco, the Fire Department petting zoo scandal, the Department of Education chalkboard thefts, the Parks Department murder-for-hire ring, and all the rest, we've been through twelve different grand juries. We have over three hundred and fifty thousand city workers. At any given time, at least one of them is doing something they shouldn't. So when is it not about us?"

"It's about Nick Denevito."

Abby lets off a deep sigh. Maybe this truly is a free pass; maybe she can get a few chits with Julia, be mildly helpful and keep Julia away from fucking with her boss—and by extension, her—for a little while. "Off the record, I worked with Nick on Hillary's first Senate campaign. Never liked him. Smug motherfucker. Not nearly as charming as he thinks he is. Not a big fan of his protégé, either. Lisa something. She's not nearly as smart as she thinks she is."

"I'm hearing that SDNY is looking at him. Guessing, pay to play? Usually is. But it could be something else. I don't know yet. Wondering what you've heard."

Abby puts her feet on her desk and feels relaxed for the first time today. Nick getting hung out to dry? She could get behind that. The oxytocin hit will last until the next email or phone call from another reporter. "Very interesting. But it's the first I'm hearing of it."

"If you make some calls to your colleagues in law enforcement, I'm pretty sure you could learn a lot more. If, you know, you think getting me out of your hair for a while might be helpful." Julia pauses. "Or, I could go back to that investigation on why the last six multimillion-dollar procurements all went to major Navarro donors. That's a fun topic. I believe you still owe me some FOIAs on it."

That's the last thing Abby wants to deal with. She doesn't control who gives Navarro money. She doesn't control who receives City contracts. She just has to clean up the mess, day after every fucking day.

Abby smiles ruefully, hating her job sometimes, still wondering why she takes so much shit for a boss she doesn't even like, but also appreciating how good Julia is at the game. "I'll start making some calls."

CHAPTER SIXTEEN

NEW YORK CITY

U.S. Attorney's Office for the Southern District of New York

Cy walks down the hall to the office that investigates public corruption. For as long as he's worked here, the office is so bland he can sometimes still get lost if he's not paying attention. Just a sea of gray—flimsy gray walls, gray carpet, gray light.

Brendan McClain, the Public Corruption Unit Chief, is sitting at his desk, feet up, scanning something on his computer. Looks like the *Atlantic*.

"Oh no," Brendan says when he sees Cy.

"Why does everyone always assume I have bad news?"

"Because you almost always do. What's this one about?"

"Are we investigating Nick Denevito?"

"I don't know. Who's that?"

"Political consultant," Cy says. "Really connected. Julia from the *Post* called me about him. Said she's heard we're looking at him."

McClain shrugs. "I'll call over to the Bureau."

After a series of phone calls and texts, Agents Wheeler and Rosario are standing at one end of a conference table, Cy and

Brendan sitting on the other end. As Wheeler starts laying out the investigation, both Cy and Brendan are only mildly interested. A rich consultant defrauding rich clients isn't that exciting. It's not even really public corruption—it's just regular business fraud.

But then they see the video with Viktor Velonova. It's always a bit of a jump start to find yourself dealing with one of the biggest criminals in the five boroughs—Cy didn't know Viktor was also a confidential informant. And he probably should have.

"Holy fuck," Cy says, pushing a palm into his forehead, which still aches a bit. "Now I get why Julia thinks this is public corruption. Velonova means taxi medallions. That means campaign contributions. Which means this could go deeper than just some consultant."

Wheeler feels completely validated. "Exactly! Who knows where this could lead?"

"But now that the *Post* knows, the clock is ticking," McClain says. "Cy, how long can we stall them?"

Cy thinks, shrugs, thinks again, then says, "A week tops if we can come up with a few things from our end that make the story more interesting. But Denevito isn't that big a deal. This is still a one-day story. So we don't need to get too worked up yet."

"Exactly," McClain says. "Denevito is a decent enough score. And if Viktor slips up, that'd be the best thing to come out of all of this. Maybe we get really lucky and find some politicians sticking their hands in the cookie jar along the way. Cy—keep stalling with the *Post.* Buy these guys as much time as you can. Maybe this leads to something useful." McClain turns back to the agents. "This isn't going to hold for much longer."

Wheeler and Rosario both nod, knowing better than to talk at this point, and take their exit. They get it. Bring in Nick's scalp, along with a few others if possible, and do it before the *Post* blows the whole thing up.

***

As the agents exit the conference room, Wheeler turns to Rosario. "That was good, right? Except they want Velonova, which isn't really what we promised him when we asked him to give Nick up."

"Does he have it in writing?"

"No."

"Then fuck that guy. He doesn't deserve any lenience from us. Being fair to Viktor isn't our problem. Our issue is timing."

"How so?"

"If the *Post* knows, we're going to have to make something happen a lot faster than we planned. Which means moving a lot harder on Lisa. No matter what we have to threaten her with. Get a wire on her, get a meeting set up with her, see what we can sort out. I think she'll come around."

"Ah, shit," Wheeler mutters. "I'm going to have to sit down with my calendar."

"Is there a problem?" Rosario asks.

She wonders if Wheeler is having second thoughts—this was all her op anyway. At first, Rosario didn't think Nick—even with Velonova involved—merited their time. She already had a career full of running down shitty tips from jackass confidential informants that invariably led to nowhere. But Wheeler saw something, pushed hard, and Rosario finally relented.

"Wait," Rosario says. She realizes that Wheeler means this could interfere with her schedule for the International Federation of Competitive Eating. "This fucking thing again?" Rosario asks.

"It's a big one," Wheeler says, a little desperate. "If I do well in the next competition, I could make the mayonnaise eating contest in Tampa, or maybe even the sliced bologna eating contest in Anchorage."

"What's the contest this time?" Rosario dutifully asks, though Wheeler knows she's exasperated by it. Not just because of how many work breaks Wheeler has to take to maintain her IFOCE ranking, but also because she manages to somehow keep the weight off.

"Poutine. I'm flying up to Montreal Monday night. Contest is Wednesday. Big annual tradition in Canada. Almost like a national holiday. Every February twenty-eighth—unless it's a leap year. I'll do my last-minute training on Tuesday, recover Thursday, and be back at work first thing Friday morning."

"And how much do you need to eat to qualify?" Rosario asks.

"The record is twenty-eight pounds in ten minutes. But you know, that's Joey Chestnut. The GOAT. No one can touch him. But I think if I can eat eleven pounds, that should keep me in the game."

Rosario stops her at the elevator before they press the button to go down. "Remember when you came into my office? Told me about this thing with Denevito? Said it would open the door to uncovering a whole new world of corruption? I gotta say, kid, after all that, I'm not thrilled to hear you're more worried about your next meal."

Wheeler looks at her incredulously. "It's a slippery slope, Sarah. If you miss the poutine competition, next thing you know, you're missing fried Oreos. Then samosas. And then tacos de lengua. At that rate, I'll never make it to Coney Island."

Rosario is annoyed. Really annoyed. Wheeler is young but has pretty good instincts—instincts Rosario has sometimes wondered if she lacks. Eighteen years in the Bureau and still no big notches in her belt. The best cases always went to the boys' club, the golfers and the bar buddies, and she's gotten stuck with the scraps.

But that's never going to change. So they need to make a dollar out of fifteen cents. Which is what Wheeler promoted when she made the case for Denevito: there are bigger fish in these waters. Who knows where this could lead?

"Yeah, you're right," Rosario says. "I guess waiting a week won't matter. If the *Post* hits before then and we can't get the rest of the evidence we need, no big deal."

Rosario is sure that Wheeler is smart enough to recognize reverse psychology—but that doesn't mean it's not effective. "Look, okay, I get it," she says. "But there's something here. All these failed startups Denevito kept investing in. On-demand toothbrushing. Create your own emojis. Buy Dogecoin so Elon Musk can shoot more cars into space. They're all fucking stupid. I'm not surprised that Denevito lost money on them. Honestly, I don't even care whether or not Denevito pays the loan sharks back by double-dealing his asshole clients or not."

"But?" Rosario asks, like she's hopeful that maybe the trip to Montreal can wait.

"This feels different from the usual political corruption, you know? It's politics and tech combined. Maybe this starts to send a message. At least show them we're watching."

Rosario ponders her next move. "You know, you're absolutely right. We bust Denevito and show everyone all the stupid shit he was investing in, maybe it shines a light on how the whole tech industry sells the public a bill of goods and rarely delivers. And with tech taking over everything these days, that's important." Rosario pauses. "It's almost as important as poutine."

Wheeler arches an eyebrow but doesn't say anything. She makes Rosario wait a little longer. "Okay, fine. I'll just have to train even harder for shrimp cocktail."

"Do you dip them in the sauce during the contest?"

"No time."

"What do you do with the shells?"

"I just eat them. Faster that way."

Rosario makes a mental note to take a sick day when Wheeler returns from shrimp cocktail.

Wheeler stops and turns to Rosario. "Call Lim. Let's get working on that wire."

CHAPTER SEVENTEEN

NEW YORK CITY

Times Square

As Lisa walks through the front door of the Times Square Alliance, a text comes in from her dad. There's no message—there almost never is—just a Facebook link to the profile of someone she went to high school with and hasn't talked to in a solid fifteen years. She clicks the link anyway. Brenda Janowitz got a new Volvo. Great. What's she supposed to do with that information? Why doesn't her dad ever text her about something actually relevant? Even a quick "how's it going?" would work. Instead, it's all passive aggressive complaining that Lisa didn't pursue a career he thinks is sufficiently secure, even after all these years. The fact that her younger sister became a dentist certainly doesn't help either. And the fact that Lisa is considered a rising superstar in her industry matters even less.

Lisa briefly considers responding, but she knows her dad. Even before her mom died, anything emotional was strictly off limits. Logistics and current events only. If you need someone to move a desk chair from point A to point B? He's your guy. But anything that involves feelings? He runs for the hills.

Rosario keeps texting her, wanting to know exactly when she's meeting Nick. Lisa knows that ignoring an FBI agent can probably get her into trouble, but she didn't break any laws. They don't have anything to arrest her with. She has paying clients who need her attention. And right now, she has more immediate issues to deal with.

Something to distract her, at least.

When local business leaders created the Times Square Alliance in the bad old days of the early nineties, the group's founders never would have imagined that their biggest problem thirty years later would stem from the literal Disneyfication of the neighborhood—people dressed in cartoon character costumes harassing tourists for money. Being assaulted by Minnie Mouse or Buzz Lightyear is a relatively new problem for Times Square, but even if it's coming from Goofy, assaulting tourists is still a problem.

And for the last few months, it's been Lisa's problem.

Lisa takes a seat at the head of the table in the Alliance's conference room. Everyone at the table is still in character: SpongeBob, Dora, the crew from *PAW Patrol.* Except all the costumes are cheap knockoffs. The colors and details aren't right. The stitching is shoddy.

"You took it too fucking far." Lisa has been trying to amicably resolve this issue for too long—she's done being nice. "Asking tourists if they want to take a photo with you and then accepting a tip is one thing. Jumping them to demand a photo and then assaulting them if they don't tip is another. You put yourself in this position. I warned you. And then I warned you again. You didn't listen."

Muffled sounds come from Elmo. Lisa shakes her head. "The ACLU's not going to save you this time. Disney wants nothing to do with you. Neither does Universal. And I don't think you realize how pissed off City Hall is. Navarro can't even keep people safe from Scooby fucking Doo? Do you realize how embarrassing that is? Especially for someone as insecure as him?"

The Scooby Doo character at the end of the table hangs his head in shame. It's so weird that they won't take their masks off for these meetings, but she's come to accept it.

Elmo tries to protest, but Lisa presses on. "Sure, you can go to court and say the law that the City Council's about to pass—the law that bans you completely—violates the First Amendment. Who knows? Maybe it does. And in three or four years, the City's Law Department will probably settle the case."

Lisa looks hard at everyone. "None of you will be here by then. You'll all be back in Toledo. If you're lucky."

Iron Man and Sonic shake their heads. Muffled sounds come from one of the Power Rangers.

"Will one of you please communicate like a human?"

Dora takes off her head. Finally. It's a young white guy with long, matted dreads. "So what's your alternative?" he asks.

"We set up a zone where you can take photos and accept tips. You don't leave the zone. Tourists enter. Voluntarily. As long as you stay in the zone and don't assault anyone, we're good. The minute you do, NYPD picks you up and takes you straight to the Tombs."

"Give us a minute," Dora says.

The characters all huddle in the corner of the room. Lisa thinks they're finally going to take their heads off; instead, Dora puts his back on.

Spider-Man looks upset. Garfield has to talk him down. Finally, Pikachu walks over to Lisa and extends his paw.

Knowing to never risk snatching defeat from the jaws of victory, Lisa says thank you and gets out of there as quickly as possible.

Plus, she doesn't want to make Nick wait.

Suggesting to Nick that they meet up on the corner of Forty-Fourth and Broadway was a terrible idea, but Lisa knows that Nick wouldn't want to meet her inside the client's office and risk having to pretend that he's actually been following their campaign on a minute-by-minute or even day-by-day basis. The street is packed with tourists, as usual, but Lisa's innate aura of annoyance sends a force field across her personal space, causing everyone to give her a wide berth. She finds Nick easily, standing against a parking meter like he doesn't have a care in the world.

Like he's not double-dealing his clients.

Like he's not facing imminent violence from a cadre of loan sharks.

"How'd it go?" Nick asks.

Lisa considers saying something. Warning him—or bracing him. Something. She wants to say it's the smart play to keep a lid on things, but the truth is, she just doesn't want to deal with the confrontation. "At least we delivered for one client," she says.

Lisa suggested lunch as a way to do some of her own digging. Maybe there are extenuating circumstances to Nick's activities that explain everything. Maybe she can exonerate him. And if not, the better she understands what Nick has been up to, the more likely she is to get Rosario and Wheeler what they need and get this over with. It's worth the effort either way.

They walk into a high-end sushi place on Forty-Eighth Street that Nick frequents. No sign out front, only a few tables, and no menu, so it's omakase or nothing. The Kosher Mexican Korean food truck is parked outside. Lisa realizes how dumb it was of

Wheeler and Rosario to choose that. The weird food combination may keep people away, but it's easy to spot and remember.

Nick stops for a second and looks at the truck. He scrunches his face up like he's about to ask Lisa whether she's been noticing the same truck around a lot lately too, but Lisa quickly intervenes with a "we're late for our reservation" and Nick heads inside.

After they're seated and have sorted out what type of water they want, Lisa jumps in. "So, I've been working at Firewall for around four years now."

Nick nods, seemingly more concerned with picking out the right sake from the small printout handed to him by the waitress.

"And I think I'm starting to get a sense of how the economics of this business works."

Nick lifts his face from the menu and looks worried.

"Don't worry, I'm not asking for a raise. I'm just trying to figure out how to move to the next level."

"Well," Nick says, "you're already the most senior person at the company after me. And trust me, elevating you over people like Allison and Alphonso, who have been there for a lot longer, wasn't easy..."

"I know and I appreciate it. But I'm thinking broader. Bigger picture. Firewall is a client services business. We charge high fees and they can add up, but it's still ultimately the same as what they say about lawyers and doctors and consultants—live well and die poor. What I'm wondering is—is there a way to do better than that?"

Nick's expression remains passive. "Like what?"

"To make fuck-you money. Look, from everything I've read and heard, you can't do that by getting paid by the hour or by the month. You need your money to multiply on its own, overnight, in the markets. Make money while you're sleeping."

Lisa leaves the important part to her unsaid. Yes, she's fishing for Wheeler and Rosario. But it's not just that. Like it or not, a big payday would resonate back home in Alexandria. Not that her dad needs money. His pension from the water department is plenty for his modest lifestyle. Thirty-three years of going along and getting along paid off fine for him. But if Lisa could offer him a six-figure gift, at least he could brag to his friends at the senior center instead of sending her links about babies and Volvos and not-so-secretly both hating and fearing that Lisa's entire job seems to revolve around pissing off powerful people.

Nick nods slowly. "We took equity from a few startups a while back. Before you started. Didn't really amount to much and required a lot of paperwork and lawyers, so we went back to all cash fees."

"Sure. But that doesn't close the door entirely. I know that what you see on *Shark Tank* doesn't necessarily reflect reality, but the lesson to me is that to make real money, you have to get in on these high-growth companies really early. When they're just starting."

Nick nods in agreement, smiling, like he's suddenly noticed something about Lisa. "That's how I see it too. Always have."

"I try to save my money. That's why when you're always hassling me about getting a better wardrobe or living in something nicer than a cramped one-bedroom in the East Village, I resist. But thanks to that, now I've got a nest egg. I'd like to invest it in something that can make me real money."

"Fuck-you money," Nick says.

"Fuck-you money," Lisa agrees.

Lisa stops and takes a deep drink of water. She can feel herself getting overzealous. Trying too hard to sell. Nick isn't dumb, and he's going to notice if she overplays her hand.

"There's a lot of risk in doing that," Nick says. "Most startups go to zero."

"But if you have an inside angle, if you have more information than most people, in other words, if you have the investment equivalent of us? That risk goes down."

"What do you have in mind?" Nick seems focused and intrigued for the first time that afternoon. For the first time in a long time.

"I don't know. Find some tech startups that we think have a really good shot at making it. Maybe companies who could use our expertise. And get in on the ground floor."

Nick shrugs, pulling back a bit. "What do you need me for then?"

"I feel like I've got the right idea here. And I have cash to invest. But other than a few of our clients, I don't know anyone in tech. You know a thousand times more people than I do. So I figure if anyone knows what to do here, it's you. Plus, you know, you're also my boss."

Nick takes a sip of sparkling water. Then two sips of sake. "There's this tech expo I like going to sometimes. You see some cool shit. If you want, we can go together and see if we find anything interesting."

***

Rosario flinches when Wheeler yells, "Fuck yeah!" so loud, she's worried the pair can hear it in the restaurant.

But Rosario also can't help but smile. "This is good. We get her wired up for that tech expo, make sure she knows what to ask and where to lead the conversation, and I bet we get what we need."

Wheeler doesn't respond. She's busy polishing off chicken wings from the Styrofoam container on the cramped table in front of her.

"Case closed," she finally mumbles.

Rosario looks over at her partner, her face covered in orange wing sauce. "Case closed on Denevito maybe. But it's not enough. You heard what McClain said—a big win here is getting Viktor or getting some corrupt local pols. Just nailing a consultant? We can do better than that."

CHAPTER EIGHTEEN

LOS ANGELES, CA

FlightDeck HQ

"You are sure we have got it this time?"

Yevgeny is grilling two engineers, both of whom are too tired to even feel nervous anymore. He wishes he could remember their names but, at this moment, he's so tired that he's blanking.

Everyone is tired.

"You are absolutely positive?" he asks, drawing out the word "absolutely" nearly to its breaking point.

"Yes," the taller engineer says again. "We've tested the simulation over six thousand times, and the sensors have worked consistently. Trust me. We're good."

Yevgeny has lost count of how many times he's been told they're good and it turned out they weren't. "You know how much these vehicles cost? They're very expensive."

Both engineers nod.

"You know that if we test this in real life and the sensors do not work, we are not out just another million and change. Since this is the final prototype that has not blown up yet, we would have to start the build all over again."

Both engineers nod again.

Yevgeny still isn't sure that going forward with a live test is a good idea, but they're right—the simulations have been successful. Susan is demanding a finished product. He can't get her that if they can't get the sensors right. And they can't know if the sensors work until they're tested in the real world.

"Okay. Fire it up."

Yevgeny and the two engineers climb the stairs to the asphalt roof, where the latest FlightDeck prototype is stationed. The other fourteen members of the engineering team are already assembled.

Yevgeny slowly walks around the vehicle, not sure what he's checking for but wanting to procrastinate for as long as possible. He notices someone wrote "Susan" on the side of the car, but then someone else crossed it out and replaced it with "The Milano." Even if Susan were more popular with the engineering team, it's hard to compete with Star-Lord.

He stalls, nervous about pulling the trigger. By the fifth lap, he knows there's only one path forward. So he shrugs, says, "*Persse*"—"fuck it" in Estonian, which no one has caught on to yet—picks up the oversized control panel, and starts pressing the buttons. The car hums deeply, throws off a gust of air as the engine engages, and lifts vertically around thirty feet. It glides smoothly through the air, turns, then twice, then three times. Everyone cheers and high-fives.

A bird flies towards the roof and the sensors spot it and shift the car out of the way. Everyone cheers again. A plane takes off from LAX and the sensors know it's too far away to matter. It's all going surprisingly well.

Until the drone shows up.

The car isn't sensing the drone. Yevgeny has no idea why the car can sense a bird and an airplane but not a drone. Most of the engineers didn't see it coming either. It could be a reporter or another tech company trying to get some intel on what they are doing, but realistically, it is probably some dumbass in a park nearby playing with a new toy.

And since it isn't registering on the control panel, Yevgeny knows there is nothing he—nor anyone—can do about it.

Except get everyone off the roof before the fucking thing explodes.

"Drone! Drone!" Yevgeny screams. The reverberations of the takeoff are still so loud, no one can hear him. He thinks about making a run for the exit, but leaving fourteen people to certain death doesn't feel quite right.

Yevgeny starts screaming, "Go! Go!" and physically pushes engineers towards the fire door on the roof. When the group sees the first few running for the door, the rest get the message and quickly follow. The last engineer barely squeezes through the stairwell door before the car hits the roof and bursts into flames.

The building shudders, and for a moment, Yevgeny worries the roof might cave in.

But it holds long enough for them to get inside.

And it seems to be holding as they watch from the parking lot, black smoke coiling off the roof.

After the Burbank Fire Department finishes extinguishing the flames, Yevgeny goes back to his office, dreading what will come next. Susan will probably threaten to fire him and the whole team. She'll threaten to confiscate their stock options. She'll threaten to expose them as incompetents. Or something worse. He doesn't know what's worse, but he knows Susan will figure it out. Yevgeny knows far too well that Susan's anger can be incredibly creative.

Which only matters, Yevgeny suddenly realizes, if she has power over him in the first place. Sitting back at his desk, he calms himself down by going through a twenty-pack of scratch-off tickets (two winners totaling six bucks).

Then he braces himself and calls Susan. She's in San Francisco, meeting with new investors, asking for more money.

She's surprisingly calm as Yevgeny relays what happened over FaceTime. This isn't what he was expecting. He was ready for cursing, yelling, screaming—normal Susan behavior. He was ready to quit. Now it's harder—even though the conversation itself is a lot easier.

But Susan keeps working him over. "Yevgeny, I understand how hard this has been on you and your entire team. And how hard it still is. But think about what's at stake here. Think about what it means for our lives if we succeed. Think about what it means for society, for the environment, for the future of cities. The stakes are too high not to keep going. I don't blame you for being frustrated. I am too. But we can't not pursue this—and we can't do it without you."

Yevgeny knows that seeking pity is an unattractive trait, but sometimes he can't help it. "You cannot do it with me, either. It is not working. No matter how hard we try."

"Sure it is. We're so close. So what, the sensory issue is still sort of an issue. Fine. But you said it detected a bird and an airplane before it didn't notice the drone. Clearly, we're on the right track."

"But we are not there yet. And we cannot launch until we do." Yevgeny knows his decision to test now almost killed fourteen people. He's not willing to go through that again.

"Of course not. Of course not! We won't put anyone at risk," Susan assures him. "I promise. You have my word."

Yevgeny grunts but doesn't say anything.

"So what's it going to take? I can't afford to lose you. Wait. Hang on." Susan disappears for a moment. "Carol agrees."

Yevgeny had rehearsed this conversation with Susan in his head a dozen times while he was playing the scratch-off tickets. But no matter how many times he gamed it out, it never once occurred to him that rather than yelling and screaming, she'd simply ask, "How much?"

It takes him a second to respond. "I want it in writing that you will not try to deploy the technology before it is safe. That way, if the police come, we are clear on who did what. I am not risking my green card for this."

"No problem. Done."

"And an extra million shares."

Susan starts punching numbers into her phone's calculator. "At our Series B valuation? That comes out to eight point two million."

"I also want to work from home the day after daylight savings time. It takes my body clock a while to adjust."

"Yevgeny—work from wherever the fuck you want. I don't care. I just need something to show investors that we're for real. And yes, I know we need to build a new prototype for that to happen. But as long as we can get that done in the next sixty days or so, we can raise a new round and live to fight another day."

What Susan doesn't say—but what Yevgeny notices loud and clear—is the inverse.

If Yevgeny can't get a new, fully functioning prototype up and running, it doesn't matter how many more shares he just received.

A million shares of zero is still zero.

CHAPTER NINETEEN

NEW YORK CITY

Firewall HQ

It's 8:30 p.m. and Lisa is still at the office, sitting in a windowless room with Pinky Fonseca, Firewall's chief opposition researcher. Everyone else at Firewall works in the bullpen, open-plan style, but they keep Pinky away from the group—and from the clients.

Lisa tries to avoid Pinky's office as much as possible. She has always hated collections of things—stamps, coins, baseball cards, Appalachian pottery. To her, it feels like pointless clutter. Pinky lives for them. In his tiny, formerly-storage-room office, he keeps the seventh-largest private holding of butterflies in the Mid-Atlantic, set behind glass frames that cover all four walls. Plus a widely coveted set of Bundini Brown memorabilia, and his three favorite antique prosthetic limbs from the much larger stockpile he keeps in a storage unit under the FDR. Lisa finds the limbs to be insanely creepy, but when Nick tried to gently ask Pinky to get rid of them, Pinky demanded to sit in the bullpen with everyone else. Nick retreated.

Pinky looks relatively normal. Basic, good-looking white guy with shortish hair and clothes from Bonobos that would make him a great decoy in a police lineup. And he comes off as quasi-normal too.

At first.

But as Lisa learned the hard way in her first week on the job, if you talk to him for fifteen minutes, you learn about his morbid fascination with the "undisclosed chapter" of Celine Dion's late adolescence, you hear his theories on why the multiverse explains the Mets' trouble with left-handed relief pitching, you get the details on his fish-sandwiches-for-lunch-every-day-except-Fridays diet—and then you remember he shares the office kitchen with you.

"Got some decent intel," he starts. "The unions, not surprisingly, have faced several recent federal corruption investigations. None of the Socialist leaders attacking us have paid their own taxes in years. Shocker. Navarro has a graveyard's worth of skeletons in his closet, but what nobody seems to have noticed yet is that his niece got a DUI on the Bruckner two months ago and the charges mysteriously disappeared. Mayor Pearce just put an addition on his beach house in Galveston. Not sure how he paid for it. I also booked a house on City Island for three weeks this summer."

Lisa looks at him. "What does that have to do with Pearce?"

"Beaches."

Lisa silently shakes her head and sifts through the dossier. There's useful material in there that could make each politician more amenable to their bill and knock each opponent back on their heels.

"We should probably poll too," Lisa says. "Show how angry voters will be if they're denied their God-given right to use flying cars."

Pinky looks skeptical, but he plays along. "Is this a poll where we want to know what people actually think? Or a poll that confirms what we already think so we can turn around and say we were right?"

"The former."

"Okay, and what are we testing? Just how voters feel about flying cars?"

"As a baseline, yes. But we need to know how they feel about it in the face of the opposition. In the face of being told they can't fulfill their dream by a bunch of politicians. We've got all these people making noise around us. The voters need to think that flying cars are so fucking cool, none of the practical objections really matter. They need to think that even if there are a thousand more pressing things that government should be doing right now, this is still a top priority because they just fucking want it. We need to see if we can win their hearts, even when their heads are telling them something different. That's what we have to figure out."

"Quantify hearts. Got it."

"And also, do the thing you do with the weekly and ethnic newspapers."

"You mean buy a lot of ads and get them to editorialize in support of our bill?"

"Unless they've suddenly become less transactional."

"Nope," Pinky smiles. "Media is changing these days, but being able to buy off the weeklies is something you can always count on."

As Lisa starts planning her escape, Pinky asks one final question.

"Want to hear something weird?"

"As if everything you say isn't weird?"

"I tapped into the local NYPD red light cameras to keep an eye on our friend Viktor Velonova. Thought it might be helpful given all this. And the footage was a little blurry, but I could swear I saw Nick walking into Turgenev."

Lisa pauses. She finally blurts out, "Nick has one of those airline-pilot, every-man type looks. Happens to him all the time." Then she realizes that if he saw the video, he saved the video. "Call it up."

Pinky taps a few keys, and a window on his computer opens.

Lisa studies it, watching Nick stride right into the tacky belly of the beast. She turns to Pinky. "Yeah, that's not him." She looks at her watch and starts putting in her AirPods. "Shit, I've got a call at nine. Nice work, Pinky. We'll catch up more later."

The agents knowing is one thing. Having the office's designated conspiracy nut know is another. Word is going to get around. And it reminds Lisa that Nick put everyone else at risk—to the point where she's getting at-home visits from the FBI.

Despite their sort-of friendship, despite Nick sometimes expressing genuine pride in her, despite Nick generally being tolerable enough to work with, Lisa realizes what she wants to be able to say when she's up on the witness stand: I didn't know, and when I found out, I did the right thing. That's why she wore the wire. And why she will again.

CHAPTER TWENTY

NEW YORK CITY

Coney Island Boardwalk

Nick isn't sure when it's a good time to stroll along the Coney Island boardwalk. In the winter and spring, it's too cold. In the summer and fall, it's too crowded. But Nick is sure that walking alongside an unhappy Viktor Velonova is the worst possible option. The winter wind coming off the water is cutting into them, but Nick's blood would be running cold even if it were the middle of July.

"Nick, you promised me the bill would die a swift death. Now I'm hearing that Navarro is thinking about supporting the bill?" Viktor asks.

"We're working on it. It's complicated."

"It's not complicated. If the mayor wants something to happen, it usually happens. He has all the power."

Nick shoves his hands into his pockets. Putting on gloves would make him seem weak to Viktor, who isn't even wearing a coat. Nick fondly remembers the time he bullied FlightDeck's board. Maybe that's the right play again? Then he remembers who he's standing next to.

"This is a big issue," Nick says. "It's going to have momentum on both sides. Sometimes it'll feel like the bill is inevitable. Sometimes it'll feel like it's dead on arrival. You know how campaigns work. Especially something high profile like this. It bounces back and forth."

"I know that this campaign is still alive. And I know that it's picking up support. I know that all the local papers in Brooklyn are suddenly demanding it. *Brooklyn Pravda* almost wrote an editorial supporting it—and I own that newspaper. Lucky for you, I happened to be in the office that day." He swipes a finger across his throat and makes a ripping sound.

Nick doesn't want to even imagine the conversation he'd be having with Viktor if that had happened. This is the problem with playing both sides against the middle—Nick can't instruct his own team to back off without making it obvious. He can only undercut the campaign in subtle ways. Which requires patience.

Which is not typically an option with Viktor.

So he improvises. "Think about it this way. If the bill just dies, all of a sudden and out of nowhere, it's a problem. It needs to be fully debated, considered, evaluated, and *then* rejected. The sponsors need to see that no matter how hard they tried, no matter how much they spent, the politics don't line up. The defeat needs to not just be a defeat—it needs to send a message to other cities, to other flying car startups, to other political consultants, that this thing is toxic. A near miss just encourages them to come back again and spend twice as much."

Viktor says nothing in response. They walk in silence, Viktor's bodyguards trailing a few feet behind.

Nick fills the void to cover up his own anxiety. "I mean, Viktor, if you want me to just kill this thing right now and take the risk that it rears its ugly head again in six months, that's fine. Totally fine. It's your call."

Of course, the sooner the bill dies, the sooner FlightDeck stops paying Nick.

But while Susan is a lot of things, she's not dangerous.

At least not as dangerous as Viktor.

"By the way," Viktor says, "you're welcome."

"For what?" Nick asks.

"All rivers lead to the ocean, Nick," he says. "And I am the ocean. All those people you owed money to, I took care of. You now owe it to me. Two million. Nice and simple. Not as much to keep track of."

Nick stops dead in his tracks. "Viktor…"

"Think of it like this," Viktor says. "Instead of the vig compounding on several debts, it's only compounding on one. You save a little money." He pats his chest and smiles. "I get to know that I am doing a favor for a friend. And…" He shrugs. "…now I know you are properly motivated."

Nick's head spins. He figured that's what Viktor was floating during their last meeting. And sure, he considered it—in very dark, desperate moments. Like maybe if he pulled this off for Viktor, the marker would be made to disappear.

But just as Viktor said, he doesn't like to pay retail.

"C'mon, Nick?" Viktor asks. "What do you say?"

Nick mumbles a "thank you," suddenly feeling like a child.

As they approach the aquarium, Viktor says, "You are very welcome, my friend. That's all. You can go now."

Nick doesn't need to be told twice. As he trudges back to Surf Avenue to jump in an Uber, he contemplates his next move.

But he can't think of anything. His mind is blank, save for the terror of spending the next forty years wearing a colostomy bag.

This just went from "bad" to "apocalyptic."

CHAPTER TWENTY-ONE

NEW YORK CITY

Tech Expo, Midtown Sushi Bar

Lisa assumed that a tech expo would be like any convention where the participants are intensely passionate about the topic at hand—comics, UFOs, sex dolls. But this is more than she expected.

The room is loud, packed, carnival-like. People are frantically rushing from aisle to aisle. Two guys are riding around on electric scooters, another on a Uniwheel. Everyone's displaying their wares. Everyone's working everyone. And while they're all kind of in on the joke, Lisa can tell that they also see themselves as part of something bigger—as part of the vaunted tech community.

They're special. They're changing the world. Making it a better place. And that makes their gatherings carry an air of self-importance.

"This is awesome!" Nick shouts, bounding around like a toddler in an amusement park. "Do you love it? You do, right? Told you you'd love it."

Nick's right—the more they walk through the crowd, the more infectious the energy becomes. "Look at this! A whole display dedicated to drone deliveries. And did you see over on aisle eight? AI systems that can predict your REM dreams with ninety-three percent accuracy. Eight months ago, it was only sixty-three percent." Nick spins around. "Oooh! There's that psilocybin lip balm everyone keeps talking about. The only thing they don't have here is flying cars, right?"

"No one has flying cars," Lisa says. "So when you decide to invest in one of these startups, how does it actually work?" This is the one question Wheeler and Rosario instructed Lisa to ask, and she delivers it verbatim, feeling minor pangs of guilt as the words come out of her mouth.

"It's like a giant auction," Nick says. "You go up to a booth, listen to what they have to say, and if you like what you hear, you make an offer."

Someone keeps yelling, "If our terms were good enough for Larry King, they're good enough for you!" Nick and Lisa step up to a booth. The founder looks like he's trying out for a YouTube spot starring a tech founder: fleece vest, medium length hair, branded T-shirt, and bright red Allbirds.

"Hi guys, welcome to Cleaner.ai. As I'm sure you already know, we're at the dawn of a new frontier when it comes to robotic window washers. Imagine a machine sliding up and down the building, self-cleaning every window, all day, every day. It used to take four months to wash every window in the Empire State Building with hundreds of workers. We can do the whole building in four days—with zero human beings. We can do a normal building in eight hours. Every real estate developer in America is going to want one of these."

"How much?" Nick asks.

"Raising seven on twenty-three-pre, thirty-post."

"For your A?"

"No, my man. This is the seed. By the time we do the A, we'll be looking at three times that."

Nick whispers to Lisa. "It means the company is valued at thirty million now, but he thinks the next round will be at ninety million. So if we invested a hundred grand now, it'll be worth a little over three hundred k in a year or so. And then, depending on how the company does, it grows from there." He shrugs. "Or it goes to zero. That's the game."

Lisa whispers back. "I get the math. But what do you think the odds are?"

"Do you think windows are going away anytime soon?"

Lisa shakes her head.

"Do you think people will suddenly start preferring dirty windows?"

Lisa shakes her head again.

Nick smiles. "Then it's not a hard decision. Now you see what I love about this. Especially when you can get in before everyone else. Only the people in this room are able to invest in these new startups. And trust me, getting into this room is not easy."

Lisa is no venture capitalist, but she's pretty sure it takes more analysis than this. She turns to the founder. "Okay, so I invest now and what happens next? When do I get my money back?"

The founder gives Nick a look like, *Come on, dude, you should have explained the rules to her before you guys got here*. That infectious energy is starting to wear off.

Nick turns to Lisa. "They use the initial money to build the product. After a year or so, they'll raise a new round of financing, which will make your investment more valuable, but only on paper. The actual cash comes when they either go public or sell to a bigger company. It can be a while. But fifty grand could easily become five hundred grand—or even five million. It's risky—I'm not going to pretend otherwise. It's your call, but we both know you can afford it. I mean, you still live in that crappy studio on Avenue C."

"It's a one-bedroom. On Avenue B." Lisa pauses. "But point taken." She pauses again. "Fuck it. Why not?" Turns to the founder. "I'm in for twenty-five k." Who knows? Maybe spying for the FBI will make her rich.

"Okay, cool. I'll throw you in an SPV with some other randos."

After trading contact info with the window washer, Nick and Lisa head to the food court area to try some of the free Lingonberry Soylent. "I knew you'd dig it," Nick tells her. "The tech, not the Soylent."

Lisa nods, her mouth full of a substance that isn't quite liquid and isn't quite solid, either, but still tastes like perfume. The effect is quite disturbing.

Nick keeps talking, particularly fond of being able to mansplain a topic. "Just so you know, there's one more trick to all of this. You don't really need to pay the twenty-five k up front."

Oh shit, Lisa thinks, suddenly realizing—this is it. She can practically feel the wire brushing against her skin under her blouse. She's suddenly afraid Nick might be able to see it. She wonders what would happen if she got up and left right now.

Rosario and Wheeler would make her do the whole thing all over again.

"How so?" she asks.

"There are these guys I know you can get it from. It's like having a line of credit."

"I don't need a loan," are the first words out of Lisa's mouth before she remembers that these people and their line of credit are what Wheeler and Rosario have her here for in the first place. So she pivots. "Or maybe I do. Can't hurt to have options."

Nick nods. "I'll introduce you."

***

"That's step one, motherfucker. Connecting you to the loan sharks. Here we go." Rosario pumps her fist so hard she ends up punching the sidewall. Any harder and she would have broken her hand.

As she curses to herself, they hear a loud banging on the other side of the truck. She peers out the window and sees two very angry Hasidic guys in full garb. Rosario opens up the serving bay, which, given this is a cover vehicle, they haven't actually tried opening yet, so it takes a minute to figure out.

"Can I help you?" Wheeler asks, when they finally get it safely latched.

One of the Hasidic guys raps his knuckles on the side of the truck. "Where's your OU certificate?"

"My what?"

"You're selling kosher food," the guy says with a slight Yiddish accent. "Where's your certification to prove the food is kosher?"

Rosario and Wheeler give each other an "oh fuck" look. "It's back at the office," Wheeler says. "We'll bring it in next time."

The second Hasid moves forward aggressively, even though he's currently about three feet below them. "There isn't going to be a next time. This is our turf. All food trucks on Forty-Seventh

Street pay us for their certification and then pay us again for rent. Every week. You haven't done either."

"You don't even look Jewish," the first Hasid says, edging in closer.

"I am," Wheeler insists.

She's not, Rosario thinks, *but nice try.*

"What day does Purim begin?" he quizzes her.

"Guys, guys," Rosario jumps in. "This is just a misunderstanding. No one meant to step on your turf. We'll move the truck."

"You bet you fucking will," Hasid two says. "And if I ever see you two ladies here again—"

"Step off, asshole," Wheeler says, suddenly matching their aggression with her own. "You don't know who you're talking to."

The man is surprised. Even vague threats cause most people to meekly back down. Either he's an idiot or he's badly misjudged the situation. He's about to find out.

"What the fuck is wrong with you," he says, escalating the tone. "Don't you know who we're with?"

"Guess who we're with," Wheeler says, moving her coat aside to reveal the holstered pistol at her hip.

Their eyes pop. Rosario pushes Wheeler back a little. "Guys, I'm going to stop Justine from shooting you. And you're going to walk away. Okay? You might have guessed we're not exactly in the food business. We'll move the truck."

The two of them consider it for a moment, nod to each other, and disappear. Rosario wants to scold Wheeler, but she's not sure which she's more annoyed by: flashing a gun at a civilian, or the piles and piles of cabeza tacos Wheeler's been wolfing down for the last hour, which have made the inside of the truck—already stuffy, and somehow humid despite the cold—smell like a slaughterhouse.

"Back to work?" Rosario asks, which feels a lot easier than talking about the gun or the smell.

Wheeler nods and returns to her tacos.

CHAPTER TWENTY-TWO

NEW YORK CITY

Midtown Sushi Bar

When Nick and Lisa arrive at the omakase place, their guests have already been seated. Both guests come off like they're trying to look like characters in *Narcos*—gold jewelry and very, very shiny shark-gray shirts. They've got sake glasses in front of them, and the bottle is almost empty.

They approach from behind, and Nick claps them on the back. They look startled, like they don't like being touched. Nick doesn't notice. "Chris, Tony, meet Lisa Lim."

Everyone shakes hands. Nick and Lisa sit down.

"I hear you're both serious startup investors," Lisa says.

"Yes, I like to think so," Chris responds. "I mean, more on the Bitcoin side for me personally. Invested in a few ICOs back when crypto was just getting going. Worked out pretty well. A little less well now, admittedly."

"I'm long Postmates," Tony offers.

Lisa wants to give Nick a look, but Chris and Tony seem a little too close and a little too buzzed to risk it.

"Just to put it out there again," Nick says, "if you guys ever want to partner up and convert your cash into equity, I'm open to that." Both men shake their heads no. They're not quite as dumb as they look.

"So how does this all work?" Lisa asks.

"It's pretty simple," Tony explains. "You borrow the money from us. Vig is seven points a week."

"Which is below market," Chris points out.

"At least given our proximity to the New York Fed," Tony adds.

Lisa plays dumb. "But these startups usually don't hit for a long time, right? Sometimes not for years. Sometimes not ever."

"But when they do hit, they hit big," Tony exclaims. "Gain on the investment should easily outweigh the vig. That's your take, right, Nick?"

"And then some. One winner can be a hundred times the size of twenty losers. That's why I reinvest in something new every time there's a liquidity event."

"This window cleaning opportunity sounds interesting," Chris says. "Me personally? I'd do it if I were you."

Lisa doesn't need to borrow twenty-five grand. Especially from them. Political firefighting pays well, and she's been frugal with her earnings.

Nick turns to Lisa. "Look, no pressure. You decide what you want to do. But I've been doing business with these guys for a while now, and I have to say, every time, they've been true to their word." Lisa can't tell who Nick's trying to be helpful to—her so she leverages her money better, or these men so they have a new "client." Knowing Nick, since only one of those two options is in his self-interest, it's the latter.

Lisa doesn't know what else she's supposed to try to get on the wire, but it feels like she's now spent more time with these men than advisable. She taps her Apple Watch and turns to Nick. "I've got a call at one. We're getting those polling results back today."

"Good," Tony says, staring at Nick. "We have to talk about the other thing."

Nick smiles at Lisa. There's something off about the smile.

Lisa doesn't wait to find out what it is. She leaves the restaurant, turns the corner, and heads to the Kosher Mexican Korean food truck. Wheeler's standing outside of it, waiting for her. They go inside. Rosario starts removing the recording device from Lisa's bra.

Lisa looks at both of them. "We're good, right? I did what you asked. Got Nick on tape talking about his tech investments. Got those other guys. Got everything you need. In a perfect world, we never see each other again."

"Well..." Wheeler says with a shrug.

"You know..." Rosario adds unhelpfully.

Lisa knows where this is going. She reprimands herself for being naive enough to think that they'd let her off the hook this easy.

Wheeler confirms it. "You did great. Seriously. Really great. You should be proud. You served your country."

"But?" Lisa asks.

"But we still need more evidence that Nick is throwing the FlightDeck campaign. Proof that he's sabotaging the whole thing. This is a really good start. You're on the right track. Keep at it."

In other words, we're not even close to done.

Like everything else, Lisa realizes, ratting on your boss turns out to be harder than it looks.

CHAPTER TWENTY-THREE

NEW YORK CITY

Firewall HQ

Lisa and Pinky are sitting in Firewall's main conference room, talking to their pollster, Dennis Bennis. Bennis is the rare pollster who can both keep the client happy and deliver accurate numbers almost every time. Bennis is also a dead ringer for Philip Roth in his prime: big wireframe glasses, balding pate, tweed jacket.

"It's all about the framing," Bennis explains. "When we ask people if flying cars is a good idea in the face of all the opposition, they overwhelmingly say no. But when we ask whether we, as a society, should be able to think big enough to make dreams like flying cars a reality, eighty-seven percent say yes." The charts showing what Bennis said pop up on the flatscreen monitor attached to the far wall.

"So it's totally aspirational?" Pinky asks.

"Yes. But you want to pass these bills now, right? You don't have a few years to build a brand."

"We need this done in the next twelve weeks," Lisa says. "Susan told her investors we'd be legal by then. I don't know what actually happens if she misses the deadline, but she's made it clear that if we don't meet it, we won't be around to find out the rest."

"Then you need to show the voters that the future is already here."

Lisa mutters thanks and walks out of the conference room. She turns to Pinky, who's right on her heels. "Call all the local papers we're funding. We need each of them to write that the technology for flying cars is already here so it's a question of having the political will to move forward," she tells him. "And once the clips start coming in, have the graphics team turn them into mailers and maybe some digital ads on Facebook."

"Mailers? Really? Physical mailers? Don't you mean digital ads and infographics? Who does mailers anymore?"

"Maybe some digital ads for Facebook. But the baby boomers still check their mailboxes. I want to rile up the elderlies. Get them marching on City Hall. You know, so we can help them actualize their childhood dreams. Like Bennis said. Put the future first."

Pinky looks a little confused. "Uh huh. Actualize childhood dreams. But...I don't know...do baby boomers really scream the future to you? Maybe it's just me, but I don't usually equate incontinence with cutting-edge technology."

"Old people vote, Pinky," Lisa says.

Pinky nods. "Got it. Okay. Let me run this all by Nick and we'll be good to go."

"Actually," Lisa says, talking faster than her brain can keep up, "Nick is on board with all this. We've been texting." She holds up her phone, like it's proof.

Pinky furrows an eyebrow, as though he's trying to remember if he saw Lisa texting. She's playing a dangerous game, acting as if she has approval that she doesn't, but she's worried that if Nick gets his hands on this, he's going to change or manipulate something to suit the needs of whatever game he's playing.

And she just wants to do her fucking job.

"Got it," Pinky says. "Off to the races."

Lisa sighs with relief as she slips her phone back in her pocket.

CHAPTER TWENTY-FOUR

LOS ANGELES, CA

FlightDeck HQ

Everyone has a boss. That's what Yevgeny thinks to himself as he walks by the large glass conference room occupied by Susan and the entire FlightDeck board. He's met the board before at a reception, so he gives a half-wave through the glass as he passes by. But before he can get to his own office down the hall, he hears Susan yelling, "Yevgeny! Yevgeny!"

He stops, and before he can turn around, she's already behind him. "Hi," he offers, unsure what this is all about.

She's a little out of breath. "I need your help."

He pauses for a moment, considers running, but knows Susan is probably faster, even in stilettos. "What can I do?"

"I need you to go in there and convince the board not to fire me. Carol would usually do it, but her dog has a callback today."

Fire her? Sure, it's something Yevgeny has fantasized about more than once. But it never seemed actually possible. "They are thinking of firing you? Seriously?"

"Well, we don't have a flying car yet, and I told them we would by now."

Yevgeny pays close attention to Susan's tone, anticipating the blame shifting to him mid-sentence. But it doesn't. She's owning it.

He has to give her that. Maybe he was too harsh on her. He was so afraid of her blow-ups that he entered every conversation ready to fight back or shell up and defend himself. But she isn't all bad. She's smart—the bat thing proved that. She can be kind (or at least kindish, when it suits her interests). And right now is the most human he has ever seen her.

She looks scared.

"When I tell them to be patient, to give us a little more time, it falls on deaf ears," she continues. "They're tired of hearing the same thing from me. But if they believe that the new prototype works and is just around the corner..."

Even when she's scared, she has an angle.

"So you want me to give them an update?" Yevgeny asks.

"I want you to convince them to maintain the status quo."

For half a second, it occurs to Yevgeny that if the board fires Susan, maybe they'll make him CEO. How cool would that be? But then another half a second later, he realizes that it's a lot more likely that he just gets fired by whichever one of them decides to be the new CEO. So he agrees and follows Susan into the conference room.

Susan speaks to the group. "Everyone here knows Yevgeny Kolnikoff, our chief engineer. Since we're talking about the status of our prototype, I think it makes sense to ask the person who's actually doing it."

The board freezes for a moment. Beating up on people like Susan—entrepreneurs and strivers who are solely focused on money—is standard operating procedure. But to seriously question Yevgeny, you need some background in how flying cars actually work. And no VC is comfortable revealing how little they understand about the technology they're investing in.

But Susan's suggestion is too reasonable to dismiss, so now they have to try.

Walter Lee, managing partner at Platform Ventures, steps in. Lee is older and handsome, face weathered and hair gray. He's also the only board member who studied computer science in grad school, so he doesn't look completely lost.

"So Yevgeny," Walter says, trying to think of and ask a question at the same time, "I understand our final working prototype exploded last week."

"Yes." Talking to billionaires is not Yevgeny's usual Tuesday afternoon, so he decides to be as concise and straightforward as possible.

"And that means that our flying car not only doesn't work, but that we also now have to spend another one point eight million to build a new one."

"Yes."

"And if you can't solve the sensory issues Susan told us about, it doesn't matter if we develop a new prototype or not. The car still won't work."

"Yes."

"So it seems like we're stuck. We can't launch a flying car that doesn't work. We can't shut the whole thing down—not after all the money we've put into this." The entire table nods in agreement. "Other than making a change at the top, I honestly don't know what else to do."

The word springs from Yevgeny's mouth, almost as soon as it enters his brain. "Hackathon."

Everyone on the board knows what a hackathon is.

No one on the board wants to do a hackathon.

It's a last resort. A lame PR stunt usually intended to make it look like whoever the host is cares about the community by soliciting their ideas for new technology. The winning ideas from hackathons never actually turn into anything. But it would be a way to buy a little goodwill, and some extra time.

If Yevgeny had a better play, he would have gone for it.

But he doesn't.

"I think we need a little more than a carnival right now," offers Andy Albanese from 720 Ventures, who looks barely out of college.

"When the last prototype crashed, its sensory mechanism wasn't a complete failure. It sensed a bird. And a plane," Yevgeny reminds them.

"But not the drone," interrupts a middle-aged white dude whose name Yevgeny can never remember.

"Right. Not the drone. But everything else. So look at it this way—we are like ninety-eight percent of the way there. None of our competitors are even at fifty yet. You could change all the senior leadership at the company and see if a new team does better. But we may be able to solve the remaining two percent in a fraction of the time it will take you to fire everyone and hire a new team."

"Okay, but why a hackathon?" Albanese asks.

"We have tried everything we can possibly think of. Maybe someone who is not in the weeds can see whatever it is we're missing. This is a way to generate outside knowledge to solve our problem. And the winner gets, I don't know, ten thousand dollars? Twenty thousand? Peanuts."

The whole room is silent. Finally, Stephanie Stevens from Tahoe Ventures speaks up. "Hackathons are easy to put together.

We can see whether or not we get anything useful from it pretty fast. Probably just a matter of a few weeks."

Removing a founder is always a tricky problem for venture capitalists. Wait too long, and your investment could go up in smoke. Move too fast and you get a reputation for being founder-unfriendly, and then no other founder wants your money. So delaying Susan's beheading by a few weeks to see if Yevgeny's crazy idea could work makes sense.

At least that's how Yevgeny sees it.

One by one, the board does too. Some members just say okay. Others nod. Walter asks Susan and Yevgeny to give them the room.

Once they're in the hallway, Susan expresses something Yevgeny has never seen before.

Gratitude.

"That was amazing," she says, taking one of his hands in both of hers and holding it. "I had no idea you'd be so good with the board."

Yevgeny is a little thrown by the sudden burst of intimacy. Also, her hands are extremely dry; he assumed she is the kind of person who relentlessly moisturizes. "What is that phrase you like to use?" Yevgeny says. "It has the added benefit of being true? If it worked, it is because I did not say anything I do not believe in. I do not know if the hackathon idea will be successful—I made it up on the spot. But it at least buys us some time. And who knows? Maybe someone else can see something we cannot."

Walter steps out of the conference room and pulls Susan into the hallway.

Yevgeny watches through the conference room window. Lots of nodding. It doesn't look like an execution.

After a minute, she comes back out. "We're safe. For now."

CHAPTER TWENTY-FIVE

NEW YORK CITY

Inside City Hall, NY1 Studios

"Welcome back to *Inside City Hall.* I'm your host, Kirsten White. Our two guests today are regulars on the show—Graciela Vazquez, president of the New York Democratic Socialists, and Roland Hodges, the former Republican state senator from Staten Island. Hello again to both of you."

Vazquez and Hodges both nod tersely in acknowledgment. It brings the temperature down a few degrees in the studio. They haven't forgotten how their last appearance went.

"A few weeks ago, we had a pretty lively discussion about legislation pending before the City Council to legalize flying cars. How do you each feel the campaign has evolved since then?"

Vazquez eagerly jumps in first. "Terribly. Everyone I know is against it. No one wants another giveaway to the rich. No one wants to make New York City more of a playground for billionaires. Honestly? I can't see this bill even making it out of committee."

Hodges cuts in, ready to rumble. "Graciela, that's because you only talk to people who think the same way you do. That's what happens when you demand safe spaces all the time—your sense of reality becomes completely distorted."

Vazquez tries to interrupt, but Hodges keeps talking.

"Personally, I think the flying cars campaign is going pretty well. I know it got off to a bumpy start, but that TV ad moved a lot of people—the poll released by Firewall shows that everyday New Yorkers want flying cars. You're also seeing strong support from the weekly papers in all five boroughs, and that's the real pulse of the city. From what my sources tell me, Mayor Navarro is now leaning in favor of the bill. And if Navarro wants it to happen, there's a pretty good chance it'll happen."

White turns to Vazquez for a rebuttal, who is more than happy to offer one.

"Navarro got whatever he wanted at the beginning, when people thought he was the crusader he sold himself as," she says. "But then we all realized he's just another pay-to-play politician. The DSA helped elect twenty-three new members of the City Council last year. They're all loyal to a progressive agenda. And a progressive agenda does not include flying cars."

Hodges tries to jump in, but White wants to speak.

"I'm not sure how closely either of you are following the campaigns in Austin and Los Angeles, but it seems like both cities are at least open to the idea. Even though it's up to the city of Austin, the governor of Texas has come out in favor of the bill. Multiple advocacy groups from the NAACP to the Cato Institute have as well. Given all of that, Senator Hodges, does it matter if New York is the first?"

"Of course it matters! It makes all the difference in the world. Think about how these bills work. Any City Council—ours, Austin, LA—who approves this is going to want something in return!"

"Can you elaborate for our viewers?" says White.

"Sure!" Hodges is happy to pontificate. "If New York legalizes flying cars and LA does not, does FlightDeck move their headquarters here as part of the deal? I would think yes. That means there are jobs at stake. Tax revenue. It would send a signal to the market that we are open for business. When corporate America thinks about our city right now, they see taxes, they see regulations, they see people giving them a hard time."

He jerks his head to the left to indicate he means Vazquez.

Hodges continues, "But if we embrace this kind of innovation? If we're the first city in the country—in the world—to do this? That tells everyone we want companies to come here. We want tech startups to come here." He turns to the camera and speaks more slowly, to emphasize his point. "We want to work with you."

"You know what, Roland?" Vazquez asks. "I know I never agree with you—"

"That's why they have us on together!" Hodges laughs, trying to cut the tension.

Vazquez smiles. "But everything you said is exactly right. If we legalize flying cars, we're sending a signal to the nation, a signal to the world. A signal that New York wants to be the home of economic inequality."

Now it's Vazquez's turn to pause for effect.

"That New York wants to favor the interests of the one percent ahead of everyone else. That New York doesn't care about affordable housing, doesn't care about social justice, doesn't care about environmental justice—just money. It does send a signal. Exactly the wrong signal," she says.

"Well," White jumps in, ready to bring the segment to a close, "the two of you have captured the argument in a nutshell.

One bill. One concept. Two completely different perspectives. If my friend Roland is right and Mayor Navarro is supportive of the bill, you have to like FlightDeck's chances. But if my friend Graciela is right, then the zeitgeist for the bill is wrong. And as we've all seen in politics, zeitgeist can be everything."

White pauses and adjusts her glasses. "Okay, we're going to take a quick break, and when we come back, we'll finally, finally, learn the answer to what happened to the chicken in Chinatown that played tic-tac-toe."

CHAPTER TWENTY-SIX

AUSTIN, TX

City Hall

"You see, Lisa," Deputy Mayor Taylor begins, "people may think that being a vegetarian is a good choice. And you know, some religions don't permit meat, and I respect that. I respect non-Christians. They're people of God too. But for the rest of us? These ribs right here? This place right here? You can't eat this and then tell me your life is better not eating meat."

Lisa is a full-fledged carnivore, so she doesn't bother to look up from her plate of ribs, potato salad, pinto beans, pickles, onions, and Wonder Bread to indicate her agreement.

At least he's talking to her instead of playing on his phone.

Taylor doesn't notice that she hasn't stopped eating, lost in his own brilliance. "Sure, some people say that cows emit a lot of methane that causes global warming. But you know, lots of things cause global warming, so you really can't just put it on the ribs. And in a city like Austin, where a steer is the unofficial mascot, blaming cows for climate change is like bringing quinoa to a Lake Travis barbecue."

Lisa doesn't watch college football, but her dad does, so she knows about the mascot. "Right. The football mascot. The cow. What's his name?"

"Bevo."

"Right, the beloved Bevo. How many Bevos have there been now? Can't be the same one from when I was a kid."

Taylor registers some surprise that Lisa knows who Bevo is.

Lisa is surprised that Taylor knows what quinoa is.

"So Lisa," he says, changing course. "How do you feel your bill is coming along?"

Lisa is surprised to see Taylor asking someone else for an opinion. He seems to only value his own. "We're definitely building a lot of support. You saw the governor endorsed the bill. But you tell me. You're the boss." Flattering an arrogant man is never a bad play.

"Well, I think it has potential. Definitely has a chance if we move it through the Council. Probably couldn't pass on its own, but if we put some real muscle behind it? I'm coming around to the idea, but I still need to learn more. Do my diligence."

Lisa isn't sure where Taylor is going with this, but she's anticipating a request for an in-person demo and wondering whether Susan is capable of delivering that yet.

But then the conversation takes a different turn. "Lot of technology conferences these days, huh?" Taylor asks.

Lisa doesn't know what Taylor's talking about. Conferences to her mean lurking the hallways of whatever hotel the Democratic Governors Association or Republican Governors Association is having their annual fundraiser in. But if Taylor's going to support the bill and he wants to talk about tech conferences, they'll talk about tech conferences. "I think so."

"I was looking at this list on the internet last night of the best tech conferences. Impressive bunch. Did you know *Fortune* has a conference in Aspen in July? The *Wall Street Journal* has one in Laguna Beach in September. And Web Summit is in Lisbon in November. They sure pick nice places. These tech folks definitely aren't stupid. I'll give them that."

Lisa digs into her second giant rib and mutters, "Uh huh."

Taylor keeps going. "Do you attend these conferences, Lisa?"

She starts to wonder if this is a come-on. Like, *maybe we could get a drink? And I could see your hotel room after?*

Wouldn't be the first older white government official to put a feeler out on her.

The muscles in her shoulders bunch up, and she puts the rib down. "Not those conferences. They're above my pay grade. From what I hear, those are for CEOs and the top politicians and venture capitalists. Not consultants like me."

"CEOs like Susan Howard?"

"Yeah. I assume so. I don't have access to her schedule or anything, but she certainly seems like the conference circuit type," Lisa responds, politely. In fact, attending conferences is most certainly *not* one of their campaign tactics. The last thing Lisa needs Susan wasting time on is hobnobbing at conferences. No one ever passed a bill in a breakout session.

"Well, you know," Taylor says, "it may help my diligence if I spend some time with her at one of these conferences. Get her take on the issue. Talk to her peers. Survey the scene. Talk to the experts."

Okay, so, he's not awkwardly propositioning her.

Does he want to proposition Susan?

Is he trying to get her to set that up?

This is getting weird.

"I mean, I don't know how they figure out who goes to these events, but I can definitely talk to them about it," she says. "I can also have her come see you in Austin whenever you want. She'd be happy to."

"I want to see her in the proper context. See her in action. Get multiple opinions. Assuming your client picks up the cost, I'm interested in attending. My wife is too. She especially loves Aspen in July. And Lisbon in November."

Ah. So there it is.

"She likes Laguna Beach in September too," Taylor says, underscoring the point.

Lisa nods, thanks Taylor for lunch, makes an excuse about another meeting, and gets out of there as quickly as possible.

Even before Lisa met the FBI, she knew that the same rule that applies to dealing with law enforcement—stay the fuck away—also applies when a client or an elected asks you to do something illegal.

Like asking for a free trip to Aspen in return for supporting your bill.

The prudent thing to do is call Rosario or Wheeler, report what happened, and let them handle it.

But then that might kill the bill in Austin.

And, she thinks, *lots of people have conversations where they're just spitballing ideas. If nothing comes of it, no harm, no foul.* Once Lisa calls the FBI, it becomes bigger. Best case, she's spending hours and hours and tens of thousands of dollars with lawyers preparing to testify.

Worst case, Taylor says she's part of it. Like maybe she made the offer first.

She wishes she could ask Nick what to do. She wishes Nick had never gotten her into this whole mess in the first place. So

Lisa does what she's been trying to do more of when she isn't sure what to do—she waits.

Wait. Think. Don't shoot from the hip.

Which, in this case, means don't report Taylor's request for a bribe to anyone just yet.

CHAPTER TWENTY-SEVEN

LOS ANGELES, CA

The Bar at the Four Seasons

Nick has never wanted to open an official office in Los Angeles. Official offices mean process. They mean paperwork. Bureaucracy. Insurance. Leases. HR. All headaches as far as Nick is concerned.

So, over the years, he's made the Four Seasons in Beverly Hills his home away from home. On a good day, he never leaves the bar area. People come to him—at least anyone below Nick on the politics food chain. That includes Jimmy Van Meter, Firewall's go-to lobbyist in Los Angeles.

Jimmy does not have good news.

"I've worked this from every angle possible. There's no way DeFrancesco budges on this. He sees this as an existential threat to the union. It's a lost cause," Van Meter says.

"And without DeFrancesco, City Hall is out of play. And without City Hall, there's no way the Council passes this," Nick adds.

Van Meter nods.

"And you're sure there's no way to get him on board? Positive? Make him a partner in some way? Offer to unionize some component of the FlightDeck team?"

"FlightDeck would let you do that?"

"I doubt it."

"So then what?"

Van Meter looks at Nick. Nick looks back. They both know the answer, even though it's a tougher path than buying someone off.

"You're gonna have to take him out," Van Meter tells Nick. "Make him so fucking toxic that everyone has to drop him. So toxic that the only way to cleanse yourself is by doing the thing he hates. By passing the bill."

"Jimmy, you know me. You know I don't mind doing that. But there's got to be some *there* there. If it's all bullshit, it won't work and we'll look even worse."

"From what I've heard over the years? There may be something there. Guy lives a pretty lavish lifestyle for a union boss. But you're the one with the oppo team. You tell me."

Nick sighs.

He's a little nervous, because the dirtier this gets, the harder it is to control. But he doesn't see any other option. If it gets LA to move, it gets LA to move. That keeps the campaign going, which keeps the fees rolling in.

"I'll call my guy," Nick says.

There's no reason Nick can't call Pinky from the bar. It's two in the afternoon, and other than three old ladies playing mahjong in the corner, no one's there.

But this is Pinky, and it's always hard to know where those conversations are going to go, so Nick decides to make the call from his room. Pinky doesn't get that many calls from Nick directly, so he answers on the first ring.

"Nick! How's it going? You're in Los Angeles? What's the weather like there? I hear it's really nice. Especially compared to here. It's freezing. I forgot to bring gloves this morning and my hands were so cold on the walk from the subway to the office. So cold. Do you wear gloves?"

This is why Nick avoids calling Pinky. He knows that if he indulges Pinky in a conversation about gloves or ferrets or the Ottoman Empire, the call will last indefinitely. So he gets right to it.

"Do you know who Steve DeFrancesco is?"

"The union leader in LA. He's against our flying cars bill. Just saw photos of him on Insta at a rally opposing it."

"That's the guy."

"I assume there's no way to bring him around?"

"If there were, would I be calling you?"

"How deep do you want me to dig?"

"To the center of the Earth. Go through his trash. Access his emails, bank records. Make up a false account and friend his kids on Instagram. Whatever you need to do."

"Does Lisa know about this?"

"I'm the boss, not Lisa."

Pinky sounds honored to be in with Nick on a conspiracy "Nick—I will turn over every leaf, every rock, every byte of data out there. And when I'm done, you'll have DeFrancesco's head on a stick."

CHAPTER TWENTY-EIGHT

NEW YORK CITY

Madison Square Park

Lisa steps out of her building and onto the street, headed toward the Madison Square Park dog run for the monthly new business meeting. The walk is twenty-five minutes if she's moving really fast, thirty to thirty-five if she's not, which means, in her case, she usually makes it in twenty.

But her living room window only looks onto a dark gray airshaft, so she never knows the weather and never bothers to check online. Turns out it's raining. And cold. Even though they're now technically a few days past the vernal equinox. Wheeler and Rosario could have at least mentioned the rain when they were in her apartment earlier fitting her for another wire.

There are no cabs in sight. She can hop in a Lyft, but it'll be at least a ten-minute wait. She sees a bus idling a few blocks down Avenue B and walks across the street to the plexiglass bus shelter. It's better than getting soaked and it's cheaper than a cab, but it means she won't arrive at the park for at least half an hour, probably longer. She wishes she had made coffee at home and makes a mental note to buy a single-cup coffee maker.

Her phone rings. The ringtone definitely does not go with her hangover. She makes another mental note to change the setting to vibrate.

"Hello?" Lisa immediately curses herself for answering a number she doesn't recognize. Another downside of operating on too much to drink and too little sleep.

"Hey, Lisa. It's Julia Alessi from the *Post*."

"Fuck me," Lisa mutters to herself. Then to Julia, "Hey. How's it going?" She starts pacing anxiously back and forth along the fourteen square feet the bus shelter offers. Nothing good ever comes from Julia Alessi. Even when you try to use her as a weapon to box other people in, it somehow comes back to haunt you.

"Good, good, thanks. Listen, real quick, I just wanted to ask you about this FBI investigation into Nick Denevito."

Lisa stops cold right as the bus pulls up. "I don't know what you're talking about." She lets the bus go by.

"Really? That's not what Agents Rosario and Peeler told me. They said you're cooperating. That you've been very helpful."

"It's Wheeler, not Peeler." Lisa cringes as soon as she says it, realizing what she's done: confirmed the story. She bets Julia did that on purpose. And if they talked to the *Post*, why the fuck would Rosario and Wheeler mention her in the first place? And why not give her a heads-up? Unless someone else talked.

"So you have talked to them. Then what's the point of lying to me? You're too smart for that. But either way, let's clarify for the record—you're officially denying that Nick Denevito is being investigated by the FBI? Are you also under investigation? How would you describe your relationship with Nick? Solely professional?"

"I'm not saying anything. On or off the record."

"How about on background?"

"That's the same thing! I'm not going to be in your story."

Lisa can hear Julia smiling through the phone. "Oh, but you are. I can say that when reached by phone, you confirmed the existence of the investigation but refused to comment. I could say you wouldn't deny being under investigation yourself. Or, you can give me a quote so you don't look quite as bad. To be honest, I don't really care either way. I just need to check the box."

Lisa slams her fist against the plexiglass. "I didn't confirm anything. All I did was say someone's name. So what? You can report that I corrected your spelling? Plus, I wasn't on the record. And even if I was, I'm not going to give you what you want."

Julia pauses. For a moment, Lisa thinks she's gotten through to her.

Then Julia says, "You already did." And hangs up.

As the call ends, one good thing does happen. A cab appears miraculously.

When Lisa arrives at the dog run only a few minutes late, Nick, Alphonso, and Allison are already there, standing under umbrellas. The rain has turned into a light mist, so getting slightly wet seems preferable to their rainy-day backup location fighting off a million tourists for a table at Eataly.

"Okay, great," Nick starts. "Everyone's here. New business ideas. Let's hear 'em. Alphonso?"

"I've got a bunch!"

Allison rolls her eyes.

"Tele-religion. On-demand haberdashery. The Hall of Very Good Players. Take your pick. All great ideas for new startups. I've got decks on all three of them. Want me to pull them up on the iPad?" Nick just shakes his head no. He calls on Allison.

"The governor still wants to close that nuclear power plant on Staten Island," she says. "Maybe we run the campaign to keep it open? Play on that classic Staten Island insecurity—it may be deadly, but it's ours."

"What's going on today?" Nick asks. "Did you guys ask the interns for ideas on your way over here, or are you just making them up completely on the spot?"

Everyone except Nick stares at the ground. "Lisa? You always have something good. Save the day for us here."

Lisa hadn't spent much time thinking of new business ideas even before the call came in from Julia. Now, the notion of soliciting new clients seems patently absurd. But since no one but her knows that the firm is about to implode, she has to come up with something. "Umm...well, they're proposing new soda taxes again in Chicago. Maybe Pepsi could hire us to fight the bill? Or Dr. Pepper maybe? I hear they pay pretty well."

Lisa wonders if the rain is making it hard for the mic to pick up everyone's sound. She edges closer to Nick. She doesn't want to have to do this all over again.

"No!" Nick yells. "None of these are good enough. Guys, guys—we have a long, bright future ahead of us. Lots of money to make. But I can't be the only one figuring it out. You have to do your part too."

"We are, Nick," Lisa replies. "We're all working our asses off. Taking shit from Susan. Shit from you. Fighting off all the opponents of the campaign."

"And you're lucky for that. You are here by the grace of my kindness and nothing else," Nick responds.

His fucking grace? Kindness? Seriously? This guy. Lisa knows what she's about to do next is wrong, but her rage outweighs her judgment.

"Nick—we're here because you need us. You can't charge people like Susan crazy retainers if there aren't people like us to do the actual fucking work. And of everyone working to legalize flying fucking cars, you're the one who's adding the least value of anyone."

Lisa desperately wants to say the final part out loud. That she knows Nick is double-dealing. That he's looking at jail time. That he's putting them all at risk.

Nick stares at Lisa. Strangely, he's not upset. But he is concerned. Does she just mean he's been too quiet in strategy meetings? Or does she know more? Lisa's too smart to take for granted. He decides to find out. It's risky, but that's never stopped him before.

"What exactly are you accusing me of?" He stares at her hard. This is where growing up in Queens offers a big advantage over the white-picket-fence suburbs in Virginia.

Shit. Lisa's not sure what to do. She doesn't like a face-to-face confrontation. She knows Rosario and Wheeler certainly don't want her telling Nick that he's under investigation. But the *Post* is planning to run with the story, probably any day now anyway, so what's the difference? Better they at least hear it from her. She turns to Nick. "You're under investigation by the FBI."

He holds back a laugh. "No, I'm not."

"Yes. You are. They tried to get me to wear a wire on you. Well, actually, they did get me to wear a wire on you."

Nick is never surprised. When he acts surprised, it's usually just that: an act. Not this time. "What'd you tell them?" He almost seems to lose his balance for a moment, steadying himself on the railing of the wrought-iron fence.

"At first, I told them that they were being absurd and there's no way you'd do anything wrong. I know you. But once they showed me the photos of you hugging Viktor Velonova? And then the loan sharks we met with the other day? And all your failed startup investments? I really didn't want to believe it, but..." Her voice trails off.

"Wait. What is this even about?" Allison asks, looking fairly panicked and even more confused.

"They think Nick is double-dealing our clients," Lisa answers. "Signing them up for a campaign and then going to the other side and asking for bribes to throw the result their way instead."

There's this expression about how when people are sick, they turn green. Lisa always thought it was some kind of exaggeration. Like when you get hit and see stars. But the more she talks, the more Nick's skin is taking on a sickly green hue.

"But why?" Allison asks. "The whole reason we do this job is to win. To beat other people. You can't do that when you're playing both sides."

Nick doesn't answer, so Lisa does it for him. "He's deep in debt. He borrowed all this money from loan sharks to invest in risky tech startups. The FBI thinks he's essentially a gambling addict. He can't repay the loans. And now the only way to get out from under it is by making double on every client. And only paying taxes on half of them."

Everyone is silent for a moment, taking in the information.

"How long have you known about this?" Allison finally asks.

"A few weeks."

"Then why are you first telling us now?"

"Because now the *Post* knows about this too. Julia Alessi called me right before I came here. She's running with the story."

"Fuck," Allison and Alphonso mutter simultaneously. Nick remains silent.

"Nick?" Alphonso asks.

Nick takes a deep breath, then makes eye contact with each of them in turn. Lisa last. "Of course it's not true. None of it is. Everything you just said is total bullshit. I've never done any of that and never would. Come on. You guys know me."

Lisa wasn't sure if Nick would crumble or turn on her. She's seen both over the years. He likes her. He respects her. He cares about her life and her career. Ninety-five percent of the time, that's the norm. But she's also still just an employee. She's there to get him what *he* needs. Firewall is a business, not group therapy. Employees come and go. Everyone is replaceable. Even Lisa. And so the caring part only goes so far.

Fortunately, she prepared for both.

"I didn't want to believe it either," Lisa says. "I told the FBI there was no way it was true. Debated them on every single point. They don't just have pictures of you and Velonova. They have audio. Trust me, I really wish it weren't this way. For your sake and ours. We're all out of a job because of you."

Nick doesn't say anything. For a guy who's always talking, always charming, always laughing, his silence is unsettling. The team waits a few moments to see if Nick has anything to say.

He doesn't.

She expected something different than this. Something better than Nick just stalling and lying. When it's clear he's not going to say anything else, she walks out of the dog run, angry at Nick for betraying them, angry at the FBI for making her wear this wire, angry at herself for not knowing how to make this all go away. As she storms off, she rips off her wire.

CHAPTER TWENTY-NINE

NEW YORK CITY

The Kosher Mexican Korean Food Truck

The wire makes a tearing sound as it scratches against Lisa's clothing, before the feed goes silent. Rosario and Wheeler both yank off their headphones.

"What the fuck?" Wheeler shouts. "She can't do that. Her job is to wear the fucking wire, not to tell the target he's the subject of an investigation. What's not clear about that? And why the fuck did she talk to the *Post*? She should have hung up the minute Alessi identified herself. We didn't fucking talk to Alessi. And we certainly didn't tell her to."

Rosario considers pointing out that they're lucky Lisa is cooperating at all, given that they have nothing on her—which, lucky for them, Lisa hasn't realized—but knows that will just lead to more grousing and outrage.

"We need to press charges against her. Or at least scare the shit out of her," Wheeler demands. "Obstruction of justice. Contempt of court. Deliberately sabotaging a federal investigation. Something. Whatever. The grand jury can figure it out."

Now it's time for some reason. "Justine," Rosario says, "let's give this a minute, okay? Yes, what Lisa did was not right. But if we charge her with obstruction, then it becomes a pissing match between us and them, rather than our uncovering corrupt behavior by a prominent political figure and stopping it."

She says it with so much conviction, she almost believes it.

But frankly, she's starting to feel like this whole thing is a wash. They should have just put all their effort into Velonova instead of bringing him on board to go after a bunch of possible political targets they aren't even sure are guilty in the first place.

Wheeler says she's going outside to vape. Rosario knows that Wheeler doesn't smoke, but Rosario is happy to have some space.

A little over an hour later, Wheeler returns, seemingly better. Whatever she did—Rosario guesses she watched competitive eating videos on YouTube on a bench by the Shake Shack in Madison Square Park before wolfing down a few burgers, because she smells like ShackSauce—it worked.

So now they can get back to focusing on arresting Nick.

As Rosario starts filling out the paperwork for a warrant to search Nick's home and office, there's a knock on the door. *Oh no*, she thinks. *Not the Lubavitchers again.*

She reluctantly flips the latch and opens the door.

It's not the rebbes.

It's Nick.

"Holy shit," Wheeler says.

"How'd you even know we were in here?" Rosario asks. "Lisa told you?"

"She told me about the investigation. I figured out the food truck part on my own. I mean, once you see the same stupid Kosher Mexican Korean food truck for the fifty-third time, it doesn't take much to put two and two together."

"We're thinking about switching it to halal," Wheeler tells him. "Otherwise, we'd have to shut down for Passover."

Rosario jumps in. "Mister Denevito, as you seem to know, you're the target of a major federal investigation. We'd love to get some answers, but you do know you have the right to counsel, correct?"

"Am I under arrest?"

"Not yet. But that doesn't mean you won't be."

"Yeah, my lawyer said that too. He said coming to see you guys is a terrible idea."

Rosario can't help but agree with Nick's lawyer. She does her best not to show it.

"But you know what?" Nick continues. "I've made it this far going with my gut. And my instincts are telling me we can work something out here. Let's be honest. As important as I like to think I am, I'm still basically a nobody. No one passing this truck outside has ever heard of me. So will arresting me get you a one-day story in the *Post*? Sure. Maybe one of you even gets quoted. You can cut out the article and have it laminated. Mazel tov. But that's the best you'll do. It won't advance your careers. But if I can help you get someone who everyone outside has heard of? A major figure? That's an entirely different ballgame."

Both agents remain silent, wanting to see what else Nick volunteers. Their instincts are to ignore him, given that he's both a criminal and a master salesman, but everything he's saying makes sense. And it's also what McClain at the U.S. Attorney's Office said would be the best-case outcome.

"Look, I know you've been listening to my conversations with Lisa. And unless you're wildly different from every other career-obsessed federal agent I've ever met, you know that using me to trade up is the right play for all of us."

Rosario tries to look skeptical but instead ends up confirming Nick's prediction. The upside is too high to ignore. "Assuming you even have anything."

Nick smiles for the first time all afternoon. "I might. I just might."

CHAPTER THIRTY

LOS ANGELES, CA
FlightDeck HQ

The fun part of the hackathon—the visitors, the glad-handing, the bagels and coffee—is over. Everyone who came for the cameras or the free food is long gone. Now it's just the sixteen teams grinding away on their ideas, competing for the first-place prize of $20,000 or the second-place prize of Susan's family's front-row Dodgers tickets (they never use them anyway). Most of the FlightDeck employees have quietly migrated back to their offices, anxious to get some real work done.

Yevgeny walks into the bathroom, goes into a stall, and as always, puts his phone in airplane mode. The door opens again, and two of the participants walk in. Through the crack in the stall door, he can see it's the twin brothers who look just as disheveled as the other hackers—hoodies, beat-up jeans, comic book T-shirts—but Yevgeny thinks being Black makes them look a little cooler than the other schlumps. They're mid-conversation.

"...I think it's all about the sensors," says Twin One, who's wearing a Thor T-shirt.

"How so?" asks Twin Two, in a Green Lantern T-shirt.

"We know the cars can take off," says Thor. "We know they can land. We know they can move forwards and backwards. FlightDeck has already revealed all of that. But the car still isn't operating in the real world. So why? Because something in the real world doesn't match what they see in the lab and they can't solve it."

"Like?" asks Green Lantern.

"Like detecting foreign objects—a flock of seagulls or a drone or a hot air balloon. But what if they installed a series of sensors at key external points that could detect potential activity and guide the car away from it? Give them a fuller picture of the surrounding area. Maybe that could solve their problem." Thor pauses, then reconsiders. "I'm sure they have it under control. Compared to the kind of engineering talent they must have in-house here at FlightDeck, I mean, what do we know?"

"Maybe something they don't," Green Lantern says. "Or else, why are we even here?"

"Yeah, maybe. Let's see if it's possible to build out my idea. See if the judges like it. And see if they still consider the cars to be autonomous if it now requires all this extra external equipment and cooperation. But if that can happen, maybe we have something useful to contribute?"

Yevgeny's eyes go wide, and he nearly drops his phone.

How did he never think of external sensors?

Yes, it'd be a nightmare to install them across the city, but it could provide the detection and navigation help they need. He tries to stay quiet, hoping to hear more. But he can't hit the brakes in time. Hearing a loud plopping sound, the second hacker swivels his head toward Yevgeny's stall.

"What the fuck? There's someone in there," says Thor.

Green Lantern drops his voice. "Could be another team listening in. We should talk somewhere more private."

"No," Yevgeny cries from within the stall.

Both hackers freeze, then try to quickly zip up and scram. Yevgeny grabs for the toilet paper but can't get it off the holder. The metal box is clanging around and now he's got paper wrapped around his hand like a mummy. Sweating profusely, he reaches back and under to wipe, then hears the bathroom door open, says fuck it, and runs out of the stall, yanking his underpants back up, toilet paper still wrapped around his hand. "Wait!"

The two hackers stop and turn around. "Eavesdropping wasn't bad enough? Now you want us to just tell you how to win?"

"No. I am not on another team."

"Dude, you should put some pants on."

"I work here," Yevgeny explains, not even bothering to cover himself, which he realizes might turn into an actionable thing, but he doesn't care. "I am the chief engineer."

Both hackers look skeptical. This imbecile can't possibly be the chief engineer.

"No. It is true. I am." Yevgeny bends all the way down to get his ID out of his pocket. Holds it up. "See!"

He tries to hand it to them. They both back away and put up their hands in disgust.

"Okay, okay, I get it. This is a little weird. But maybe not that weird when you think about it. I mean, you are in the bathroom. I am in the bathroom. We are all in the bathroom. This is what happens in bathrooms."

The hackers start backing their way to the door again.

"Fine. It is weird. Let's do this. I will clean up. I will meet you guys outside the bathroom, we will go to my office, I will prove to you who I really am, and we can talk from there. Good?" They look at each other and nod tentatively in agreement.

***

After an hour and a half grilling the hackathoners—the first ten minutes of which are very awkward—Yevgeny walks into Susan's office at the exact moment she's Googling herself again. She quickly closes out of the window when she realizes Yevgeny can see. Normally he'd roll his eyes, but right now he doesn't care.

"I think maybe we are there," Yevgeny says.

Susan stands up and walks over to the exterior window and searches the sky. "Did I just see a flock of pigs fly by?"

"Hilarious."

"I'm sorry, but I feel unprepared for this moment. Dr. Doom and Gloom is telling me that something good actually happened?"

"Fine, maybe I deserve that. But one of the groups here—"

"One of the hackathon groups?"

"Yeah."

"You're taking advice from amateur coders?"

"No. Well, yes. I mean they have a really good idea around adding sensors and cameras to external objects in the flight path. I think it solves the detection problem. And the spatial relations problem."

"Which all means?"

"That we will not keep bumping into things. And things will not keep bumping into us. Especially drones."

She pauses. "Right, but now we've got to pay for the rights to attach our sensors to buildings? The fucking permits alone! Not to mention that it would give our critics a whole new point of attack—they'll say that we're not in full control of the process if we need the cooperation of others. That we're not truly autonomous. That a building could deactivate a sensor and then our vehicle could crash. And they can try to stop buildings from installing the sensors. This is not an elegant solution."

"Think of it like a subway system, right?" Yevgeny sits and talks with his hands, outlining something. "Just like subway lines, you have dedicated flight paths instead of cars flying all over the city in any direction. This probably makes it safer too. We program the sensors to watch specifically for birds and drones. That covers most of it. Then we can do the rest—and we can work on truly solving the sensory problem—when the pressure is off."

Susan seems unsure.

"Do you prefer the alternative?"

"Depends what it is."

"No functioning product at all. Bankruptcy. Humiliation."

Susan pauses for a moment, then shakes her head. "No. You're right. This isn't the best solution, but maybe it's the only one we have. Let's get these hackathoners to sign an NDA and get them on the payroll as quickly as you can. Tell HR I said to expedite everything. In fact, I'll call them myself. Right after I see Carol at two p.m. She's postponed three times. I really hope her pen pal is doing better."

As Susan indicates it's time for him to leave, Yevgeny can't decide if listening to two dudes who showed up at a hackathon is crazy or genius.

And he can't decide if their story ends up being the one that becomes known—that two random twins from Crenshaw figured out how to make cars fly. All the work he did over the last two years...

Then he thinks about paying rent on the three-bedroom he can't afford. He thinks about the monthly payment on his new hybrid BMW. He thinks about the vacation he's already booked to Machu Picchu. He thinks about having to tell his family in Estonia that his flying car company completely failed and that he can't pay to send everyone to college in the U.S.

At least the hackathon was his idea in the first place.

"Okay," he says to Susan as she's yelling at the unfortunate person in HR who picked up the phone. "I will get them going today."

CHAPTER THIRTY-ONE

NEW YORK CITY

The Kosher Mexican Korean Food Truck

Nick pulls the silver latch, opens the door, and climbs the two stairs into the Kosher Mexican Korean food truck. As he does this, he lets out a deep breath.

He's not sure if anyone has ever used a comms strategy before as a way to change the underlying focus of an FBI investigation, but it's worth a shot.

Wheeler looks up from a full box of Hawaiian pizza that she's halfway through. There are three more boxes on the slim table next to her. "You really need to stop doing that."

He gets settled in the passenger seat up front. "Why? Are you going to add trespassing to the list? Breaking and entering?"

Wheeler rolls her eyes. "You asked for a night. You got it. What do you have for us?"

"Navarro," Nick says.

Rosario tries to hide her excitement and does a bad job.

It came to him last night: Navarro is perfect for this. Taking out the mayor is exactly the kind of score that would dwarf him. It's not like Navarro doesn't deserve it. And the best part is, he might be able to make it a package deal, so it takes a little pressure off with Viktor at the same time.

"What about him?" she asks, trying to be nonchalant.

"Is the mayor of New York City a big enough target for you?" Nick asks.

"Yeah, of course," Wheeler says excitedly. "What'd he do this time?"

"Not what he did. What he will do. With our help. On this flying cars bill."

"From what we keep hearing," Rosario says, "he's strongly in favor of the bill. You think Susan Howard would bribe him to make sure of it?"

Nick considers this for a moment. "Maybe, but that's not the right play."

"She's fucking useless," Wheeler says, shaking her head.

Nick's lawyers would not have advised him to launch into a defense of Susan. But Nick's lawyers also advised Nick to do nothing except let them handle everything. "She's not useless."

"What?" Rosario asks.

"She's not useless. What she does is hard. She may be full of shit. She may be totally tone-deaf on most things. And it's easy to sit here and list all the things wrong with her. But I haven't come up with a big idea like flying cars and then convinced people to give me tens of millions of dollars to try to make it happen. And neither have you. So clearly, it's not nothing."

"Fine. She has her strengths. Doesn't help us here," Wheeler says.

"So what then?" Rosario asks.

"Flip it around. Bribe Navarro to kill the bill."

"But the bill hurts Uber. And he hates Uber."

"That's why he's turning against all his usual allies on this," Wheeler adds. "Enemy of my enemy."

"Because he's mad. Sure. I get it. I stirred it up myself. Used the same 'enemy of my enemy' nonsense on him that you just did."

"Okay," Wheeler says. "You can't just roll up on this guy, talk him into taking a bribe, and expect all of this to be wrapped up and go away. You do understand what entrapment is, right? I thought this guy was your friend."

"First off, there are no friends in politics, just enemies you haven't made yet. Everyone is replaceable.

"Second, we all know Navarro is corrupt, and it's doubly offensive because his whole campaign was about how he was the only virtuous man left in the city.

"Third, his main concern isn't revenge. It's taking care of himself once he's out of office. He's a career politician. He's never made any real money. He's going to need income. The guy has no skills of any use outside of politics, and he's already put feelers out to me. I'm sure he's done it to others."

"So you're going to convince him to switch his position by offering him cash?" Rosario asks. "Could it really be that easy? He's not going to sell out for a few stacks of hundreds in a metal briefcase. He's not dumb. He's going to want equity. Security. Something for the long term. Something he'll tell himself is for his kids and grandkids."

Understanding self-delusion often unlocks the key to political decision-making. Rule number four: expecting politicians to do the right thing and defy human nature never works. Nick always got that.

"But it needs to be related to this bill somehow," Rosario says. "It's not like the Audubon Society or the Socialists can give him equity in something. You can't give equity in birds or useless political rhetoric."

Wheeler smiles, already catching on. "Taxi medallions."

"Ding, ding, ding," Nick replies. "At this point, after getting decimated by ridesharing, the market value of the medallions has plummeted so much, they're selling at a fraction of their original value. They can only go up from here. That's the opportunity."

And it's not like Viktor will have to pay out once Navarro goes down. Viktor will be more than happy to embarrass the guy.

"But the industry's such a mess," Rosario says. "It's hard to see who we could even bring to the table. Most of the major medallion owners from a decade ago are either broke or in jail."

"Well, I know one guy who still has a lot of medallions. Who really hates this bill. I mean, really hates it. Now, he'd never work with you guys," Nick says, milking the moment. "Or even talk to you. Not in a million years. It's not in his DNA. Not how he was raised. But that doesn't mean I can't come up with something to lure him in."

Wheeler starts tapping at buttons on her phone.

Nick keeps going. "I mean, he can never know you're involved. At least not until the very end when he gets what he wants. And even then, it'll be a tough sell given who he is and all. But you guys give me full immunity, I'll get it done. Like I always do."

"Full immunity's a big ask, Nick," Rosario says. "Especially since you're not even denying any of the accusations."

"Fair enough. But this is a heavy lift. Really heavy. There's only one guy who can make this all happen. And I'm the only one who can get to him. So ask yourself, Sarah, ask yourself,

Justine, is putting me behind bars really worth sacrificing the biggest win of your careers?"

Wheeler holds up her phone. She's connected to someone on FaceTime. It's hard to make out who it is from a distance.

But then Viktor's voice erupts from the speaker. "Hello, Nick."

CHAPTER THIRTY-TWO

NEW YORK CITY

City Hall, SDNY HQ

"I thought we had a deal," Cy yells into the phone, dangerously close to slamming his forehead into the desk again. "I told you I had to do a little rooting around on my end. And you, what, went and called the assistant?"

"Not the assistant, the second in command," says Julia. "And she confirmed the investigation. My editors are getting antsy, Cy. I was tired of waiting. And I couldn't keep begging for more time. So I did my own legwork and found out the names of the agents on the case. Honestly, it wasn't hard."

As Cy argues with Julia, he texts Rosario:

WTF
POST ON PHONE
WHERE ARE YOU
POST RUNNING STORMY
STORMY
STORY

Ducking autocorrect.

"Look, you had your chance, Cy," Julia says. "You know how this game works. I produce, or I go home. I'm not ready to go home."

Three dots appear under Cy's frantic texts.

He tries to buy time.

"What about a little professional courtesy, huh? What if I told you I would owe you..."

"Owe me what?"

A gray bubble appears on the screen.

NAVARRO ON A HOOK
OFFER OF MEDALLIONS TO FLIP
CHECK EMAIL

Huh.

"What if I told you that you could have something bigger?" Cy asks while scrambling to open his Gmail. "Much bigger. And if you run this story, the chance for that goes away?"

"How big?"

"Pulitzer-level."

"You're full of shit," she says. This does not surprise Cy one bit. It's his job to be full of shit. "My editors will say the same thing. Worse, they'll think I'm full of shit."

"Just convince them to give us a little more time. Trust me, this is a career-making story."

"I can't convince them when I don't even know what the story is."

"Come on. You know I can't compromise an ongoing investigation."

"How do you think that investigation will do once we put Denevito on the wood? Think it stays undercover after a million people hear about it? It's a slow news cycle. Plus, he's a Democrat. You don't think FOX is going to make him the lead story for at least three days?"

Cy sighs. "Okay. Fine. But this is on deep background. Not for attribution. Not for publication. Just so you know what we're dealing with here."

"Understood."

"Denevito may be in cahoots with a high-up politician. A very prominent, very high-up politician. That's all I can say right now. But if you want a bigger story, if you want this to be your story and not one about some random political consultant getting indicted, buy us some more time."

Julia is quiet on the other end.

"Do you want this or not?"

Cy knows he's offering her nothing at this point—the possibility of a big story, but honestly, he's not even sure it'll happen.

He half-reads an email while waiting for her decision.

Finally, she says, "Fine," and ends the call without saying goodbye.

Cy looks down at his phone at the half-read email showing that his boss's name ID in the latest Quinnipiac poll was subzero. Indicting the mayor would get a lot of attention. And be a lot of fun. Southern District versus City Hall. He'd get to spend most of the next year playing offense, blindsiding Navarro from every anonymous source any reporter is willing to accept as sufficiently credible. And from start to finish, only he would have the moral high ground (and the power of the federal government of the United States behind him).

For the first time in a while, Cy remembers what he loves about his job.

CHAPTER THIRTY-THREE

NEW YORK CITY, LOS ANGELES, CA

Firewall HQ, Blessed Sacrament of Windsor Hills

Nick is pissed. Viktor played him. The FBI is breathing down his neck. He needs a win. And the agents told him to keep the campaigns going. So he walks into Pinky's office supply closet. It's a much tighter squeeze than sitting in one of the five glass-enclosed conference rooms but still preferable to having Pinky out in the open any more than absolutely necessary.

"What's DeFrancesco's home address?" Nick asks.

"Nick! What are you doing here? I heard that…" Pinky trails off, not sure how to tell his boss that he heard he's a crook.

"Oh, that. It's nothing. I'm working with the FBI on it right now. I'll end up being a witness whenever there's a trial. Probably not for a few years. Don't worry about it. We just need to focus on passing the bill. So what's DeFrancesco's home address?"

Pinky peers into his laptop. Nick grabs a mini orange Mets bat off Pinky's desk and starts tossing it from hand to hand. Pinky relays the information, and Nick asks, "Where do his kids go to school?"

Pinky peers into his laptop again. "Looks like the older two are at Alliance Morgan McKinzie in Valley Village. It's a charter. The younger daughter is at a private middle school nearby. Oakwood. I hear it's a nice place. My cousin's husband's sister's mother-in-law used to teach there."

Nick starts pounding the bat in and out of his palm. Pinky winces.

"Where does he go to church?"

Pinky peers again. "Umm...Blessed Sacrament of Windsor Hills."

"Where are the nearest parks and playgrounds to his house?"

Pinky types. "Hang on... Okay, there's an LA County playground two blocks away, and it looks like there's a municipal pool maybe like six, seven blocks away."

"Where does his wife work?"

"The county courthouse. Wait. Why are you asking me all this?"

"Because we need to know where to strike."

"With what?"

Nick stops walking, stops pounding. "See all that oppo you've got sitting there in the cloud? We're gonna pick out the five juiciest items suggesting that DeFrancesco's been stealing from his union all these years, put them into a black-and-white flyer with really shitty graphics, get them photocopied, hire some aspiring actors, and have them hand them out everywhere."

"In front of his kids' schools? Really?"

"Yep."

Pinky grabs the blue mini Mets bat off his desk and stands. He mimics Nick without realizing it. Nick notices, smiles to himself, but doesn't say anything. "In front of his church?" Pinky asks. "His local playground? His wife's job?"

"Yep. All of them."

"We can't do that. He's going to go fucking apeshit. Ballistic. He'll say we're hitting way below the belt. And…he might be right. Plus, he's a union boss. A big one. Well, he's short. But big. You know what I mean. He could be violent."

Nick starts pacing and pounding again. "That's a really good point. Let's hope we're that lucky. But you're right. We should team up our leafleteers in pairs. That way, when DeFrancesco goes postal on one of them, the other gets it all on their phone."

"But…Nick…I mean…even for you…even for us…" Pinky's face then scrunches into concern. "Does Lisa know about all of this? Shouldn't we see what she thinks?"

"Who signs your paychecks?"

"You do."

"Who started this company?"

"You did."

"Who built it from a one-person show to the most profitable political consulting firm in town?"

"You."

"So do you still think we need to ask Lisa for permission? The transit union has two million bucks and over twenty-three hundred points on the air slamming our bill. They've got half a dozen lobbyists working the Council around the clock. The narrative at the moment is that our bill has issues."

Pinky can't argue there. "We need less issues."

"Right. And guess what happens once we start accusing him of stealing from his own union? At a time when most of its members are barely getting by? Once we start making it an issue where he lives? Where he literally lives? The topic changes completely. No one's going to talk about the impact of flying cars on blue collar jobs. No one's gonna talk about taxis or birds or Karl Marx. They're gonna talk about what *he* did."

"Yeah, speaking of that," Pinky says. "I can do my best to keep our fingerprints off it, but it won't be that hard to figure out. Won't we look like the asshole then?"

Nick smiles big. "Let them say we crossed the line. Let them say we're out of bounds. Let them say we're sleazy. Just get them talking about something else." He gives his palm one more emphatic whack with the bat. "Sometimes the sac fly wins the game."

***

Steve DeFrancesco, his wife, and their three kids descend the steps of their somewhat-drab but blessedly scandal-free church. It's a pleasant Los Angeles morning. The sun is out. The air is crisp, and it's still a month or two out from dry heat and air quality advisories.

DeFrancesco looks like what you'd expect in a labor leader (so, Jimmy Hoffa). His wife is better looking than he is, at least in a Los Angeles, Susan kind of way—fit, tan, white teeth, blonde highlights. His kids are teenagers, ranging in age from thirteen to eighteen. The fifteen-year-old looks as awkward as she feels. The eighteen-year-old has emerged from that phase, and the thirteen-year-old is just entering it, starting with a full complement of braces and a body that has grown into most of its height but virtually none of its weight.

As DeFrancesco is walking down the church steps, a pair of leafleteers, a man and a woman, accost him. One of them shoves a flyer into DeFrancesco's hands. He looks at the flyer. It's all about him taking junkets to Vegas paid for by the union. It asks how he paid for the new addition to his home. It asks how he affords private school for his fifteen-year-old daughter with her latest yearbook photo in full display—braces, pimples, the whole awkward adolescent package. And it ends with "Connect the dots—Steve DeFrancesco isn't fighting for working people. He's stealing from them."

"You motherfuckers!" he yells at the woman. "My family? In front of our church? On Good Friday?"

The man, holding an iPhone, starts recording. The woman starts shoving flyers into the hands of the other people leaving church.

"What are you doing? I told you to stop!"

DeFrancesco swings at the stack of flyers the woman is holding, knocking them onto the ground. She bends down, picks a few up, and keeps shoving them into people's outstretched hands. All of them now really want to know what the flyer says.

Half the church is standing there, witnessing this bizarre scene. DeFrancesco sees the crowd. He's the big shot of all the parishioners. Everyone knows that. He loves that. He sees his wife and kids. He knows they're waiting for him to do something.

So he does.

DeFrancesco tackles the leafleteer, taking her out at the knees, just like he learned in Pop Warner. She hits the concrete. Hard. He jumps on top of her, snatching the flyers away. She's screaming. He's grabbing and flailing. His wife is yelling for someone to do something.

And the other leafleteer keeps filming. Then he hits stop on the recording, emails it to Pinky Fonseca, and makes a quick dash toward a Honda Civic idling halfway down the block.

CHAPTER THIRTY-FOUR

NEW YORK CITY

Lisa's Apartment

Pinky, as instructed, sent the footage of DeFrancesco's meltdown to every local TV station and posted it on YouTube, Instagram, Facebook, Twitter, and TikTok immediately.

But instead of invalidating the powerful labor leader and his opposition to flying cars, it makes him sympathetic. DeFrancesco is savvy enough to talk to every reporter, every blogger, and say that he was defending his wife and kids and would do it again in a heartbeat.

DeFrancesco's angle works. And the coverage reflects it.

Lisa snaps her laptop shut after watching the fourth consecutive story talking about FlightDeck's dirty politics.

How was she not consulted on this? And what the fuck is Nick even doing? He's still running the FlightDeck campaign? For which side? Rosario and Wheeler told her to stay the course. Status quo. Any sudden changes could disrupt the Navarro sting.

Sure. That may work for them, Lisa thinks. But it doesn't help the campaign if the two people running it aren't talking. If she knows Nick, he is too ashamed to talk to her. But not too ashamed to take DeFrancesco's head off. Always easier to shoot down clueless strangers from afar than deal with unhappy colleagues up close.

She still wants to win this. Without Nick.

Fuck Nick and fuck his double-dealing. She's learned everything she can from him anyway. Good riddance, assclown.

The only way to change the trajectory of this thing, she realizes, is to get a quick win. Put some points on the board, and then the political world starts taking you seriously.

And there's only one outlet for a quick win in any of the three cities. It bothers Lisa to even think about it. But maybe a few free trips to tech conventions could be passed off as legitimate government due diligence. One woman's corruption could just as easily be another's standard operating procedure.

That arrogant sleazebag Hal Taylor? He's so gross, Lisa thinks.

But she realizes that his grossness is the only reason she has a chance to pass the bill in Austin in the first place.

It's a risk, but if she wants to save the client and the firm after Susan finds out what Nick did, it's her only play. She finds Taylor's number at the bottom of an old email and picks up the phone.

CHAPTER THIRTY-FIVE

NEW YORK CITY

Upper West Side, Brighton Beach

Nick keeps a houseboat docked in the Riverside Park boat basin for two reasons. The first is that it's a great place for a very private meeting. The second is that whenever his marriage or latest relationship invariably falls apart, he always has somewhere to go.

On a pleasantly warm April evening, Nick and Navarro are sitting on the deck. Navarro's police detail is standing guard on the dock, wondering what they're doing there. An attendant serving drinks is in the corner of the cabin below deck. Nick and Navarro head down below.

Navarro looks around at the cozy wood-paneled room. "This is romantic."

"Had a client once who couldn't pay," Nick says. "He had this boat to get away from his wife. When he realized he couldn't just stiff me like he does everyone else, I ended up with the boat." As Nick says this, he realizes that maybe he shouldn't be telling this story with the FBI listening in, given that he never reported the boat on his taxes.

"Try collecting campaign contributions," Navarro says. "So I've got my team whipping votes in the Council like crazy. I think we have a real shot at this. What's your whip count saying?"

"Actually, Joe, I think I may have a better option."

"To get to twenty-six votes in the Council?" Navarro asks.

"Better than that. There are a lot of moving parts here. I think I have a way to make flying cars safely ensure all of our futures. My future...and yours."

Navarro raises an eyebrow.

"You've been in office now for how long?" Nick asks. "Twenty-five years or so, all in all?"

"Thirty-two total if you include the Assembly, the State Senate, and two terms as AG."

"So you've got your pension. That's good. Should at least take care of all your incidentals. But we talked about it last time we met—you're getting down to the wire. What's your plan post-City Hall? Finally put that law license to good use?"

Navarro shakes his head. "I never took the continuing education classes, so I think I'd have to take the bar exam again to renew my license." It took Navarro three tries to pass the bar the first time around.

"That'd be pretty fucking funny if you show up to take the bar exam and you're sitting next to the former mayor of New York."

"It'd be pretty fucking pathetic if you're the former mayor."

Time for Nick to throw out the opening salvo. "Doesn't have to be that way."

"How so?" Navarro asks. "What, I'm going to become some hot shit stockbroker at the age of sixty-three?"

"I'm not sure stockbrokers even still exist. I was thinking more like a long-term equity play."

Navarro peers at the bartender.

"It's okay. She's my guy," Nick assures him. "Doesn't even really speak English. All good."

In response, the bartender rolls her eyes and mutters something in Spanish.

Navarro relaxes. "So you were saying."

"Who loses if we win this FlightDeck thing?"

Navarro raises his hand in a "come on, stop asking me stupid questions" way. "Uber. That's why we're doing this," he says.

"True. But not just Uber."

"How many times do I have to explain this to everyone? You think I give a fuck about birds? Or the Socialists who don't know the first fucking thing about making the trains run on time? Or the transit workers, who can't make the trains run on time either? Fuck 'em. Fuck 'em all." Righteous anger has always come easy to Navarro.

"You know who you're leaving out. Our friend down in Brighton Beach."

Navarro tenses up a little at the mention of Velonova. "I've been good to Viktor. He's been good to me. We're squared away. I took care of all those library fines. And got him backstage passes for that Genesis reunion. I don't owe him anything on this."

"Of course you don't. But that doesn't mean we can't all help each other out."

"Won't work," Navarro shakes his head for emphasis. "Taxis are a dying industry. Even if we bail them out and ban flying cars, sooner or later the medallion price will go down to zero."

"You sure about that? Right now, they're trading at around a hundred and thirty k."

"My point exactly."

"But that's actually good for us. I'm not sure there's much more room to keep going down. There's still a limited number of them. They still have intrinsic value. If someone were to take, say, a hundred basis points in, I don't know, two hundred medallions, what might be worth three-sixty today could easily be worth three point six million in a few short years."

Navarro raises his eyebrows. "You think the price goes up tenfold just because we don't allow flying cars?"

"It's part of the equation. The price goes up tenfold if you engineer a new cap on the total number of medallions. The price goes up if you make Uber and Lyft pay a congestion surcharge and taxis don't. The price goes up if you reclassify all Uber and Lyft drivers as full-time employees. The price goes up if you restrict access to EV charging facilities to yellow cabs. The price goes up if you only give autonomous licenses to the yellow cabs. There are lots of ways to make the value go up. Killing this bill is just the beginning."

"And why would Viktor be willing to hand over so much equity if the future is so bright?"

"What choice does he have?" Nick says. "The future is only bright if you make it bright. Flying cars may not be as big of a problem as he thinks, but he still needs you for all the other stuff. You being his partner is the best thing that could possibly happen."

Navarro considers this for a moment. "Okay, fine. Let's say someone were to accumulate around one percent in a couple hundred medallions. How would that someone cover the purchase price?"

"That someone might have a friend who could partner with him, or maybe even get Viktor to waive the initial buy-in."

"And how would that someone ensure he actually then gets the equity in the medallions?"

"Silent partnerships always require trust," Nick knows this truth firsthand.

"I don't know." Again, Navarro looks skeptical. Or maybe that's just his default posture when he's around Nick.

Navarro starts to say something, then stops.

"Look, we don't even have to kill the bill," Nick tries. "We need to build in a cushion that helps Viktor. The bill could still legalize flying cars. It just can't take effect until, say, the transportation commissioner authorizes it. And you know what a stickler for safety the transportation commissioner is."

"So what? I'm out of here in less than a year. The medallions are going to need more time than that to recover."

"Okay, so it's not just up to the mayor. It's up to an independent commission appointed by the mayor, the speaker, and the transportation commissioner to decide. You each get one appointee. Terms are a fixed four years. Six years even."

"So the new mayor can't remove them?"

Nick nods.

Navarro continues, gaming it out. "If I get one and my DOT commissioner gets one, that means I get two. As long as I keep them loyal."

Nick nods again.

Navarro keeps going. "So...we still pass flying cars legislation. Because, you know, it's groundbreaking. Innovation. The future. We believe in the future. That's what I keep telling my staff. But we also build in a four-year head start for Viktor. That works." He pauses, then asks, "What about Uber?"

"What about them?"

"They win, I lose."

"Not necessarily. Even if they develop their own flying car, they're still gonna need a permit from the independent commission. A commission that you control, even long after you leave office. So what are the odds of that permit ever being granted?"

Navarro smiles. He's on the hook. Nick sticks out his hand. Navarro shakes it. Nick hands the bartender some cash on the way out. She thanks them for the tip.

Navarro nods goodbye to her.

Agent Rosario nods goodbye back.

***

Nick doesn't waste a moment. He's got the Uber app open the minute Navarro leaves the boat and has already typed in Viktor's address in Brighton Beach. He takes a moment to note the irony and then gets in the car, leaving Wheeler to clean up. Traffic is light, and Nick gets to Turgenev in record time.

But then he spends the next two hours sitting at an empty table, waiting for an audience.

When Viktor finally emerges from the back and sits down at Nick's table, Nick has to remind himself not to show how annoyed he is by the wait.

"Nu?" Viktor asks.

Nick doesn't speak Yiddish, but he's lived in New York City long enough to know what that means. "I think Navarro's in."

"You think he's in or you know he's in?" Viktor lights a cigarette in full violation of New York City's laws on indoor smoking.

"Look, it was a conversation on a houseboat in Riverside Park. It's not like we signed a contract or anything. But yeah, he's termed out and needs a way to support his lifestyle once the door to Gracie Mansion shuts behind him."

"What did you offer him?"

"One percent ownership of two hundred medallions."

"And he said yes to that?"

"He shook my hand."

Viktor starts shaking his head. "I always forget how unsophisticated these...buffoons are once you take them out of their element. If that works for Navarro, fine with me." Nick decides not to mention that he told Navarro they could pass the bill but with some modifications. He'll break that to Viktor later.

"Okay, Viktor, just so you understand, a whole process will still have to play out. The bill needs to be heard, debated, seriously considered—and then killed or amended one way or another by Navarro. If it dies tonight, everyone will know something went down, and a bill like this will pop back up in no time. So when you see the campaign for flying cars, don't get nervous."

"The campaign you're running for flying cars? Or the campaign you're running against flying cars? And Nick, don't ever say again that I get nervous. Nervous is when you piss off Putin and they're about to send you to a re-education camp in Siberia. Nervous about a City Council bill doesn't exist in my world." Viktor pauses. "But if that bill goes the wrong way? You, my friend, should be very, very nervous."

CHAPTER THIRTY-SIX

NEW YORK CITY

Gracie Mansion, City Hall

As the butler lays out his four daily newspapers in the specific order he prefers (first the *Post*, then the *Daily News*, then the *Wall Street Journal*, and finally the *New York Times*), Joe Navarro unfolds his cloth napkin, places it in his lap, and nods to the waiter to pour his coffee and grapefruit juice. He gruffly dismisses the butler with the wave of the back of his hand. The butler is used to it.

Once the mayor finishes breakfast, works out in the in-house gym, and uses the sauna and six-headed steam shower, he hops into his motorcade flush with lights, sirens, and three NYPD vehicles.

A team of aides meets him at the steps of City Hall, and every action he takes over the next twelve hours—until he returns to the comforts of Gracie Mansion—will be designed specifically to maximize the mayor's time, convenience, and preferences.

As he walks into his massive marble-and-gold-leaf-adorned office in City Hall, he tosses his suit coat onto the purple velvet couch. It misses and hits the floor. He just leaves it there (someone will pick it up). He looks up at the countdown clock—an idea he stole from Bloomberg that lets everyone know exactly how many days, hours, and minutes remain in the term. For Bloomberg, the point was to motivate everyone to work quickly. For Navarro, it's mainly a reminder of how radically his life is about to change.

Sure, his two-bedroom, one-and-a-half-bathroom apartment in Mill Basin in deep Brooklyn is perfectly fine. So is the cream-colored 2013 Lincoln he bought before the campaign started.

There's no butler, but he can afford to have a cleaning lady come by once a week. He put aside money for a down payment on a condo in Fort Lauderdale before the first mayoral campaign and can probably still get something, although he's heard prices have skyrocketed over the last few years.

There's absolutely nothing wrong with Joe Navarro's upcoming life as a civilian. It's perfectly fine. Better than 90 percent of the city even.

Well, this is New York. So maybe more like 65 percent. Definitely better than 95 percent of the country, 99 percent of the world.

But if Joe Navarro wanted a regular life, he never would have run for office. And never would have worked like an animal to do whatever it took to keep running and keep winning.

And yet, he walks away from all this with little more than a pension and some trinkets given to him by local organizations? Too-big T-shirts, a few plaques, and some shitty arts-and-crafts projects from kids who have no clue who he is?

Some bureaucrat is sitting across the desk from him, going on about building-permit reforms or new senior centers or bike lanes. Doesn't matter. Navarro is never running for office again.

It's time, he realizes, to shift his focus. Time to accept that he can't go back to Mill Basin, can't go back to a 2013 Lincoln, to a small condo in Fort Lauderdale.

He'll die of depression and boredom within a month.

And yet for all of his success, he's never worked a single day in the private sector. Always been on the public dole.

Sure, he could become a lobbyist and beg and plead the same low-level councilmembers and commissioners—people he doesn't even acknowledge now, people like the numbskull sitting across from him—to do favors for the grubby clients paying him seventy-five hundred a month. Hustle enough and it can add up to a decent living.

But every moment would be humiliating.

So what then? Try for a spot on CNN or MSNBC? He asked his press secretary to look into it awhile back. Turns out they only pay contributors a nominal fee and no one seemed interested in having him host a show. He could probably force St. John's or Fordham to make him an adjunct professor. So that gets him what? Another twenty k?

Fucking Uber. Those motherfuckers. Sure, in retrospect, doing Viktor's bidding and trying to ban ridesharing in New York City was a mistake. He underestimated Uber's wallet, its will, its political team. Well, his staff did. They screwed it up. He's just the one who suffered for it. As usual. His approval ratings tanked and never fully recovered. Which has pretty much made his post-mayoral opportunities toxic.

It'd be nice to go out on a high, with a knife in Uber's chest. And some long-term security in the bank.

He yells for his secretary, Anna Griswald, who has been with him since the very beginning. She's the only staffer who has stuck with him from day one. Everyone else abandoned him.

He can't live without her. And he can't afford to pay her if the government isn't picking up the tab. At least not in his current situation.

"Anna, get the legislative team in here ASAP. I don't care if they're in a meeting or whipping votes on the Council floor or taking a dump. I want all of them in my office in the next ninety seconds."

He wonders which of them he can trust to work directly with Nick.

CHAPTER THIRTY-SEVEN

AUSTIN, TX

The Bar at the Hotel Saint Cecilia

Lisa needs to see the mayor. And she needs to see him in a private setting—showing up at City Hall would tip Taylor off immediately.

There are a handful of local lobbyists who owe her. And even more who would like to be on Firewall's payroll. After three calls, Luis Acevedo, a longtime, beloved Texas lobbyist, fixer, influencer, and dealmaker, promises he can make it happen. An hour later, it's set. The mayor will be at the bar of the Hotel Saint Cecilia at 4 p.m.—two hours from now.

The Saint Cecilia bar is always quiet because it's only open to hotel guests. And at 4 p.m. on a Tuesday, especially just a few weeks after South by Southwest, no one else will be there. Perfect for this type of meeting.

Lisa gets to the bar at 3:45 to scare away any tourists looking for a late afternoon cocktail. There's no one to scare away. At four on the nose, Mayor Pearce walks in, one member of his security detail in front of him and two trailing behind.

Don Pearce is young and ambitious. He's square-jawed, has a great hairline, and looks like the dream of every centrist Democrat. Since Lisa is the only person at the bar, and since Pearce was told to look for a Chinese-American woman, she's not hard to spot.

"Mister Mayor," she says.

"You must be Lisa," he says, with a practiced politeness that still says *this better be important.*

"I am. Thank you so much for meeting with me. It's really an honor. I've been following your career for years. Always been a really big fan." Again, flattery works.

"Any friend of Luis is a friend of mine." The way he says it makes Lisa wonder if they're actually friends.

"As Luis probably mentioned, I'm a political consultant based in New York. We run lots of campaigns for different tech startups. One of them is a company called FlightDeck. I'm not sure if you've ever heard of it."

"Of course I have. How could I not? You tend to notice when your city is one of only three they're trying to launch in. Especially for something as high profile as flying cars. Being put up there with New York and LA says something about how far we've come under my leadership."

"Exactly," Lisa says, placing her phone on the bar. "Now imagine if you beat New York and LA to the punch."

"So this is just a lobbying pitch for a bill? I didn't need to leave my office for that, and you didn't need to meet with me. I have staff for that. Luis said it was really important and that I—personally—needed to be here."

Lisa puts her hand on the phone and moves it around the polished wooden bartop. "Well, what I want to tell you is related to the FlightDeck bill. But this isn't a pitch for your support. Not specifically. It's what I uncovered as I was seeking your support."

Pearce looks confused.

Lisa continues. "Your deputy mayor, Hal Taylor, oversees aviation and economic development, right? I went to him first. Followed protocol, met with staff. But what he then asked me for in return for your support for the bill is something you should hear for yourself."

Lisa's not sure if recording someone in Texas without their consent is legal. Frankly, she didn't look it up because she didn't want to know. It's a problem for another day. Getting a meeting with Taylor was easy once she mentioned she had good news on the trips. Getting him to restate his request for a bribe was easy. And the recording app on her phone worked a lot better than she expected.

Once she had the recording, the question was what to do with it.

She could play it for Taylor and force him to move the bill at the risk of her leaking the tape. She could play it for local prosecutors, but that wouldn't do much to advance flying car legislation.

Then she got a better idea.

She could use it to make the mayor a hero.

The mayor uncovers corruption in his own administration. Reports it himself. And to prove how virtuous he is, he passes the bill that Taylor was holding up for a bribe. Along the way, he becomes the first mayor, and Austin becomes the first city, to legalize flying cars. He gets a ton of press, and that launches his campaign for attorney general.

Not totally crazy, she thinks. And it's got enough good intention built in—drum out a corrupt staffer while advancing a non-lunatic politician statewide in Texas—that she would be able to sleep well.

She hits play. "*Okay, Hal, I talked to Susan. She agrees that having you at these conferences by her side could be helpful, provided it means you're already on board with the bill.*"

"*Well, I certainly could be,*" Taylor responds.

Pearce's face drops.

"*She wants to know which conference of the three you mentioned—Aspen, Laguna Beach, and Lisbon—is your first choice.*"

"*All of them,*" Taylor replies. "*My wife said it would be good to get the fullest picture we can.*"

Lisa stops the recording. The look on Pearce's face says he's annoyed but not surprised. "So this is, what? Some kind of shakedown? You get my guy on tape asking for a bribe and then you play it for me to force me to support the bill?"

Lisa smiles. "I wouldn't quite put it like that. I'd say that you have a significant problem in your administration, especially for someone planning to run statewide for a position that requires so much trust like attorney general. I'd say the likelihood that I'm the only one Taylor's ever solicited a bribe from is extremely low. I'm just the first person who had the balls to tell you about it."

Pearce leans back, suddenly alarmed.

"Sir, as far as I can see it, there are two paths here. The first is letting everything take its course."

"Meaning you extort me to support the bill?" Pearce asks.

"Not at all. The first path is I give the recording to the district attorney. He's up for reelection next year, so we both know he'll jump all over this. In fact, it could even help him replace you as the frontrunner for the Democratic nomination for AG."

"And the other path?" Pearce is very good at identifying what's in his self-interest.

"We solve multiple problems at once. You do what you think is best with the recording. You want to expose it yourself and look like a moral hero? Great. You want to bury it? Your call."

Lisa pauses and presses a few buttons on her phone. "I just texted you a copy. Hope it's okay—Luis gave me your cell."

She continues doing her best to wipe the smirk off her face. "But you have an opportunity here to put Austin on the map. Globally. You do something New York City couldn't do. You do something Los Angeles couldn't do. You become the first city in the entire world to embrace technology that will completely change the way we live. This isn't like getting some professional lacrosse team to come to your city or getting HP to open a new plant. That's the usual blocking and tackling for any mayor. This is historic. And on top of that, you clean out a corrupt member of your administration? That writes your ticket, not just for AG, but way beyond. Senator. Governor. You could be the one who turns Texas blue. Well, purple."

Lisa knows she's not the first person to appeal to Pearce's vanity, his ambition, his insecurity. Any political operative worth their salt knows to do that. But the great thing about politicians is they never learn. They're so desperate for validation, for affirmation, that they fall for it every single time.

And she's right.

"So tell me how you see this playing out," Pearce says.

"You fire Taylor, and then endorse the bill publicly. Then you work the bill in the Council. That gets you there first, before LA, before New York."

"Have you met the members of this City Council? Half of them make Bernie Sanders look like Genghis Khan."

"They're still politicians. They still have to run for reelection. They still have to deliver for their districts. And just like you, they really, really want to stay in office. You'll figure it out. You have tools at your disposal. Grants. Support for bills they care about. Endorsements. We only need five votes plus you. It's totally doable."

Pearce sits still for a moment, then nods his head. "What are you going to do with the original copy of the recording?"

Lisa pretends to think about it. "I'll hold onto it for safekeeping."

Politicians do this, she thinks, *because they need the attention. Can't live without it.*

Operatives do this because taking someone out makes them feel safe. They were always the nerds in high school who got bullied by assholes like Hal Taylor and Susan Howard. Not anymore.

She isn't sure who's worse.

CHAPTER THIRTY-EIGHT

TORRANCE, CA

Testing Site

Finding a testing site that is urban enough to simulate the actual environment but quiet enough that, if the car crashes, it probably wouldn't kill anyone is quite a challenge.

But after two weeks of scouting, Yevgeny's team finds a location in Torrance that seems to fit the bill. It's a mostly abandoned stretch of strip malls that fades into half-empty suburban streets—a poor neighborhood where the cops only come out when they're called, and even barely then.

Yevgeny's team is jealous of its two new colleagues, Thor and Green Lantern. Even though Yevgeny learned their names—Todd and Shawn—he still thinks of them like that. The rest of the team, though, thinks of them as amateurs who have no place working at a cutting-edge tech startup like FlightDeck.

Yevgeny has given the same answer all week to their complaints and insinuations: "For all your brilliance, all your degrees, all your credentials, none of you have solved the sensor problem. If you had, they would not be here right now. But you did not." He left the last part unsaid: *So shut the fuck up*.

Grumbling aside, they get the message and work together to install external sensors on nine dilapidated buildings along a single corridor. They look into getting permits but realize if they go ahead and install the sensors without telling anyone, no one will notice.

The launch site is a parking lot in an abandoned strip mall that used to house an Autoworks, a Kids "R" Us, a Circuit City, and three competing frozen yogurt franchises (they all lost the competition). Yevgeny isn't worried about liftoff. They've gotten that part right a few dozen times. The problem begins once the car starts moving in a particular direction.

The car itself could be a problem too. With all the latest models destroyed and no time to rebuild, Yevgeny had to dust off the first prototype, which is bigger and boxier than he would like. Definitely more than Susan likes. When she first saw it, she said *Blade Runner* wasn't the aesthetic they were looking for.

But this was all they had left, and he worked like hell to get it looking halfway decent. It would fly fine; it just isn't pretty.

The route is fairly simple. Yevgeny wants to see if the basic external sensor concept works. If it does, they can start making both the tests and the digital simulations more complicated.

It rarely rains in Torrance, but it's cloudier than usual. Yevgeny is standing with his two new prize pupils. He turns to them. "Are you worried about the weather? Do you think it's an issue?"

Thor and Green Lantern look at each other. What do they know? Three weeks ago, they were contestants in a hackathon. But if they've made it this far… "Yeah, we're good," both of them reply in unison.

"Okay. Let us fucking *do* this, then." After an entire childhood of watching bootleg DVDs of bad Steven Seagal and Jean-Claude Van Damme movies, Yevgeny has always wanted to say that. He signals to his launch engineer, and around thirty seconds later, the car takes flight.

Liftoff is smooth, as expected.

So far, so good.

The car hovers around three hundred feet and starts flying straight. Again, nothing new. But if they complete the run without any interference—without any birds or drones or helicopters—they might not get the confirmation they need.

That's why they've brought their own drones.

The car flies down the corridor and back without any problems. It lands smoothly, but Yevgeny and his team know it means nothing. Not until the sensors are truly tested.

So they do it again. But this time, after another smooth ride of around six hundred feet, Yevgeny throws a finger in the air, and one of his engineers launches a drone directly in the flight path. They can see the external sensors light up on their laptops.

Whether the car sees the drone is another story.

It does, sort of. As the drone approaches the vehicle, the car moves about six feet to the right, narrowly avoiding contact. And it misses the closest building by a good ten feet. Everyone cheers. Yevgeny does too, excited to see the progress.

But he also knows a narrow miss isn't good enough.

So they try again. And again. And again. Four hours later, the data is clear: it avoided the drone twenty-three times and took four direct hits, none of them deadly.

It's not ready for prime time just yet. But maybe this external sensor idea isn't so bad. Maybe the hackathon was a good idea—and let's not forget it was Yevgeny's idea in the first place.

As they drive in horrendous traffic back to LA, Yevgeny drafts an email to Susan half a dozen times crowing about their success. But each time, something tells him not to press send. If Susan thinks they're even halfway good to launch, she won't hesitate to do so—even if the tech isn't completely ready, or even mostly ready.

Keeping her on a need-to-know basis, Yevgeny realizes, is probably a lot safer for everyone.

CHAPTER THIRTY-NINE

NEW YORK CITY

Pegasus Club

Navarro stands at the foot of the table in the vaulted, stately dining room of the historic Pegasus Club. Which, lucky for them, is empty. A place like this, people know when the mayor walks in—and they talk about it. But Nick picked it because the kitchen has been closed while they fix a gas leak in the basement.

Nick extends his hand, but Navarro says, "Pull up your shirt."

"Buy me dinner first?"

"C'mon, I'm not an idiot," Navarro says.

Nick sighs. Grabs the hem of his pastel-pink Neiman Marcus dress shirt and pulls it up, showing his bare midsection. "I've been slacking on the Pilates. Don't judge."

Navarro nods, satisfied, and sits down.

***

Rosario breathes a sigh of relief from the large storage closet across the room, where she's sitting with headphones and a laptop. About ten minutes ago, Nick decided to pull the wire, thinking Navarro might check for one. His instincts were right.

But that also meant they had to scramble for a backup. She slipped a mic pack into the planter next to the booth. It was picking up audio just fine, but she had to be nearby to record.

Not ideal, but better than nothing. It's also not ideal that Rosario is there in the first place. The plan was for Wheeler to take this one, just to reduce any chance of Navarro noticing anything, since Rosario was on the houseboat. But after Wheeler spent the previous evening training for the deep-fried turkey competition, at least one morsel in the six pounds she consumed wasn't cooked all the way through (the pink hue might have given it away if not for the thick coating of lard). Vomiting on the mayor seemed like a bad idea, so Rosario is back in the saddle.

Rosario curses Wheeler's hobbies and obsessions—not for the first time—as she watches the wavy lines of the voices recording on her laptop.

***

"What's so urgent that we had to meet right away?" Navarro asks. "I'm busy on Wednesdays."

"I know," Nick says. "The legendary gin game in the presidential suite. Always wanted an invite."

"Good luck with that."

"Viktor's pressing me. He says your team is pushing just as hard as before to pass the bill, without any amendments. I thought we had an agreement."

"I'm for the bill," Navarro says. "Everyone knows that."

Nick wants to reach across the table and give Navarro a light smack on the side of the head. What the hell is he doing? "You're for the bill as proposed? Or the bill with the amendments we discussed?"

"I'm not sure what we discussed still holds. Sounds like Viktor thinks he's gonna lose."

"That doesn't worry you?"

"Viktor's not my problem. You obviously have something going with him, but it's got nothing to do with me."

"So you're gonna let the bill pass and let this whole opportunity pass you by? When are you going to have another chance like this? Especially before the term runs out? Flying cars are literally a once-in-a-lifetime kind of thing."

Navarro does his best to exude an air of indifference. "Considering what you're asking of me, I'm not sure the opportunity's really what it should be."

Nick needs a second to read that one.

At first, he's afraid that Navarro has suddenly developed a conscience. That he's not going for the carrot. Which has the potential to fuck Nick even harder if the mayor reports him for this.

But there's something on Navarro's face, a slight squint to his eyes, a slight demand in his voice, that makes Nick realize what this really is.

A negotiation.

"What if it were two percent of two hundred medallions?" Nick asks.

Navarro pauses. He asks, "How many medallions does Viktor own?"

"Four hundred and twenty."

"Three percent of all of them should do."

Well, Nick realizes. There's nothing to be worried about after all. Navarro doesn't just want a taste. He wants the pie. "Two percent on two-fifty."

"Two point five on three hundred and twenty-five."

Nick can live with that. Hell, it's not like Navarro will ever see it. This is like playing with *Monopoly* money. He sticks out his hand to shake on the deal.

Navarro shakes his head. "Let's have a drink and toast to it. I'm superstitious that way. Scotch all around?"

Nick realizes this is a problem. They cleared the room of any actual club employees just in case things got ugly. Rosario pokes her head out of the storage room, and Nick calls, "Two scotches, please! Macallan 18, neat, dash of water." Before Navarro can turn, Nick pulls out his phone, figuring that anything that speaks to the riches Navarro might see coming will hold his attention. "Joe, have I ever shown you photos of my ski house in Jackson?"

A few moments later, Rosario walks up with two crystal tumblers. Nick does his best to keep Navarro's focus.

But then Rosario fucks up.

"On the house, Mister Mayor," she says.

Navarro is looking at his phone. He glances up at Rosario, then does a double take.

Nick hopes that Navarro is the kind of guy for whom service industry workers disappear from his brain the moment he can't see them anymore. But service industry workers are voters, at least sometimes.

And from the smirk on Navarro's face, Nick doesn't think he's going to be that lucky.

"You know, Nick, thirty-two years in office gives you a good memory for faces," he says.

"I'm sorry—what?" Nick stammers.

"That's the same waitress from the boat," Navarro says, standing up and backing away. "You motherfucker."

"Really? That would be an insane coincidence." Nick is supremely confident of his ability to talk his way out of anything, but this may be a lost cause. "Coincidences happen. That's what you have to do to make it in this city, right? Work three, four jobs. City that never sleeps. You know what I mean. Shit, you run it."

Navarro bends down and speaks into the bowl of nuts on the table. "Just for the record, I absolutely will not compromise my principles on this or anything else. I strongly support the flying car bill as originally written, and I find your offer of a bribe to be illegal, unethical, and offensive. I intend to report it to District Attorney Weinstein immediately."

Even though the mic is in the potted plant behind them, speaking into the nut bowl is probably close enough to be picked up on tape.

Navarro storms through the lobby and out the front door.

Nick approaches Rosario. "We were literally inches away from getting him. Inches." Then he calms down, almost instantly. "Well...hopefully what we got is enough. Is it?"

"No," she says. "Probably not."

"So what happens to us?"

She straightens up. "There's no us here. You're going to prison. Me and Wheeler get busted down to desk duty. Navarro lives to corrupt another day. I should have fucking known something like this would happen."

"Navarro's not really going to the DA with this."

"Probably not. But he's *definitely* not doing a deal with you. Which means we're not either."

She starts to say something, and then stops. Nick is hoping it's "I'm sorry." Instead, she stalks off, presumably to the food truck.

Nick sits there, stunned. He knew he'd been playing a dangerous game.

Not just with this—for the last couple of years. Getting in deeper and deeper. And it always felt like the next thing—the next startup, the next campaign—would be the thing to pull him out, and it always turned into the thing that dug the hole deeper. The stress was intense but also kind of exciting. Until now.

For a minute, Nick accepts that this is the end of the road.

But just for a minute.

Then it hits him.

He pulls out his phone and scrolls through the As in his contacts. He pushes the green button. She answers immediately.

"Julia? Nick Denevito. I think I've got a story for you."

PART THREE

CHAPTER FORTY

NEW YORK CITY, LOS ANGELES, CA, AUSTIN, TX

All Over the Place

Joe Navarro walks into Gracie Mansion's formal dining room to find his bowl of oatmeal with walnuts, raspberries, and raisins waiting for him. A tuxedoed waiter hovers anxiously in the corner. The stack of newspapers is there as usual, except in a different order.

He checks his phone and sees a bunch of missed calls late last night from his press secretary. He knew she was calling. He knew there had to be a problem. But he figured it was just a normal problem like a water main break or another out-of-control brawl at the Dave & Buster's in Times Square. His time in office is almost done. He's over all that. Let someone else deal with it. That's why God invented staff.

The *Post* is shoved underneath the *Times*, *Daily News*, and *Wall Street Journal*. He fishes it out from the pile with one hand as he sprinkles brown sugar on his oatmeal with the other. He sees the headline on the wood and freezes. "Top Political Operative Accuses FBI, Mayor Navarro of Corruption."

The mayor flips to page three, where the full story is, and scoffs at the byline. Julia Alessi.

> "*Top political operative Nick Denevito yesterday went on the record and on the attack, accusing both New York City Mayor Joe Navarro and the United States Federal Bureau of Investigations of engaging in political corruption. Denevito said that the FBI forced him to try to set up a sting operation on Mayor Navarro and that the mayor was on board with taking bribes to change his position on pending legislation to legalize flying cars.*"

Navarro puts his head in his hands, muttering, "Oh fuck," over and over and over again. He thought he had this solved when he caught Nick in the act of trying to entrap him. It never occurred to him that Nick would flip the whole thing on its head by telling the unvarnished story to the *Post*. It's a kamikaze move. So ballsy he'd respect it—if this didn't mean the end of his career.

The waiter slips out of the room as quietly as he can.

***

Agents Wheeler and Rosario are sitting in the food truck. It's a mess—food wrappers and debris all over the floor, Wheeler's gun on a rickety table. They look like they haven't slept in days.

Rosario has barely spoken to Wheeler since the incident. The older agent is furious—Wheeler let her obsession with the eating competitions screw a case. A case that was supposed to make their careers. Get them off the Bureau B-list.

The first thing Rosario thought when Wheeler came to her with this idea was: here's another young and hungry agent with eyes bigger than her stomach. Rosario had no idea how correct that snap assessment would turn out to be.

They'd been working overtime to try and salvage something from this investigation.

Now, it doesn't even matter.

> "*Denevito said that the FBI threatened to indict him on charges of defrauding clients of his political consulting firm, Firewall, and that the only way to avoid prison was by getting someone higher up the political food chain to incriminate themselves. That someone was Mayor Joe Navarro.*"

Rosario is sure she's going to get fired any minute. She checks the balance in her Citibank account and the Fidelity account that houses her pension. She scrolls through the rules around early withdrawals, doing the math in her head on how long she can go without a paycheck.

Wheeler just looks pissed as she gnaws on her fourth scone. Feeling betrayed, no doubt. But Rosario hopes the younger agent also recognizes that her competitive eating obsession destroyed the best opportunity of her career.

***

Susan is at the 4:30 a.m. SoulCycle in Santa Monica. The instructor sounds like he just did a rail of coke. While she's spinning, Susan sneaks a peek at her phone. There's an email with the subject line, "Holy Shit!!!"

She opens it, stops cycling, and walks to the lockers, wishing Carol weren't so busy coaching the Joint Chiefs of Staff. The only upside is Carol doesn't know she's skipping not only the daily 4 a.m. cold plunge but also the fourteen daily minutes of hanging upside down.

She sits down on one of the benches and starts reading. She doesn't believe it. More than that, she doesn't think it's true. And quite frankly, even if it is true, Nick is on his way to getting the bill through. With the mayor's support. If Nick got a little extra on the side, if Navarro got a little extra on the side, so what? What does she care? Maybe this thing is still salvageable.

She tries calling Nick, but it goes straight to voicemail.

***

Yevgeny's still at FlightDeck headquarters from the night before. He looks disheveled, but not that much more so than usual. His assistant, Bryon—decked out today in a neon-pink hoodie that, at this hour, is offensive to Yevgeny's eyes—is glued to his phone, a look on his face like a bomb went off. After a few moments, he hands the phone over to Yevgeny, who sits down on the floor to read it.

> "*Denevito said he was under investigation by the FBI for working both sides of campaigns: his firm would work for one side of the campaign and then Denevito would privately shake down someone from the other side of the fight and offer to throw the result if they paid him. Denevito admits to the double-dealing, saying, 'I was deep in debt. It was the wrong thing to do, but it was my only play.'*"

Yevgeny doesn't follow politics and quite frankly has no idea what to make of the story. But he knows the article likely means two things: one, the risk of putting people in flying cars that can't actually fly now seems a lot lower; and two, the chance of his equity turning into overflowing riches is a lot lower too. He can't quite process all this in real time, but some part of him knows this is a trade-off he can live with.

***

Pearce is at his home in Clarksville. A nice, regular house—and he likes it that way. It means people are less likely to ask questions. When he takes meetings here, he looks more like a man of the people. And nobody suspects what he keeps in the basement.

He's reading the *Post* story on an iPad after the Politico breaking-news email came through.

> "*According to Denevito, Mayor Navarro offered to switch his position on the flying car legislation in return for equity in 325 taxi medallions owned by shadowy Russian entrepreneur Viktor Velonova. The flying car legislation has caused controversy nationally, with Los Angeles labor leader Steve DeFrancesco recently accusing FlightDeck of unethical business practices.*"

Pearce thinks about his own potential legal mess and then immediately starts thinking about what kind of job he could get in the private sector. Maybe management consulting, something that involves public policy. Lobbying his former colleagues and subordinates would be too embarrassing. Maybe he could join a national firm like Firewall. He emails his scheduler to set up a call with Lisa to discuss. True to his profession, it doesn't occur to Pearce that she might have better things to do that day than calm his nerves and map out his financial future.

***

Viktor's at the nightclub, sun blaring through the front windows, drinking black coffee and reading a hard copy of the *Post*. The janitors are still sweeping up from the crowd that left just a few hours ago. There's a pile of newspapers in English, Russian, and Mandarin in the middle of the table (plus the dog-eared, ever-present copy of Phil Collins' groundbreaking memoir).

> "*Denevito said that when he learned he was under investigation by the FBI—led by New York City–based agents Sarah Rosario and Justine Wheeler—they discussed ways to reduce his potential prison sentence. Together, they hatched a plan to convince Mayor Navarro to switch his position on the bill in return for a substantial bribe. If the mayor took the bait, the FBI would then recommend a more lenient sentence for Denevito.*"

Viktor can't help himself and starts laughing. He knows that, for him, all press is bad press. He knows that investigators from the Taxi and Limousine Commission are about to go through the financial structure of every one of his medallions with a fine-tooth comb. He knows that Nick just caused him a lot of tsuris.

But despite all of that, he can't help but admire Nick's ability to turn things inside out and wreak total havoc in the process.

***

Lisa's on the subway heading to an ophthalmology appointment on the Upper East Side, reading the *Post* on her phone.

> "*Denevito said that Navarro was on board with the bribery scheme but backed out at the last minute when he became suspicious that their conversation was being recorded. 'To be clear,' Denevito told the Post, 'Navarro was one hundred percent on board with the plan. He negotiated the bribe himself. He just backed out when he realized something was up.*'"

Lisa says, out loud, to no one in particular, "Fuck me."

Then she smiles. Nick's clearly going down, but at least he's doing it on his own terms.

There's something admirable in that.

Her phone dings. A text from her dad. Probably some kid she went to third grade with won the Nobel Peace Prize or bought a state-of-the-art dishwasher.

Isn't that your boss in the paper? the text asks instead.

Now you pay attention? Lisa shakes her head and deletes the text.

***

Pinky's in the storage closet. He's got the story up on his desktop, reading as he polishes an antique wooden prosthetic hand.

"'This is a blatant attempt at entrapment,' said top white collar defense lawyer Jay Hirshenbaum. 'The FBI can't just concoct scenarios to try to put high-profile scalps on the wall.'

"Southern District spokesman Cy Berger declined to comment on the investigation, citing grand jury secrecy rules.

"Denevito also said that Navarro offered to pass various laws and regulations to artificially inflate the value of the medallions, including imposing fees on ridesharing vehicles but not taxis, capping the total number of medallions, orchestrating a city-funded bailout for taxi medallion owners, reclassifying Uber and Lyft drivers as full-time employees, and other measures."

Pinky is floored. Nick is his hero. Nick has always been so nice to him. Even called him "hotshot" a few times—the only nickname anyone has ever given him. But he knows one thing: if anyone can figure a way to make this all work out in the end, it's Nick Denevito.

Nick's his guy.

That's not changing.

***

"It is unclear at the time of this writing whether Navarro's alleged discussion with Denevito is sufficient to bring an indictment against the mayor. Sources expect Denevito to be arrested as early as

> *today and charged federally with wire fraud, corruption, extortion and mail fraud."*

Wheeler turns to Rosario. "So who should we arrest first?"

"What do you mean? I'm worried someone's going to arrest *us*. This whole thing was a bad idea."

"Not if we get out ahead of this. We should do exactly what Nick did. Go on the offense. If we don't, then it looks like we totally fucked this whole thing up. But if we do, then this is just another rough-and-tumble case where everyone got a little beat up. Not ideal, but, hey, this is New York. Everyone gets beat up sometimes."

"You don't think we should check with someone first?" Rosario asks. "Before this gets even messier? Before we get beat up even more?" She knows that trusting Wheeler is the last thing she should do, but she also knows that Nick's Hail Mary may require one of their own too.

"Come on. We ask for direction, we know exactly what they'll say. Stand down. Do nothing. And then guess who's on unpaid leave while some inspector general investigates? Fuck that."

Rosario realizes who Nick has reminded her of this whole time. Wheeler! At this point, either she bolts from the food truck and begs her bosses for mercy, or she puts her trust in her partner.

Fuck it.

Rosario's face brightens for the first time all day. "Let's track down Nick."

CHAPTER FORTY-ONE

NEW YORK CITY

Firewall HQ

Nick is dragging the solid oak podium they use for press conferences out from the actual supply closet at the Firewall office. It was made for a science fair in Altoona, Pennsylvania, in the late 1950s, and he bought it at a flea market six years ago. He loves any chance to use it. But he doesn't usually move it himself and had forgotten how goddamn heavy it is.

He's wearing a suit and is somewhat worried about sweating through it. The press should be there in an hour or so. He announced the presser via Twitter, which he knew would draw an overflow crowd.

When he finally has the podium where he wants it, he retreats to the back conference room with the comfortable leather couch with the stuffing coming out while he catches his breath and waits for showtime. Before he sits, he takes off the jacket of his navy Tom Ford suit so it doesn't wrinkle. The suit is custom-cut and the one he looks best in. Should at least make the mug shot a little less bad.

He looks at the endless list of missed calls. No reason to respond to any of them. It'll all get settled in the press conference. Except the three calls from his ex. Who hopefully didn't show the paper to their son. She probably did. Another way to even the scales. *So what? Just one more mess to clean up*, he thinks. *Put it on the list like everything else.* But he knows it's not just one more mess.

Forty-five minutes later, the room is jammed with reporters and TV cameras. Nick waits ten minutes past the presser's call time and strides to the podium at the front of the bullpen. He steps up, running his hands along the smooth, gorgeously faded veneer.

"Thank you all for coming today. As you know, I raised several concerns about our mayor and about the Federal Bureau of Investigations in today's *New York Post.* I know those allegations are shocking to some, so I wanted to give everyone the chance to ask questions. I'm fully willing to answer any question you have, including those about my own legal issues. I'll stay here as long as you want."

Nick understands that sometimes no spin is the best spin, that transparency and candor will go further with reporters than any clever retort, any creative excuse, any justifiable defense. He surveys the packed room of reporters all chomping at the bit and recognizes this is one of those moments.

"Who's first?" he says, catching Julia's eye and smiling wryly. He makes an "I'll call you later" motion with his head, which she gets and then leans back, ready to enjoy the show.

Every hand in the room goes up.

Pete Lauder from the *Daily News* goes first. "Nick, did Mayor Navarro ask you for a bribe to change his position on flying cars?"

"Yes. Actually, to be fair, I offered a bribe. He accepted it."

Mary Kim from NY1 jumps in next. "What specifically did you offer him?"

"I offered the mayor one percent of the value of two hundred taxi medallions—"

Susie Moss from the *Staten Island Advance* yells, "Medallions owned by Viktor Velonova? How much is that worth?"

"Around three hundred and sixty thousand dollars. He accepted it. Then later, the mayor went back on his word and asked for two point five percent of the value of three hundred and twenty-five medallions—"

"How much is that worth?" screams half the room.

"Oh, a lot more. Let's see." Nick dramatically pulls out his phone and opens the calculator function, even though he already knows the answer.

Nick holds up his phone. "According to this, a bit over one point four million. In today's dollars. The plan was to pass laws to artificially inflate the value of the medallions, so that could have easily turned into ten or fifteen million. Anyway, I was about to accept his counter when we were interrupted, and then he realized the conversation was being recorded."

Richard LaFarge from the *Times* goes next. "How did he realize it? And why were you interrupted?"

"Well, for one, he's smarter than people think. That's why he's the mayor and we're not. But specifically, it was when he realized that one of the Pegasus Club workers was the same person as the houseboat bartender from the first time we met about this."

"And who is that person?" LaFarge asks.

"Agent Sarah Rosario from the Federal Bureau of Investigations."

Ralph Howitzer from *AM New York* jumps in. "Why was she dressed as a houseboat bartender or a hotel worker?"

"Because she was working undercover, recording our conversations."

Jocelyn Guttierez from NBC: "Why did Agent Rosario think that the mayor was likely to take a bribe?"

"Because I told her that I thought Navarro would be into it. I figured he was only in favor of the flying car bill because it screws over Uber. If his position was solely based on vengeance, that meant it could be flipped by a better offer."

Jed Jefferson from ABC goes next. "So Agents Wheeler and Rosario asked you to set up the mayor?"

"I offered Navarro. But they made it clear that giving them someone bigger would help me in the long run."

Marsha Sunstein from CBS chimes in. "Why'd you even make the offer?"

"Because I don't want to go to jail. Because I'm under federal investigation and was looking for a way to trade up and reduce my sentence. Navarro is leaving office and already put out feelers to me on whether there was a way I could help him maintain his lifestyle. And we all know how he plays the game. So, it didn't come out of nowhere."

Mary Kim from NY1 again. "Do you consider what the FBI did entrapment?"

"I'm not a lawyer. But it felt pretty sleazy to me."

LaFarge again. "Haven't some of your actions also been sleazy?"

"Absolutely. That's why I understand it so well."

Mary Kim gets one more in. "Did Mayor Navarro's actions feel sleazy to you?"

"Of course. He negotiated a bribe. Just because he was smart enough to back out at the last second doesn't make him any less guilty. Trust me, smart and sleazy are not mutually exclusive. Especially in this business."

Rajinder Sethi from WINS radio jumps in. "Why exactly are you under federal investigation in the first place?"

Before Nick can answer, there's a rustling in the back of the room. A group of people wearing FBI windbreakers aggressively pushes through the crowd and approaches Nick at the podium.

Agent Wheeler walks up to Nick. Nick holds out his wrists. Wheeler slaps the cuffs on and walks him out. The press keeps screaming questions at Nick and the agents. The agents refuse to answer. Nick smiles for the cameras on the way out.

His smile gets even bigger when they step outside and the entrance is surrounded by folks in bird costumes, cheering his arrest.

"Having fun yet?" he asks Wheeler.

"Shut the fuck up," she says, dodging a leggy flamingo.

CHAPTER FORTY-TWO

LOS ANGELES, NEW YORK CITY

FlightDeck HQ

After Susan's call to Nick goes straight to voicemail, she tries Lisa. Susan has never seen Lisa as anything more than Nick's assistant, and whenever she deals with Lisa, she feels like she's not being given the first-class treatment she deserves.

Her call to Lisa goes to voicemail too—but a little while later, Lisa calls back.

"So we're dead?" Susan asks immediately, in lieu of "hello" or "how are you."

"Honestly, Susan? I'm not sure. At first glance it seems like we are. But when you dig into it a bit, it could play out a few different ways."

"Such as?"

"Well," Lisa says, "right now, our bill is associated with a corrupt consultant and a possibly corrupt mayor."

"That's not good."

"No, it's not. But—if you're Joe Navarro, what's the best way to prove that this is all bullshit? What's the best way to show that you're innocent and always were?"

"Pass the bill."

"With a transparent public debate, and without amendments. Which makes our lives easier. So he has to prove his integrity by doing our bidding."

Susan pauses for a moment, thinking. "How do I know you're not just trying to keep me from firing you? Carol warned me about this."

"Of course I'm trying to keep you from firing us. And look, you could decide that we're way too toxic and get rid of us today. I'd get it. That'd be the prudent thing to do."

"But?"

"But I think starting over doesn't help you at all. Look at where we are. In New York, the mayor now has to use every resource he has to pass the bill—"

"Is he still powerful enough to pass the bill?"

"I think so. He's definitely a lot weaker than he was twelve hours ago. But in New York, if you make a pie chart of where all the power sits, like ninety-plus percent of it would be with the mayor. He controls everything—jobs, grants, infrastructure, policies, programs. And while Joe Navarro may not be the world's most honest guy, he knows how to work the levers of power as well as anyone I've ever met. So yeah, I think he can still get the bill through."

Susan pauses again, formulating her next question. "Let's say, for the sake of argument, you're right about Navarro and right about New York. Fine. That's still just one of three. What about Austin and LA?"

"LA is still a total wildcard. We're making less progress there than we are in the other cities, even though it is your hometown. But—I haven't told you this yet—we have kind of a similar situation in Austin."

"Their mayor is corrupt too?"

"No. Well, maybe. I'm not sure. Depends on your definition of corruption, I guess. But let's say that like Navarro, he has a powerful incentive to pass our bill."

"Jail?"

"Not for him directly. But it's messy enough that meeting our needs is his best play. By far."

"Well," Susan says, "if we can get two out of three, that's enough to start with."

"Exactly. And then when you show that the product works, how great it is, we'll be able to get new cities on board a lot faster and a lot easier."

"I hope you're right," Susan says.

"Me too."

"So what's the plan for now?"

"Assuming you're still good with moving forward? Nick resigns from Firewall. Makes it clear no one else had anything to do with this—"

"Is that actually true?"

"Yes. And then once we're in the clear, we leverage Navarro and Pearce in exactly the ways we just discussed, lobby the councilmembers like crazy, and pass our bills. Launch as fast as you can—I'm assuming you've got all the tech issues figured out. And then we roll from there."

Susan knows that continuing to do business with a firm led by a guy who's about to go to jail is incredibly risky, at best. But she knows Yevgeny has solved—or mostly solved—the sensor issue, so it's really now or never.

"Okay. The goal here is to win. So yeah, I'm willing to play out the string a little more."

"That's great, Susan," Lisa says. "Thank you."

"But Lisa?" Susan adds. "If you don't have these bills passed in the next couple of weeks, not only are you fired, we're going to sue you and every member of your team personally for fraud, misrepresentation, and anything else our extremely smart and aggressive lawyers can think of. For every penny you've got—and every penny you'll make for the rest of your career."

Susan ends the call before Lisa has a chance to respond.

CHAPTER FORTY-THREE

NEW YORK CITY

City Hall

Nick's in the back of a black Suburban with Rosario and Wheeler. The cuffs are still on. Another agent is driving. The car looks and feels brand-new, and Nick is half-tempted to ask the driver how it handles.

"What the fuck, Nick?" Rosario asks. "Why would you go to the *Post* like that? And why would you hold a press conference?"

"What choice did I have? You told me I was going to prison. So if that's the case, I figured I should at least get out ahead of it. Tell my side of the story. Plus, it's hard to see the FlightDeck bill passing in light of all this. That solves at least one of my problems."

"Nick, you're literally on your way to jail," Wheeler says, turning around from the front seat. "Who cares about the bill?"

"I do. I owe Viktor two million dollars, and the interest is growing by the day. If this story kills the bill, at least I might go into jail free and clear of any markers. That's a lot better than making myself a target every time I step foot in the yard."

"Don't worry about the yard," Wheeler reassures him. "Viktor's going to be in the cell right next to you."

"Why? He was just doing his civic duty helping you. That's not a crime. In fact, I'd call it a public service. A mitzvah even." Nick pauses. "So…do you guys think you can still get Navarro? And if so, does that mean I still get off with probation?"

Rosario speaks for both of them. "Shut the fuck up."

***

Navarro is about to hold his own press conference at City Hall. He's in the antechamber, preparing with his team. The room is filled with anxious staffers furtively surfing LinkedIn. Navarro may be the calmest of all of them, which isn't saying much.

Abby, Navarro's press secretary, speaks first. "Joe, are you sure this press conference is a good idea? Counsel hasn't spoken to SDNY yet. We really don't know what we're facing. Charges. Arrests. Indictments. We're totally in the dark here. Maybe it'd be safer to wait a little—"

"I'm on the front page of the *New York* fucking *Post* being called a criminal. It hit like a fucking dirty bomb and you guys weren't able to do a damn thing about it. I can't just sit around and wait for you to figure things out. I'd be voted out of office if I listened to you."

Navarro decides that more conversation with his staff is a waste of time and pushes forward, storming into the Blue Room. It's just as packed as the press conference in Nick's office. Maybe even more so. Local and national media are all there. International too. There are a solid twenty cameras on the back riser. It's unclear if the riser can even handle that much weight.

A cameraman yells, "Heads up," as Navarro enters, and everyone quickly stops talking.

Navarro goes straight to the podium and starts. "Where I come from, when someone accuses you of something that's not true, you don't hide under a rock and hope it all goes away. You come out and tell the truth. And the truth here is very simple. This entire story is completely, entirely, unequivocally false."

Michael Rao from NY1 interrupts. "So you didn't ask Nick Denevito for a bribe?"

"No. Of course not."

"Yeah," Navarro says. "You—with the nose ring."

"Thank you. Joanna Montez from the Daily Beast. How can you deny asking for a bribe when Denevito's saying they have it on tape?"

"Great. Let's hear it. He seems to have no problem making things public."

Eduardo Simeon from *Noticias* jumps in. "But why were you dealing with someone like Denevito in the first place?"

"We had the same agenda. Or so I thought. I support flying cars. It's the future. We need the jobs. And we need the tax revenue even more. Next year's deficit is looking like seven billion. So whenever someone is running a campaign aligned with an issue I care about, we work with them."

Helen Simmons from NBC is next. "Why didn't you just let your staff deal with it? Then you wouldn't be in this situation."

"Because that's not how I do things. I'm the mayor, not them. The people voted for me. So if the best chance of getting something done requires me to be involved, then I'm all in. That's what New Yorkers expect. They have every right to."

Shelley Samuels from the *Daily News*: "Is the flying cars bill now dead?"

"Why would it be dead?"

"Because it's now wrapped up in a major scandal."

"The question before the Council is whether to legalize flying cars, not whether to validate lies from a dirtbag political operative looking to squirm out of trouble. I'm confident that when the Council sees all of the facts at hand and when my administration has finished making the case in support of the idea, it will pass. Handily."

Abby yells out, "Last question!"

Julia Alessi. She goes in for the kill in front of everyone. "Have you been interviewed or approached by the FBI? Do you expect to be?"

Navarro winces. It's barely perceptible, but it's there. "No and no. Thank you everyone."

Navarro and his team walk out, ignoring the questions still being screamed at them, and head up the stairs. They stop halfway up.

Abby asks, "What happens when the tapes are made public?"

"They won't be," Navarro answers.

"What makes you so sure?"

Navarro stops walking. "Because everyone's going to want this to go away. The FBI has egg all over their face because they let a few low-level agents try to entrap the mayor of the City of New York. There's no case against anyone because I didn't accept a bribe. This is not that complicated. We pass the bill, the FBI announces there's no credence to the *Post* story, we declare victory and move on."

CHAPTER FORTY-FOUR

AUSTIN, TX

City Hall

The *New York Post* story was a wonderful source of motivation for Mayor Pearce to pass FlightDeck's bill—and bury Lisa's recording of his own deputy mayor soliciting bribes.

He called Lisa personally that morning to ask her to help them get the desperately needed five votes in the City Council. The *Post* scandal had created problems everywhere. But Lisa thought that getting a call from the mayor directly was still kind of cool. That kind of call usually went to Nick.

Six hours and one JetBlue flight later, Lisa is in his office.

Pearce and Maura Kasman—Pearce's legislative director—are already going through the bill strategy when Lisa walks in.

"You're here! Fantastic. Let's get to it. Maura, where are we on the roll call?" Pearce asks.

Maura is an older woman whose style is retro-chic—a gray beehive and thick, cat-eyeglasses. She looks a little like Lisa's fourth-grade teacher, the one who told her parents she had an "enthusiasm problem," which immediately puts Lisa on edge. "As of right now, we've got three solid yeses, four solid nos, the other three are up for grabs, plus you're the tiebreaker. So we need two of the three."

"What did you give the three who are with us?" Lisa asks.

"For Johnson, nothing. He's just for the bill."

Pearce and Lisa both give a "who knew?" kind of expression. It had never occurred to either of them that someone could take a legislative position without first getting something in return.

Maura continues, "Espinal didn't take a major push either since he's young and likes technology. I told him we'd support his recreational drones in wildlife bill. Not that we have jurisdiction over much wildlife, but if it makes him happy..."

"Fine. Sure. Whatever," Pearce says.

"Addabbo was lukewarm on the bill but, shockingly, the new senior center we funded in his district is somehow running over budget. So we'll use our discretionary capital budget to fill the gap." Pearce and Lisa nod appreciatively.

"Any of the opponents flippable?" Lisa asks.

"Probably not," Maura says. "Some of them answer to the Socialists. Others still take campaign money from the taxi guys. We can go after them if we have to, but I'd rather pick off the undecideds instead."

"So how do we get two of the final three?" Pearce asks.

"Well, Rosenthal, as you know, still wants a ban on plastic products of any kind."

"I mean, in theory, sure," Pearce says. "Who wouldn't want that? But in reality, that's not feasible. Everyone loves the environment until they can't get what they need at Target. What if we create a blue-ribbon commission to explore how to make it work?"

"She's smart enough to know blue-ribbon commissions are bullshit."

"Task forces too," Lisa adds.

"What if we put someone serious in charge of the commission?" Pearce asks. "We put in some real staff resources. Show her it's a priority. Actually, let her decide who runs the commission. It becomes her thing."

Maura looks down at her phone. "Texting her now."

"Menino?" Pearce asks.

"She needs more convincing," Maura says.

"On the merits of the bill?" Pearce asks.

"On the value of having you owe her," Maura replies.

"Fine. Have her come in for lunch today. I'll bring her around. What about Skelos?"

"Where he always is—looking to sell his vote to the highest bidder."

Pearce shakes his head. "Lucky guy. The freedom of representing the one swing district in Austin. Where you can actually make decisions based on something other than what the handful of left-wing nuts who bother to show up for the primary think."

"Wouldn't be a problem if we had mobile voting," Maura responds.

"This again?" Pearce wanders to his desk to avoid hearing the same lecture for the three-hundred-and-thirty-fifth time.

Maura has been urging Pearce to back mobile voting for two years now. He's ignored her every time—he has power already, so why make it easier for someone to take it from him? She corners Lisa instead.

"How much do you know about mobile voting?" Maura asks. Lisa is standing in the corner of Pearce's office, looking for a polite escape route.

"Umm...not that much. Voting on your phone, right?"

"Right. Think about what we're dealing with here. Are all of the councilmembers actually left-wing nuts who hate tech and jobs and business? No. Some of them are, but not every single one of them. But other than Skelos, do any of them have the actual freedom to behave in a reasonable, centrist way? Also no."

"Because of primary turnout."

"Exactly. Just about every district in every city and every state across the country is gerrymandered. A handful of people like Skelos have competitive general elections, but they're few and far between. So, in reality, the only election that usually matters is the primary. I assume you know what average primary turnout is?" Maura rarely gets to introduce this topic to someone who knows politics as well as she does, so this is fun.

Lisa stops looking for the door and starts to enjoy the conversation too. Maura may be overly passionate about this, but it is interesting. "Low. Lower than we think in fact. I'm gonna say twenty-five percent. Maybe even twenty."

"Even lower. More like ten to fifteen percent on average, especially for non-presidential primaries. And do you know who that ten to fifteen percent is?"

Lisa nods. "The crazies on both sides of the aisle."

"Right. And what do the crazies want?"

"Moral purity at all times."

Maura makes a gun with her thumb and index finger and points it at Lisa. "You got it. So the elected official is doing what they need to do to stay in office. Obviously, they all"—she lowers her voice so Pearce can't hear—"put themselves ahead of anyone else. But we know they just respond to the incentives they're given. They don't actually believe in anything except their own need for constant validation."

Nick's rule number one, Lisa thinks. Every policy output is the result of a political input.

"So let's say turnout in a primary were forty percent instead of fourteen percent," Maura continues. "Take assault weapons as an example. Seventy percent of Americans would tell you that we should neither confiscate everyone's guns nor should we make it so easy to buy an AK-47. Even here in Texas. Well, Austin at least. But that seventy percent never votes in the primary. So their views don't matter. Same with immigration. Most people would say we shouldn't deport everyone here illegally but we also shouldn't have wide open borders. But those people are irrelevant because they don't vote in primaries."

"But if they did—" Lisa says.

"Right. Then the incentives shift. If you want to stay in office, you'd now support an assault weapon ban if you're a Republican. You'd now support stronger border security if you're a Democrat. Because at forty-percent turnout, your primary voters just became a hell of a lot more moderate. And they want things to get done."

"They don't see talking to the other side as a crime. And the only way to get that kind of turnout is by letting people vote on their phones," Lisa deduces.

"Yep. Regular people are not going to miss taking their kid to school or be late for work or inconvenience themselves in any way just so they can vote in a State Senate primary or a City Council primary, or, hell, even a mayoral or congressional primary. But if they could vote securely on their phones? If they could vote from anywhere with one press of a button on the supercomputer already sitting in their pocket? A lot more of them would. And that, my friend, changes everything."

Pearce gets bored of not being paid attention to. "Lisa, is it true that you have Sharpton on board?" Pearce asks, steering the conversation back to himself. "It may help if he could make a few calls."

Lisa smiles ruefully. "We're still working on it."

Everyone's silent for a good forty seconds, trying to figure out what to do about the missing votes.

"What if we flipped it around?" Lisa asks. "Have someone accuse Skelos of soliciting campaign money to support the bill and then force him to be for the bill to prove he didn't do it."

Kind of a Jedi political move. Not unlike what she did to Pearce. Pearce arches his eyebrows. "Force him to disprove a negative. Not bad. Probably kills our relationship with him for anything going forward, but if we don't survive this, there is no going forward."

Pearce gives Lisa a searching look, hoping that maybe Lisa will jump in and say that she'll never release the bribery tape no matter what happens with the bill. Lisa pretends not to notice and buries her face in her phone.

Pearce gets the message—pass the bill or become the next Joe Navarro. "How about this? Maura," he says. "Get a drink with Skelos tonight. Actually, get him a lot of drinks. Float the idea of my supporting his next campaign—even float the idea that he should succeed me as mayor. Then press him on the bill. If he commits, great. If he doesn't, we can still claim he solicited a donation. If you get him drunk enough, he won't know for sure whether he did it or not."

Maura looks down at her phone. "Rosenthal seems open to the commission. Menino's coming in for lunch at noon."

"Okay, this is good," Lisa says, rubbing her hands together. "We can work with this. Don, you do your thing and make the sale to Menino. Maura, you figure out, one way or another, how we get Skelos there. You both come through and we'll have the votes."

Lisa knows that with her boss in handcuffs, and the Taylor recording burning a hole in her phone, neither Pearce nor Maura is sure they should trust anything she says. But at this point, this far down the road, she can bank on one thing: believing that Lisa is a political genius is their only path left.

***

At 11 p.m., Maura arrives back in the mayor's office. Pearce and Lisa have been there the whole time, eating take-out fish tacos from Gueros and devising second- and third-tier strategies in case the current plan doesn't work out.

"Skelos is in," Maura tells them proudly.

"Just like that?" Pearce asks.

"It took seven appletinis. But yes."

"How many did you have?"

"Two vodka sodas. And five club sodas with lime."

"What'd you have to give him?"

"Specifically? Nothing. Just talked up what a great mayor he'd be. How he embodies sensible centrist progress, represents the future that Austin needs, and that's the kind of thinking that embodies the flying car bill. How it's easy to see the whole Austin tech community rallying around him. Maybe even do a victory lap in Silicon Valley after the bill passes. He already has some ideas for what his mayoralty could look like. Including entrance music."

"What?" Pearce asks.

"He likes the idea of having someone with a boombox, or I guess these days a phone and a portable speaker, always walking a few steps ahead of him so whenever he enters a room, his theme song plays."

"Like 'Hail to the Chief'?"

"He mentioned Kid Rock, but yeah, like that, except on a continuous loop."

"I already feel bad for his staff, and he's not even a candidate yet," Lisa adds.

"He's never going to be mayor, so thankfully, this is only a theoretical problem. How did you get him to yes without a give?" Pearce asks. "Very unlike him not to demand a specific transaction."

Maura smiles. "He may be shallow. He may be transactional. He may be corrupt. But he's still a politician. Which means ego comes before anything else. Spin enough fairy tales about being mayor one day, add in half a dozen or so stiff drinks, sprinkle some pixie dust, and it overcomes all rational thought."

Lisa breathes a little sigh of relief. This one went down a little cleaner than she thought it would. She instinctively reaches for her phone, to call Nick and tell him the news.

And then she remembers: *Oh, right.*

Sure, she had to play a little fast and loose with Taylor, but he had it coming. When the first passenger steps into the first flying car, she can take pride in knowing that, for once, this is her victory.

CHAPTER FORTY-FIVE

LOS ANGELES, CA

FlightDeck HQ

It isn't every day that a midsized city like Austin, Texas, becomes the first in the world to legalize cutting-edge technology. So not one, not two, but three local TV stations carry the City Council vote live.

Susan's in her office, watching the livestream on her desktop. Yevgeny walks in just as the local KVUE reporter is breathlessly reporting on the outcome.

"Thanks, Jeff," says the anodyne blonde, blue-eyed reporter. "An epic day here at City Hall. By a six-to-five vote, with Mayor Don Pearce casting the critical tie-breaking ballot, Austin today became the first city in the world to legalize flying cars. Let me repeat that. Austin just became the first city in the entire world to legalize flying cars."

"Brooke, is this a surprise?" Jeff the dead-eyed anchor asks. "It seemed like the bill was headed for defeat."

"Exactly. Insiders expected the bill to narrowly fail, but Councilman George Skelos surprised everyone and sided with Mayor Pearce at the last minute, bringing the vote to a five-five tie and allowing the mayor to cast the final vote in favor of the legislation. And with that, Mayor Pearce made history. A big day here at City Hall. We'll be coming back with updates and live shots all day long, so stay tuned to KVUE."

Lisa gave her a heads-up, so Susan knew the call was coming. But it is still thrilling when it does. She praises her good judgment in allowing Lisa to keep running the campaign after Nick's arrest.

The cell phone buzzes. A voice comes through on the other end: "Hi. I've got Mayor Pearce for Miss Howard."

"Mister Mayor!" Susan says. She thinks about patching Carol in, but there's no time.

"Susan! How are you?" Pearce says. "I have good news."

She puts Pearce on speaker. "We watched the vote on the livestream. Really exciting. Incredible." Even at a moment like this, it doesn't occur to Susan to say thank you.

"Exciting for FlightDeck too! But now we need to show people this is real. As you saw, the floor debate was tough. A lot of people think we can't do this. They think it isn't legit. We need to prove them wrong."

"We're ready to go," she says. "We can be operational as soon as..."

She looks at Yevgeny. He shakes his head no. "One week from today." Yevgeny throws up his hands in a *what the fuck?* motion.

"Great. Have someone come by my office. We'll have the permit waiting for them."

Susan hangs up with a big grin. Yevgeny's face is the exact opposite.

"What the fuck, Susan?" he yells, in case all of his hand motions hadn't already made the point. "We have only run a few successful practice tests so far. In Torrance! We are not nearly ready."

Susan's grin turns to a hard stare. "If I listened to you, we'd never be ready. We'd test and tinker all day for the rest of eternity. I understand where you're coming from. It's why we're a good team. But I'm a thousand percent positive that there was someone just like you telling Edison they weren't ready, telling the Wright brothers they weren't ready, telling Musk they weren't ready, telling Ford they weren't ready, telling Jobs they weren't ready, telling Oppenheimer they weren't ready. The world needs flying cars now. And that means I have to push through, even when people like you tell me not to. That's the responsibility of greatness."

"Oppenheimer? Really?" Yevgeny asks. "Well, I will not do it. Neither will my team. So you can launch whenever you want. But I hope you know how to operate your own flying car, because no one is going to be there to help you."

Susan pauses, then smiles. "Really? Because to me, that sounds a lot like insubordination. Which, if you bothered to read your employment contract, you'd know is grounds for termination. And you know what that means, my friend? You lose everything. No equity. No options. Not even a positive reference when some community college calls to see if they should hire you to teach Introduction to Coding 101."

Yevgeny's face drops. She has him and she knows it. Susan doesn't pay much attention to other people, but she still understands that Yevgeny is relying on a big payday as much as she is—actually more, since her ample trust fund will still be there no matter what happens to FlightDeck.

And of course, Yevgeny hadn't read his employment contract.

No one does.

Yevgeny is still silent, standing there, face red, hair a mess, clearly not sure what to say.

"Let me make this easy for you," Susan continues. "I'm not saying we launch commercial service in Austin next week. Or even the week after. But we need something to show the world that we're real. It doesn't have to be a long flight or a complicated route. But we need something. Once we have that, we can secure more funding. And you get the resources you need to finish this."

She knows what Yevgeny is thinking. Something is better than nothing. And if he can control the test flight, it should be okay.

She knows she's right when he nods, turns around, keeps his mouth shut, and leaves the room.

CHAPTER FORTY-SIX

AUSTIN, TX

The University of Texas Campus

Pearce's communications team decided to hold the event on the University of Texas campus: lots of landmarks, lots of pretty buildings, lots of well-kept lawns. Lisa thinks it makes sense—good visuals, plenty of open space for reporters and onlookers, a place where they can install a plaque commemorating the launch of the first ever flying car. The timing is perfect, because mid-May is the last safe window before Austin turns into the surface of the sun.

For a moment, she even thinks about whether there's a way to put her name on the plaque along with Pearce's and Susan's. But she's staff. A consultant. Never going to happen. That's the plight of this job. Never any glory. Always backstage.

But she's still the one pulling the strings.

The clock tower's sordid history as the site of Austin's first mass murder has long faded, and now it's just a pretty visual for the takeoff. All the money the trustees spent on public art is paying off too, with Sol LeWitt, Michael Ray Charles, James

Turrell, and a host of others available to adorn the backdrop for TV live remotes.

Yevgeny is on site, scouting the area for the launch. Lisa's happy to see him. Like her, he's staff. And like her, he matters. Even if no one else notices.

Lisa approaches him. "Hey! You ready for this?"

Yevgeny frowns, but maybe that's just how he always looks. "Not really. We could use more time."

"Really? Susan said you were good to go."

"Does that surprise you?"

Lisa shakes her head. "Not at all actually." Then she continues. "But either way, we've announced the launch, so it's happening. How do you see it all working?"

Yevgeny walks over to a particular area of cement. "We launch from here," he says. He points his arm and finger in the air, tracing the direction of a flight. "Car goes up twelve hundred feet, then straight for about eight hundred feet, then lands right over there." He points to another patch of cement that doesn't seem all that far away from where they started.

"Wait, that's it? That's like right up and down."

"That is what I am comfortable with."

"Look, Yevgeny, I'm sorry, but that's not nearly enough. It'll look like this whole thing is a joke."

It's clear Yevgeny wants to start screaming, but he takes a moment and does a few breathing exercises. *He must think I'm as bad as Susan*, Lisa muses.

"What do you need to make it work on your end?" he asks.

"The takeoff area seems fine. And I have no idea how high in the air the car should go. That's your department. But it needs to go a lot farther than right over there." Lisa points to the cement patch not too far away.

"How far?"

"Can it go over the clock tower?"

"No."

"Can it do three or four loops around the campus?"

"No. It needs to travel in a straight line."

"Okay, so how far can it go then? Just up and over the football stadium and down?"

Lisa can tell Yevgeny wants to object. But she also knows that he can't keep saying no to everything without seeming totally unreasonable. He nods.

"I think we can do that. We just have to get the sensors up."

"Sensors?"

"That's the problem. We need external sensors. It limits the flight paths of the cars, but it gives us a fuller picture of the surroundings." Lisa sighs. "Well, that's a regulatory nightmare. But I guess it's a not-right-now problem. Where do the passengers deplane? We need cameras there. Lots of them."

"What passengers?"

"What do you mean 'what passengers'?"

"We cannot put people in this!" Yevgeny says.

"What the fuck do you mean you can't put people in this? That's the whole point! Otherwise, you're basically just a big drone."

"Lisa, we are not ready for that yet. Do you want blood on your hands? I know I do not."

"Well, the car can't be empty. That defeats the whole purpose."

Yevgeny thinks. "Could you put a dog or something in there?"

"Not iconic enough. Plus, people love dogs. If anything goes wrong, they'd go crazy. We'd be better off killing a few people." Lisa realizes she shouldn't have said the last part out loud.

"So what then?"

Lisa ponders for a few moments. She looks at the football stadium, and she remembers her conversation with Taylor. "What about a cow?"

Yevgeny shrugs. "A cow?"

"Yeah, a cow. There's a big one here." She looks it up on her phone because she can't remember the name again. "Here it is. Bevo. The official mascot of the University of Texas football team. He's a steer."

"Not a cow?"

"Says steer."

"What's the difference?"

"I have no idea. But either way, what if we put Bevo in there? That feels like we're marking the occasion properly."

"How much does he weigh?"

Lisa checks her phone again. "Umm…according to Google, sixteen hundred pounds."

Yevgeny says nothing, so Lisa keeps pushing. "The car is equipped to handle up to twelve passengers, right? That has to total more than sixteen hundred pounds. Especially here in Texas."

Yevgeny puts his head in his hands. "Yeah, sure, but you have to think about weight distribution. Twelve passengers are evenly distributed throughout the space. This is not. What if it shits all over the interior? Not to mention I'd have to remove a row of seats just to make it fit…"

Lisa is having second thoughts when Susan and Pearce stroll up.

"Did I hear something about Bevo?" Pearce asks.

"We're trying to figure out what to put in the car for the flight, and we threw out Bevo, but now…" Lisa starts.

Pearce jumps in. "That's brilliant! Think of the photo op. What do you think, Susan?"

Susan smiles. "It's very Texas. Yevgeny, make it happen."

"But..."

"Yevgeny," Susan says again, sharper. "Make it happen."

And after a moment of silent protest, Yevgeny nods.

Bevo it is.

CHAPTER FORTY-SEVEN

AUSTIN, TX

The University of Texas Campus

It's launch day. The turnout from the city's distinctively oddball population—skateboarders, frat boys, musicians, screenwriters, day laborers, tech geeks, barbecue aficionados, Silicon Valley expats, hill people—only adds to the vibe. Even the bird nuts, ca-cawing louder than ever, don't feel like a problem. Frankly, some of them look excited.

Everything's perfect.

Even Yevgeny is having a hard time feeling otherwise.

Lisa pulls Pearce, Susan, and Yevgeny off to the side. "Once the press is totally set up, we'll do a countdown," she says. Pointing at Susan and Pearce, she continues. "The two of you will press this big red button right here, and the car launches."

Yevgeny wonders if he should point out that the red button actually does nothing and it's him who's doing the launching, but whatever judgment he has left tells him to keep quiet.

"Bevo's ready?" Pearce asks.

"We showed him the vehicle this morning," Lisa says. "So he's acclimated and shouldn't freak out too much when they lock him in. Plus, they gave him some Xanax."

"They make Xanax for cows?" Susan asks.

Lisa shrugs. "Or it's just regular Xanax. Like a whole bottle of it."

"But what about when the car lifts off? Won't he freak out?" Pearce asks.

"It'll be so loud, no one will be able to hear him," Susan says.

Nothing left to review. The moment's here.

Yevgeny's nervous, anxious, concerned. But still pretty excited. *This is,* he thinks, *the first official launch ever of a flying car. That he designed. And he built.*

Not bad.

Bevo's handler gently leads him into the flying car. The cow—or steer, whatever—is pretty docile. It doesn't struggle, doesn't think twice. The fit is a little tight. Yevgeny actually had to remove two rows of seats. But it was in the middle so he figured it would help distribute the weight.

Once the door is secured, Pearce and Susan turn to the podium. They lock hands and raise them and yell to the crowd, "Is everyone ready?!"

The cheers are so loud they drown out the bird nuts.

Susan starts counting down from ten, and the crowd follows. After they reach "one," Pearce and Susan press the oversized red (ceremonial) button, and Yevgeny presses the real button.

The flying car lifts smoothly into the air and makes its way east towards the football stadium.

People are cheering, filming; little kids are jumping up and down.

It's their generation's moon landing.

The car evades a flock of grackles, and people cheer even more. Even the bird-people finally stop their ca-cawing and look on in speechless wonder.

Susan appears at Yevgeny's side. She seems to be reaching for him, like she wants to give him a hug. But then Yevgeny sees something that stops his heart mid-beat.

"Oh shit."

"What do you mean 'oh shit'?"

Yevgeny points to the sky. "What's that prop plane doing there?"

Susan peers into the sky. "Fuck if I know. It's Texas. People have private planes. Carol's from Plano. She never flies commercial."

"But we cleared this all with the FAA. That's what Lisa told me."

"What do you want me to say? It's there. It's fine. We're good. You installed the sensors everywhere, right?"

A question, not a statement.

Yevgeny nods and shrugs at the same time, omitting that prop planes were not one of the items anticipated and programmed for.

"So why do we have a problem?" Susan asks.

"Because it looks like it is flying right at us."

CHAPTER FORTY-EIGHT

NEW YORK CITY

Nick's Apartment

The new trends around bail being what they are, Nick got out a few hours after he was taken into custody. He's allowed to roam free, provided he doesn't leave the state.

So it's not like he could have gone to Texas. Not that they'd be happy to see him at the launch anyway.

But he is watching the livestream. He's excited by the moment because it's historic and he had something to do with it. He's nauseated by the moment because it means flying car legislation will end up passing everywhere—when one city falls, the rest follow, not wanting to be left out—which is the exact opposite of what he promised Viktor. He knows what breaking a promise to Viktor means.

He knows he screwed Lisa—and everyone else on the team—when he started playing both sides of the coin. He can justify it to himself as taking money from rich clients who deserve to pay a little more anyway. He can tell himself he's the Robin Hood of political consulting. He can say he was doing it in the name of innovation, funding fledgling tech startups.

But he knows it's just stealing.

And doing it actually feels good. Because it's a secret. Because it forces him to be clever. Because it raises the degree of difficulty.

Because he's good at it.

So, not quite sure how he feels about flying cars at the moment, he settles in as the event begins. It's a little early in the morning for a cocktail and a few vape hits of sativa, but realistically, what else does he have going on today? Might as well enjoy the show.

Nick sees what everyone watching live, across the globe, sees. Susan and Pearce beaming, pressing a button that obviously wasn't the actual launch mechanism. He watches the car lift smoothly into the air and start flying.

Including Bevo was a stroke of genius. Makes the event even more iconic.

He taught Lisa well.

The crowd is cheering. The TV anchors are breathless.

But the wide camera shot shows Susan and Yevgeny conferring. Yevgeny is gesturing anxiously. Susan bites her finger to keep from screaming.

Something's wrong.

The anchor confirms it. "There appears to be an unidentified object in the air. It looks like a small prop plane advertising something, and it's flying directly toward FlightDeck's car. It's hard to make out what it says. Let's see if we can get the camera to zoom in. Frank?" the anchor says to the cameraman. The shot gets closer and clearer. It says, 'The Sky Is for Birds, Not Cars.'

"I'm not sure who paid for this or how they got in the airspace," the anchor says, "but it is another reminder of just how controversial this issue is."

Nick shakes his head. It's not just another reminder. It's an actual problem. Yevgeny and Susan wouldn't be arguing otherwise. And Pearce, who was doing media hit after media hit, is suddenly pulled away by his staff.

Thirty years in politics. Thirty years of trying to make things happen and thirty years of watching shit go wrong. Nick's not sure if he wants to see what's next. But then he looks at the bracelet on his ankle.

And he hopes for a disaster.

CHAPTER FORTY-NINE

AUSTIN, TX

The University of Texas Campus

Lisa notices the argument between Susan and Yevgeny. She walks over to see what's going on.

"Everything okay?" she asks.

"No!" Yevgeny says before Susan can offer whatever spin she's concocting. "That prop plane is a problem. What is it doing there?"

Lisa peers up. "I don't know. It shouldn't be there. We cleared the route with the FAA like ten different times. No one else is authorized to use this airspace."

"It is coming straight for us."

Her stomach drops when she sees the banner it's carrying. This isn't an accident. It's sabotage. "What do we do? Call the cops?" Lisa directs her question to Yevgeny, knowing that not only will Susan be useless in this context, she'll probably just make things worse.

"We need to hope that the sensors we installed on the top of the football stadium will help the car dodge this obstruction," Yevgeny says.

"I thought you solved the sensory issue."

"We did. But that does not save us from a direct collision with a plane trying to hit us."

"Maybe we'll be fine," Susan offers. "Things usually work out for me."

The car is still proceeding east towards the stadium. It successfully senses and dodges a flock of purple martins. It's clear the car can sense something else is nearby too.

The prop plane starts making a loop around the stadium, eager to show off for the cameras at the landing spot, moving closer to the FlightDeck car. *Fuck*, Lisa thinks. *We thought we were the great disruptors, but these bird nuts are the ones disrupting us. With a fucking prop plane.*

The car suddenly lurches unsteadily about ten feet to the left. The prop plane veers right. The two are coming very close.

"Yevgeny! Do something!" Susan commands.

He pushes some buttons on the tablet, but mainly for show.

A volley of thoughts hit Lisa at once.

Maybe Susan's right and it'll be fine.

Maybe we'll have a close call but can still show the technology basically works.

Maybe we can blame the whole thing on the Audubon Society. Call for criminal charges. Domestic terrorism. Make them the focal point.

Or maybe this will just confirm what people already suspect—cars can't fly.

The car quickly drops in altitude as the prop plane sails overhead, eliciting a gasp from the crowd.

"What's happening?" Susan screams right into Yevgeny's already red and flustered face.

"The car needs to clear the upper deck of the stadium. It is sensing that there is something else nearby, and it is trying to avoid it. But it is processing too much at once. It does not know how to react."

"Can't you make it go up higher?" Susan demands. "Do something! Use the joystick!"

"I am trying. This is like playing a video game backwards and upside down. The whole thing would have been a lot easier if we had a pilot."

The flying car tilts upwards, and for a second, it looks like it might barely clear the upper deck. The prop plane keeps heading towards it.

Just before contact, Lisa remembers the cow. *The steer. Whatever. Shit.*

Killing a beloved mascot can't be good.

Maybe they have some backups on the farm. Who could tell them apart anyway?

Lisa holds her breath. It's going to be a matter of a few feet either way.

There's always a moment right when an accident occurs when everything slows down and you can see everyone's reactions in a split second. Horror and shock are the main two emotions Lisa notices. She can make out smiles on the faces of some of the protestors behind the French barricades. They know what's coming—because they planned it.

Susan is staring at the scene without any reaction or emotion on her face whatsoever.

And then the car flies straight into the top tier of the stadium, crashing into the wall behind the upper stands.

It's loud. So fucking loud.

The vehicle starts smoking and spiraling downwards. Quickly. Luckily no one is directly below.

Then it crashes into the parking lot.

The crash is even louder. Overwhelmingly loud. Makes the crash into the stadium almost seem like a whisper. Lisa thinks she can feel the ground shake a little too.

There's smoke everywhere. Sirens are blaring. Cops start running in circles, knowing they should do something, but, never having dealt with a flying car crash before, not sure what that something is.

Little kids are crying, more scared by the noise and smoke than because of the actual loss itself.

But the adults—they remember.

Bevo.

The state's most beloved mascot. The spirit animal of UT football.

Lisa wonders for a second if there's any way Bevo survived the cash. If so, maybe her career can survive too.

Then the acrid smell of smoke and burnt flesh hits her. It makes her think of the barbecue place she went to with Taylor.

This is going to be really bad. She reaches for her phone to call Nick before remembering he's off limits. She considers calling her dad, but he'd probably make her feel worse.

She walks towards the crash site, resolved to deal with whatever comes next—on her own.

CHAPTER FIFTY

NEW YORK CITY

City Hall

Navarro is in his office at City Hall with Rodolfo Cini, his legislative director, and the rest of the team. Most of the staff are afraid to leave the room in case they're needed, but they're also afraid that any interaction they might have with Navarro is being recorded, so they all hover around eight feet from the door. They're counting votes. Passing the bill is now critical to proving Navarro's innocence, or at least the optics of it.

"We had a lot more leverage before the *Post* story came out," Cini complains, smoothing out his slicked-back hair.

"I'm still the fucking mayor. I'm still relevant. A lot I can do for them. Or to them."

"True. But you're also a lame duck and your post-mayoral endorsement may not be so valuable if this Denevito thing doesn't go away," Cini responds. "I'm not saying we can't pass the bill. I'm just saying it's tougher."

"Let's focus first on getting it out of committee. We need seven votes out of the transportation committee, right? We can get that."

"Meyeroff, Hawkins, Adams, Cabrera, Levine, and Rose are all a yes. Even after the *Post* story. Still need one more. Given that they're holding the hearing on it right now, we're kind of out of time."

Navarro shakes his head. "It's never too late."

They study the roll call together. Navarro points at each member's name, saying, "No. No. No. No. O'Brien," jabbing his finger at the page. "He's a total scumbag. He'll do it if we offer enough. Just go up there, pull him aside, and make it happen. Doesn't matter what he asks for. Anything is fine."

As Navarro continues berating his staff, he sees all six officers on his security detail look at each other and then each step three feet back.

"Oh fuck," he says to himself as Wheeler and Rosario burst through the door of his office.

Navarro spent eight years as the state's attorney general. He knows what this means. The staff scatters immediately, as if the FBI couldn't find them if they were on the hit list. The smart ones know that once the prosecutors need more people to flip on Navarro for all his other corruption, they'll be hauled in for questioning too.

Navarro looks around the room but realizes there's nowhere to run and it would only look worse if he tried. He slumps down in his desk chair.

Wheeler turns to Rosario and says, "Sarah, why don't you do the honors?"

One Miranda warning later, Joe Navarro is led out of City Hall in handcuffs.

***

The City Council is still debating the flying car legislation. Speaker Aakash Agarwal seems frustrated. "Guys, come on. We need to bring this hearing to a close and this bill to a vote. We've been debating this all day. NY1's not covering anyone's speeches anymore, and I know none of you are listening to a word anyone else has to say. So let's wrap this thing up. I call for—"

Then a voice from the side yells, "Wait!" A rumpled young man in an oversized pinstriped suit that he clearly inherited from a much bigger older brother runs up to the speaker and whispers frantically in his ear. The speaker's eyes go wide.

"Well, according to this guy—" Sethi nods his head to the left, then turns to the kid. "Who are you again?"

"Larry. Russo. I work for Councilwoman Markowitz. I was downstairs talking to reporters at the Audubon Society protest and saw all these FBI agents storm into the building. Then they came out a few minutes later with the mayor! In handcuffs!"

Everyone's looking at their phones. The speaker is too. A few of them are present enough to realize they can just look out the window and see the same thing.

"There's more. The flying car didn't work. It crashed and burned."

After a few moments of disbelief, the speaker realizes he's still at the podium and that the Council is still in session. Not anymore.

"Upon further thought, I'm not sure any of the members currently supporting the administration's flying car bill will want to maintain their position in light of the flying car crash and the mayor's sudden predicament." The speaker knows that every member will want to be on the record as "I always hated the idea" and this lets them easily do it.

He calls for a vote. All thirteen members of the committee press the red button as fast as they can. The bill is dead.

The speaker bangs the gavel. "We're in recess."

CHAPTER FIFTY-ONE

AUSTIN, TX

Hotel Saint Cecilia

Susan knows better than to stick around at the scene of the crime. She considers heading straight to the airport but figures that would look really bad, so she returns to the hotel instead.

Before she even makes it to her room, the very hip, very exclusive, very dark, very empty bar calls to her. She picks up the cocktail menu and is about to try something new with jalapeño and Drambuie, but then says to the bartender, "Fuck it. Just tequila. Straight."

"What kind?"

"Any kind with alcohol."

Three drinks in, she's feeling a little better. Maybe this isn't the end of it all. Many founders fail, start over, and become billionaires. And many new tech products have caused far more damage—have actually killed people, like Tesla's autonomous driving mode. She just killed a cow. Sure, her crash and burn literally crashed and burned. And sure, the entire world saw it. But they also saw the car work for a while too. She can spin this to her board, to her employees. Her mother will understand. If anyone knows you have to break some eggs to make an omelet, it's her. She didn't become the parking king of Western Nevada by accident. Maybe she won't even consider Susan's startup track record to be 0–2: first Bad Shit Insurance, now this. Because this isn't a loss, right? At least not entirely. It's more like a half win, half loss, still-in-play kind of thing—and about to be a very full win. Very. The solution is right around the corner. And she'll listen to Yevgeny more next time. Definitely. The more she repeats this to herself, the better she feels.

Forty minutes and two more tequilas later, she turns to find Walter Lee, head of the FlightDeck board, sitting next to her. He already has a drink—something amber and neat in a rocks glass. How long has he been there?

"Susan," he says, when she finally notices him.

At this point, she's drunk. Very drunk.

"Walter! You came."

She moves to hug him. He awkwardly shifts away.

"So nice of you. Knowing the board really cares at a time like this..."

Walter slides a letter across the bar. "You need to sign this."

Susan starts reading. "But...I don't understand. You're terminating me? I'm out?"

"There's no time. And we're all out, not just you," Walter says. "Texas law limits legal liability for killing an official mascot to five hundred thousand dollars. Thank God for tort reform. The company has enough assets to liquidate without having to formally enter bankruptcy. The lawyers don't think we'll ultimately face criminal charges, but it's not impossible." He takes a long sip of his drink. "They love that fucking cow."

"But...the car did really well. Until the end there. The FAA had cleared the whole airspace. We were sabotaged. We couldn't have expected the Audubon Society to be that violent."

"Didn't they tie up that window washer in Brooklyn?" Walter asks.

"Exactly. Now you see what we're dealing with. But look, either way, now we know how to adjust for next time. We're just a few steps away from having it completely solved. A month, two months tops."

"You crashed," Walter says. "And burned. Literally. On live TV. Plus, you killed Bevo. Avenge Bevo is the leading hashtag on Twitter. Eight different mayors have already introduced legislation to never allow flying cars in their city. PETA is calling on the LPs in each of our funds to divest. TechCrunch is calling you the Elizabeth Holmes of flying cars."

"Again?"

"The mayor here..." Walter says.

"Pearce?" Susan asks. "Don't worry. He's with us."

"He has a press conference tomorrow morning. They say he'll resign. Unless the Council impeaches him tonight."

"Walter, take a step back here," Susan says with a slight slur in her voice. "We developed a flying car. Not a perfect flying car, but still, a flying car. It wasn't a scam. This isn't Theranos. This isn't FTX. You saw it. And we got two major cities to allow it. Well, Austin at least. New York should pass this week. Hopefully tomorrow."

"The New York bill was just defeated unanimously. They weren't even going to bother calling it for a vote after the crash and after Navarro got arrested—"

"Navarro got arrested?"

"How long have you been drinking?" Walter asks. He shakes his head. "If you sign this letter, we can wind everything down cordially. No litigation, no internal investigations, just an acknowledgment that things didn't go as planned, that it wasn't the board's fault, and that FlightDeck no longer exists."

"So my equity is worthless?"

Walter looks stunned. "Umm…yeah. When your test run crashed, everything crashed with it. Your equity. Our equity. Our ability to probably ever raise another fund. It's all gone."

Susan buries her head in her hands. He slides the paper closer and puts an expensive fountain pen on top of it. She lifts her hand, takes the pen, and signs it.

CHAPTER FIFTY-TWO

NEW YORK CITY

Coney Island Boardwalk

Spring in New York is almost always cold and wet, so other than a few sun worshippers over on the beach pretending they're having fun, the Coney Island boardwalk is still pretty desolate.

"So you cut a deal?" Viktor asks.

"What choice did I have?" Nick says. "The feds had all the pieces they'd need for a conviction. No way I could win in court. A New York City jury isn't going to sympathize with a corrupt, rich, white, straight, middle-aged political consultant. So we cut the best deal we could." Nick knows that one piece of evidence against him was provided by Viktor himself—or at least enabled when he let the FBI bug their first meeting—but he also knows better than to mention it.

"When do you go in?" Viktor asks.

"My lawyer asked the judge to start the sentence as soon as possible. Sooner it begins, the sooner it ends."

"And you're out three years from now?"

"With fifteen percent off for good behavior."

"I'm not sure I'd count on that if I were you. You've always been good at getting yourself in trouble."

"You never know." Nick pauses. "Speaking of, we're good?"

"With what?" Viktor says, like he doesn't know.

"My marker. The two million I owe. The bill failed. Went just as we discussed."

"I don't remember planning to get Navarro arrested."

"Collateral damage."

"I don't remember discussing my name being dragged into the press."

"You look like a hero. You were helping the FBI."

"I look like a scummy taxi owner trying to bribe a politician."

"So what?" Nick asks. "You don't care what other people say about you. As long as they fear you, right?"

Viktor smiles wistfully. He lowers his voice a bit and looks directly at him. "Nick, everyone cares what people say about them. Everyone." After a long pause, Viktor continues. "I'm going to follow the example of our friends in the federal Department of Corrections, *da*? Prison bureau. You behaved well. Sort of. So I'm taking fifteen percent off your marker. Now you only owe me one point seven million."

"You hired me to kill the bill. The bill went down. Unanimously."

"The bill went down because Navarro went down. And because that cow in Texas went down."

"That was a steer."

"What?"

"Bevo. The mascot. He's a male cow. Or was."

Viktor doesn't care. "One point seven."

"Viktor, that's not fair. Who cares how we got to the right outcome? We got there."

Viktor pauses for a moment. Nick realizes this is the toughest negotiation of his life—going toe-to-toe with someone who has real, actual power. And the muscle to back it up. He wonders if he should back off a little.

"I'll tell you what," Viktor says. "We won't start compounding the vig until you get out. I've never done that for anyone before."

"But..."

Viktor looks hard at Nick.

That's the best deal he's going to get.

"Okay, okay. Thank you. Maybe I'll come up with a way to make some money on the inside, start paying you back sooner."

Viktor smiles. "I have no doubt you'll try."

CHAPTER FIFTY-THREE

NEW YORK CITY

Nick's Apartment

Back from Austin, free from criminal charges so far, Lisa leaves the office and walks up the street to Nick's apartment. She is dreading the visit, but she also knows she'll regret it if they don't end things right. At least for now.

It's clear where all the money went. Compared to her spartan one-bedroom with the hand-me-down brown suede couch, everything in Nick's apartment is top of the line. There's artwork on the walls that could fund college tuitions. The kitchen looks suited for a master chef, even though Nick uses his oven as storage. Lisa has always thought of Nick as the kind of guy who would happily live in a five-star hotel, so she envisioned his apartment as something like a suite at the Crosby. Her guess is mainly right. If it wasn't triple-mortgaged, he could have used it to solve his Viktor problem.

Nick is straightening up. He seems happy to see her. And despite everything, she's happy to see him too. Four years of working together doesn't get wiped out by one bad decision, or—more realistically—a series of bad decisions.

"I don't think I've ever seen you clean something before," Lisa says.

"Lucien's coming over for dinner in an hour. Told him we could order from any restaurant in the city. Anything. Whatever he wants." Nick pauses. "So Shake Shack it is." He pauses and mutters, "Fourteen-year-olds..."

"How's he handling all of this?"

Nick doesn't respond.

Trying to lighten the mood, Lisa asks, "So how does it work? Do you pack for prison?"

"I don't think so. It's not like camp."

"I almost got you a trunk." She pauses. "I'm a little worried about you. Look, I'll be honest. I'm still really angry at you. You fucked everything up for everyone. And there are a lot of things I've never liked about you. But...I'm still worried."

"I'll be fine. Thirty-one months with good behavior. Enough time for me to get in great shape, but not enough to come out too old to take advantage of it."

Always like Nick to find the silver lining, Lisa thinks.

"You know, orange isn't really my color, grasshopper," Nick says.

Lisa takes a deep breath. Today Nick is going to prison, so what does she have to lose?

"I'm not going to miss that," she says, the words springing from her mouth.

"Miss what?" Nick asks.

Lisa feels her spine straighten as the words spill out. "The condescending comments. I know my worth, and I've done a good job at Firewall. Actually, better than you've done, apparently."

Nick sits heavily on the couch and stares down at the floor.

Lisa continues. "We can have a long conversation about the built-in sexism here, but honestly, at this point, I just want you to know that I am who I am, and I deserve more respect, and if you want to really go deep on this, remember who's headed off to jail and who isn't..."

"Lisa," Nick says.

"...And I get that's a little harsh, but we've been through a lot in the last few weeks. I've been through a lot."

Nick turns to Lisa and locks eyes with her, which is enough to break her train of thought.

"Lisa."

"What?"

"I'm sorry." Nick puts his hands together and rubs them back and forth. "I know I was hard on you. Part of it, I guess, was just teasing. I felt comfortable enough to do that with you, which, you know, I don't feel that way with a lot of people. But the other part...having a thick skin matters in this job. That's the reality of it. And if you're going to take over Firewall...I don't know, I guess there was a better way to have that conversation."

Lisa pauses. "Wait, what? Take over?"

"Of course take over. What do you think the point of all this was?" Nick gets up and crosses the room to her. "I always figured you would take it over when I was ready to move on." He shrugs. "I can't exactly run the place from prison. So...we're moving the timeline up."

Lisa struggles to find a response. She wasn't expecting this. She just figured Nick would work until he dropped dead. Her taking over never even entered her head. Maybe one day she'd start her own firm, but that's as far ahead as she thought.

"I don't know what to say," Lisa says.

Nick puts his hand on her shoulder and squeezes. "Thank you is fine."

"Thank you," Lisa says.

Nick shrugs. "You'll do a better job than I did. Just do me a solid. When I get out, consider me for a job? But not completely entry-level. I want to come in with at least an office and benefits. And no storage closet." Nick pauses. "Also, as much as I hate to say this, you should probably change the name of the firm too. It's probably pretty toxic right now."

Yeah, no shit, Lisa thinks.

Nick's phone rings. "Hang on a second," he tells Lisa. He walks to the corner of the room, gesturing with his free hand as he whispers into it.

"Lawyers?" Lisa asks when Nick returns.

"The Aryan Brotherhood. They want me to run a campaign to get rid of the warden."

Lisa shakes her head. "You're not *really* going to work with them, are you?"

"Well, I need to see what the other options are first. The Crips might have their own candidate. La Eme too. I need to see what the best deal is. Or maybe I'll just back the warden they have now. He's entitled to make an offer too. I have to be fair to everyone."

"Maybe only play one side of the campaign this time?"

"Where's the fun in that? The rules still apply."

That's it, she thinks. That's always been it—and, at least, when it comes to understanding politicians, or anyone in power, how it always will be. Nick's rules are the baseline for every campaign they've run, every fight they've won, every battle they've lost, everything they believe in. They're literally the rules she lives by. Nick may be going away, but the rules he set out might as well be written in stone.

"I can think of one more. Don't get shanked in the prison yard."

He laughs, and then she laughs. Long enough that it stops being about the joke, and more about this whole debacle being over.

Which then poses the immediate question for Lisa. What's next?

CHAPTER FIFTY-FOUR

LOS ANGELES, CA
LAX

Yevgeny is in the very plush lounge at LAX, waiting for his flight to Tokyo. He's never flown first-class this far. It's a long flight, but he's looking forward to it. A good eight hours of sleep. Two and a half John Wick movies. A perfect day.

His phone rings. Lisa. Despite himself, he smiles and answers.

"I need to get off the grid," he says.

"I don't think Tim Cook would ever let that happen."

"Privacy is gone forever. How are things going? Is Firewall still in business? It seems like your CEO getting arrested for corruption and then your biggest campaign going up in actual smoke is a bad combination."

"Sure. For now. But people are always going to have political problems. They're always going to need someone like us to take care of those problems. For as long as we have a fucked-up democracy, we'll have customers."

"Your clients aren't mad about Nick playing both sides?"

"Of course they are. But we'll rebrand. Ironically, FlightDeck held on the longest. Or at least, Susan did. But we have a pitch this afternoon, and I have some cash in the bank to get us through for a while. What's your plan?"

"Susan has this new ghost kitchen concept she is really excited about. She says no one wants to cook anymore, but restaurants also cannot keep going the way things are. Costs are too high. Margins too low. So if you deliver people restaurant food and charge restaurant prices without having the actual, you know, restaurant part, it is a lot more profitable. She wants me to join her."

"She's not mad about the whole crashing and burning and killing the football cow thing?"

"She gets over things fast."

"How's she going to raise any money for this?"

"She is a founder with a track record."

"A track record of destroying the world's first flying car."

"She made it further than anyone else has," Yevgeny says. "She will raise money. Venture capitalists are like kindergarteners. Wave a shiny object and they will come right toward it. Plus, she has her own money. And she can always just sell off some of her stars."

"Her what?"

"She compulsively buys stars from astronomy websites and names them after herself. There are over six hundred stars named Susan. And like, another thirty named Carol."

"So are you going to join her?" Lisa asks.

"I'm on my way to Tokyo to start a new job now."

"Tokyo? Woah. What's the job?"

"You are not going to believe it."

"Dude, I work in politics. Nothing surprises me."

"Flying cars."

"Holy shit. Really? But who? How?"

"Ever heard of Shinzo Taiyaki?"

"Yeah, the really crazy billionaire. The one who dyes his hair turquoise and has tattoo sleeves on both arms and like six piercings on his face?"

"Yes. He sees it the same way Susan does: the Austin catastrophe was a near miss that only proves that the tech is ninety percent of the way there."

"How'd you get connected to him?"

"He asked a friend on the FlightDeck board who did the real work at the company. He said me."

"Nice."

"Shinzo and I met over Zoom. We negotiated a contract and my first day starts when I land."

"To do what?"

"Run the engineering team. What did you think it would be?"

"I don't know. Aren't there some kind of contractual restrictions on taking any proprietary information on what you did at FlightDeck?"

"My cousin Alvar is an injury lawyer and he says that the restrictions are—what's the word he used—oh right, moot. He said the restrictions are moot since FlightDeck is in the ground. The contract died with the company. And any contractual restrictions around not taking FlightDeck materials have already been met. Shinzo respects the law." This last statement may not have been necessary, but it means a lot to Yevgeny.

"Okay. Okay. So touchy."

Yevgeny pauses.

"Hey Lisa?"

"Yeah?"

"When Shinzo needs to make flying cars legal in Japan, I'll tell him to call you first."

CHAPTER FIFTY-FIVE

NEW YORK CITY

The Kosher Mexican Korean Food Truck

At this point, Rosario and Wheeler don't even need to be there anymore, but hanging out in the truck is a way of keeping the good vibes going a little longer. This whole operation could have gone terribly wrong—and for a good bit, it did—but when an investigation ends with the mayor in cuffs, no one usually cares how it happened. Just that it did.

And Rosario finally got the scalp she was looking for. Even the members of the boys' club are treating her differently. She's picked up a new nickname: Mayor-slayer.

She likes it.

"I was thinking," Wheeler starts, popping a sweet potato pierogi in her mouth in preparation for the Warsaw competition in August.

"Nothing ever ends well when you say that."

"We can do more with this."

"We've done plenty already," Rosario says. "McClain said we're safe from furlough no matter what happens in the budget. We got our commendations. We're good. We won."

"You're thinking too small," Wheeler says. "Think about this whole FlightDeck thing. All the crime involved. Denevito working both sides and defrauding his clients. Navarro going for a bribe. The Audubon Society literally taking down the car. The deputy mayor in Austin soliciting a free vacation. FlightDeck lying about their technology. Viktor just being Viktor. That window washer abduction. Everyone was dirty on all sides."

"That's politics," Rosario says, though she's thinking too: there's a whole wide world of corruption out there.

"Some of these startups are huge. Worth billions. Tens of billions sometimes. They're disrupting every industry out there. Lot of money at stake. Lot of attention. Lot of ego. Lot of risk. And when all that comes together? People always, always, always get desperate, they get greedy, and then they do dumb things."

"So you want to investigate another case of criminal activity involving a tech startup?"

"I want to create a team that investigates criminal activity involving tech startups. Could be startups breaking the law. Could be politicians trying to hold them up for bribes. Could be illegal activity from the people they're disrupting—"

"Like Viktor."

"Like Viktor. No shortage of bad guys here. Let's go talk to McClain about it. I'm sure he'll love it. I'm sure Main Justice will love it too. It's the issue of the moment. The zeitgeist. We could do it together. What could go wrong?"

Rosario nods. Yeah. She still has a few years left before retirement. Seems like a good way to spend it. "Hey," she finally says. "Are you still going up to Vermont this weekend?"

Wheeler looks a little surprised. "For the maple syrup drinking competition? Yeah? Why?"

"You got room in your Jeep for a new fan of the sport?" Rosario asks.

CHAPTER FIFTY-SIX

NEW YORK CITY

Madison Square Park

The light turns red on Twenty-Second and Fifth, and the traffic is heavy enough to ensure even the city's most dedicated or clueless jaywalkers wait the twenty seconds. Lisa uses the time to check her phone. There's a text from her dad.

Just wanted to make sure you're ok.

What? Lisa's heart skips a beat. This never happens. Turns out maybe she just needed an epic, globally visible disaster to hear from him about something other than Jimmy Fallon and traffic on 395.

I'm fine. Actually, I'm better than fine. I'm good.
I'm now the CEO of a new company.

He texts right back, another surprise. *After killing the cow? They let you run a company after that these days? Why? Shouldn't someone else be in charge?*

Well, at least he texted. And for the first time, it occurs to her that maybe her dad's negativity about her career isn't because he's disappointed that she isn't an orthodontist or a CPA—it's because he knows this is a crazy fucking business and he worries about her. Maybe it's not that he doesn't think she's qualified to be CEO, but that holding the job itself puts too bright a spotlight on her. At least more than he's comfortable with. Fortunately, Lisa's risk tolerance is a whole lot higher. She pockets the phone and heads into the dog run in Madison Square Park.

Alphonso, Allison, and Pinky are already there. It's the first warm day of spring, sunny and somewhere in the seventies. In New York, spring weather lasts about a week and a half before summer arrives and turns the city into a pizza oven. Lisa is glad to be outside, enjoying it.

"First new business meeting in a while," Alphonso offers.

"Things have been a little hectic lately," Lisa says. "But now we're getting back to normal. Or at least the new normal for us. I'm proud to welcome Pinky to the weekly meeting."

Pinky beams.

"Okay," Lisa continues. "So…new ideas. Big ideas. We need lots of them. HyperActivity just fired us from the Penske account. They are the last ones to go, so we officially have a blank slate. Nowhere to go from here but up."

"Wait, even Southern California Tech fired us?" Allison asks.

"They were the first to cut and run. That chancellor's an asshole. Especially after our secret influencer campaign moved them up eighteen spots in the *U.S. News* rankings and he got a new contract out of it. But whatever. It's fine. Who's got an idea?"

Alphonso goes first. "I've got a few."

"Figured you would," Lisa says.

"Should I start with theater tech? I've got all these new ways to disrupt Broadway. They have it coming."

Lisa shakes her head no.

"Telemedicine for birds?"

Another headshake from Lisa. "Way too specific. Plus I hate birds."

"Tiny GPS sensors for socks? That way you never lose them in the wash. Okay. Okay. Too much? How about this? On-demand pet tigers? You can rent them by the hour. Why is this something only Mike Tyson should get to enjoy?"

Allison jumps in. "Increase the speed limit for horses on public freeways to fifteen miles per hour? Public auctions for organs? Or—oh, this is good, this is definitely what we should do—we run a campaign to allow pawn brokers to start taking prosthetic limbs again. Why can't something literally cost an arm and a leg?" Pinky really likes that one.

"We might as well run a campaign to repeal Idaho's ban on cannibalism while we're at it," Lisa offers. No one laughs. But the group appreciates her attempt at humor. You get points for trying.

Rebuilding the business from scratch isn't going to be easy, Lisa thinks, *but with this group, it might be fun.*

"Okay, I'll take a shot," says Pinky. He's deadly serious. It's not clear if he understands that most of the ideas up until now weren't. "Remember the movie *Mr. Baseball*?"

"Uh...yeah? I guess?" Lisa replies.

"They should make *Mr. Baseball 2.*"

"Okay," Lisa says as slowly as she can.

Pinky continues, undeterred. "And Flemish."

"What about it?"

"It should be the official language of Wisconsin. I've felt that way for a long time. A lot of people do. Also, do you want to hear my idea about flip-flops that are also metal detectors? I have a lot of observations about how to make metal detecting more efficient."

"Pinky," Lisa says gently, "I'm not sure you've quite gotten the hang of this yet."

She knows Pinky is used to hearing that. "I'll keep at it. How will I know when one of my ideas works?"

"White smoke will emerge from the playground next door," Lisa says.

"Or from the next flying car," Allison adds.

Alphonso looks down at his phone. "Holy shit! Just up on Gothamist. Sharpton likes the idea of flying cars."

"Not sure that would have dissuaded the Audubon Society," Lisa says.

She looks down at her phone. "Holy shit is right. Two miracles in one day."

"What?" all three of them anxiously ask.

"Carol. She's real."

Pinky, Allison, and Alphonso had been hearing about the mysterious, elusive, possibly made-up Carol. Everyone is fascinated by her.

"She finally replied to the first text I sent her three months ago. I'll read it to you: 'Hi Lisa. Sorry for the delay. Been in a silent meditation retreat without my phone. Let's set up a strategy session for next week. You can access my calendar here.'"

"Looks like Carol was more real than their tech," Alphonso offers.

"Maybe she was the key all along," Lisa replies. "At least next time we have an insanely ambitious, narcissistic tech CEO client, we know who we really need to talk to."

Lisa pauses, then says, "Which gets me to what I actually want to run by all of you."

"Big picture, I keep thinking, what was the best thing about Nick? He was up for whatever. We could be as creative as we want. We could take as much risk as we wanted to—sometimes, as it turns out, way too much risk. He wasn't afraid. I want to keep doing that—I want to lean into the tech problems even more. Forget about helping candidates run for office. They're all just desperately needy and greedy. And the money isn't that good. There's a much better model out there, waiting for someone to claim it. Think about it—no one has any idea how to regulate all these new white spaces: AI, cryptocurrency, delivery drones, self-driving trucks, machine learning, esports, facial recognition, Web3, space exploration. There are so many. And we can figure all of that out—how to legalize all of it—better than anyone. I mean, we pretty much already did with FlightDeck, give or take one unexpected prop plane. And we'll make a fuckton of money doing it."

"So we're still Firewall?" Alphonso asks.

Lisa thinks for a moment. "No. We definitely need a new name. We need a fresh start. But I don't think it's much more than that. We just need to rebrand, not reinvent from scratch. We know we're good at this. We know there's an opportunity to focus on the fights around regulating tech and build a huge business from that alone. I don't know what our new name should be. And obviously I don't know if any of you even want to join me in all this. But I do think it's worth a shot."

Alphonso looks at Allison. Allison looks at Pinky. Pinky looks at his phone. Then he looks up, too, at Allison and Alphonso. Their eyes meet. And in a rare telepathic moment where each understands what the other is thinking—*Fuck it, why not? Let's give it a shot*—they nod at each other, nod again at Lisa, and for now, the band is still together. The team heads back to the office for a pitch meeting, with nothing solid, but in better spirits. Lisa is glad about that; she was worried the rest of the team would want to jump ship. Having them on board means she has a chance.

As for the meeting, the guy who connected them was a little vague, but Lisa figured her bar for taking clients at the moment is very low, so whatever it is, it'll probably be fine.

When they get to the lobby, they see three very hippy, trippy-looking guys. Each of them looks like Jared Leto after a particularly long bender. They all head upstairs, making awkward small talk about the warm weather.

After all the pleasantries in the conference room, Lisa gets into it.

"So you want to legalize psychedelics? Any specific kind?"

The first hippie replies, "Well, whatever you think you can pass. We know this is a heavy lift."

Lisa shrugs. "I don't know. Not that heavy. There's precedent. Norms around drugs are changing fast. I think it's fair to be aggressive here."

Alphonso looks worried.

"So LSD?" the second hippie asks.

"Sure," Lisa replies.

"PCP?" hippie number three asks.

Allison is shaking her head vehemently no.

Whatever. Dream big. Lisa nods. Get the client and worry about the rest later.

"Peyote?" the first hippie suggests.

Lisa shoots back. "Easy." Even Pinky is mouthing the words "not easy" to himself.

"Ketamine?"

She nods.

"Ayahuasca?"

"Definitely."

"And just to make sure I understand this correctly," Lisa says, "we're talking full-on retail. Dispensaries. Delivery. Shipping. Advertising. Marketing. E-commerce. Unlimited quantities. Direct to consumer. All of it. The whole megillah." The hippies look thrilled. Finally, someone who gets it.

Lisa just keeps recklessly expanding the clients' expectations. But they need the revenue. And this would be a hell of a win. *Is this what it felt like for Nick?* she wonders. *Sitting in the big seat? Seeing what's possible, what isn't possible—and then doing your best to make both work?*

"Would it be legal for people to grow mushrooms in their homes?" the third hippie asks.

"It will be now," Lisa says, getting caught up in the excitement.

"And the same for making synthetics?" tries hippie number two.

"Totally," Lisa assures him.

Alphonso, Allison, and Pinky have migrated to the corner of the room.

"She's a monster," Allison whispers.

"She's worse than Nick," Alphonso replies. Even Pinky thinks it's too much.

Lisa can hear them. And she doesn't care.

"Don't get me wrong," Lisa tells the clients. "This is pretty far out there. Definitely takes the whole cannabis thing to a new level. We talked to that guy in Humboldt County pitching diet weed—"

One of the hippies jumps in. "That guy sucks."

"I know, right?" Lisa continues, her voice speeding up, her excitement growing. "But either way, we've run plenty of campaigns in Colorado before. This is crazy but it doesn't seem totally crazy." She's not sure if it is totally crazy or not, but either way, pitching these guys is fun. She sees why Nick always liked selling new clients. And why he almost always went a step or two too far to reel the fish in.

"We needed the money," she hears Nick say in the back of her mind.

Hippie number one, with his deep, heavy Southern accent, chimes in. "That's great. But who said anything about Colorado?"

"Aren't we talking Colorado?" Lisa asks. "Isn't that where...I assumed you must have meant..."

Hippie number two speaks up. "We're not from Colorado."

Hippie number three chimes in. "I've never even been there. Other than changing planes in Denver once. But I don't think that counts."

"I think you have to go outdoors for it to count," Pinky offers. "Unless you're just going underneath the airport straight to the Illuminati headquarters? Then you're only outside for like a minute. I bet they have a secret elevator behind like a CIBO Express somewhere. They must. It gets cold in Denver."

Alphonso glares at him, trying to telepathically scream, *Now is not the time for this!*

Hippie number three speaks up again. "We don't want you to legalize psychedelics in Colorado."

Then hippie number two sets them straight. "We want you to legalize psychedelics in Alabama."

"Alabama?" Lisa asks.

"Alabama?" Pinky repeats.

Lisa looks at Alphonso. She looks at Allison. She looks at Pinky. For the first time since the meeting started, the weight of what she's promising seems to finally occur to her. Maybe you don't make the sale at any cost. Maybe she should give her colleagues the deference Nick should have given her. But as she's thinking that, she also keeps tallying everything it must cost to run the business. Salaries. Benefits. Rent. Travel. Insurance. Phones. Laptops. Servers. Supplies. Subscriptions. Bonuses. Commissions. Paying for all of that has to come before anything else.

Especially once the magic words come. "And to be clear, we have all the funds you'd need for a big campaign," hippie number one says. "Whatever it takes. Anything. My dad invented the thong."

Lisa is surprised that Allison resists the urge to tell them that her dad invented the Chipwich. She looks too stunned to say anything.

Alphonso is giving Lisa a *please say no* look.

"Alabama?" Pinky says again, out loud.

Lisa's not sure. You fall flat on your face the very first time out and the business could be fucked before it even gets started. But then again, they're in pretty bad shape already. This campaign lets them live to regroup, to fight another day. And if they can somehow pull this off...

They almost pulled off flying cars. They were just one minor act of domestic terrorism away. Compared to that, how hard can this really be?

Lisa looks at Allison. She looks at Alphonso. She looks at Pinky.

They all shake their heads no.

Then she turns to the Alabama hippies and smiles.

"No problem."

TEN RULES THAT DEMYSTIFY POLITICS

(1) Every policy output is the result of a political input.
(2) Every politician values staying in office far more than anything else.
(3) Politicians are extremely rational and smart when it comes to determining what's in their best political interest.
(4) Expecting politicians to "do the right thing" and defy human nature never works.
(5) Politicians will do what you want in one of two cases: (a) they think you can help them win their next election; or (b) they think you can cost them their next election. Otherwise, you don't matter at all.
(6) Because of gerrymandering, the only election that typically matters is the primary. And because primary turnout is usually 10–20 percent, a very small group of voters and special interests typically choose both our elected officials and the policies they pursue.
(7) Politicians, because all they want to do is stay in office, will adapt to whatever policies the majority of their primary voters support, so if primary turnout expands consider-

ably, then the politician instinctively shifts to the center to accommodate it.

(8) If we want different outputs, if we want different policies, we have to change the inputs. The only thing that works is changing the political incentives. Everything else is just noise.

(9) The key to any campaign is to understand whose support you really need and what will make them feel like you can impact their next primary. This applies to every state, every county, every city, every jurisdiction, every party, every ideology.

(10) In other words, politics is far less complex than the people in the business—electeds, staffers, reporters, pundits, academics, think tanks—make it out to be. The more complex it sounds, the more impressive they seem. But it's about inputs and outputs—and nothing else.

By the way, the only way to change all of this is by radically expanding voter turnout. The only way to do that is by letting people vote on their phones. My foundation, Tusk Philanthropies, is funding and running the national effort to create mobile voting, but as you can imagine, the powers that be aren't happy about it. You can learn more about it at mobilevoting.org. We'd love your help.

—Bradley Tusk

ACKNOWLEDGMENTS

I've always wanted to write a novel and there are a lot of people who helped me along the way. First, thank you to my publishers, Gretchen Young and Adriana Senior, for taking a chance on me. Thank you to my agent Kirsten Neuhaus for exactly the same. A lot of people helped me edit this book and gave me great feedback: Rob Hart, Meaghan Collins, Bob Greenlee, Hugo Lindgren, Howard Wolfson, Amber de Gramont, Elliot Regenstein, Madeline Sturgeon, and Rich Zabel. And whether it was talking through the concept or designing the cover or helping promote and market this book or the million other things it takes from having the germ of an idea to your reading this, a lot more people helped: Chelsea Huff, Cory Epstein, Marla Tusk, Gabe Tusk, Basil Apostolo, Noa Kasman, Greg Cappuzzo, Steven Soderbergh, Bryan Buckley, Hannah Tjaden, Julie Wernersbach, Charlie Gross, Jason Hodes and Brent Montgomery. And to everyone I missed, I owe you tickets to a Mets game (or at least a decent meal).